Burning
Wings

BURNING WINGS

A mostly true story about love, light, fear, darkness, hallucinations, narcotics, spirituality, debauchery, and that thing in the desert.

KYRA BRAMBLE

First paperback edition September 2020

Burning Wings Publishing

www.burningwingsbook.com

This is a work of fiction based on non-fiction.
Names, characters, places, and incidents are either the product of
the author's experience, or are used fictitiously.
Any resemblance to actual persons, living or dead, events, or locales
are entirely coincidental, unless, of course, when they are not.

ISBN 978-0-578-75525-0

Cover & interior art by Marie Poliak
Art direction by Eli Morgan
Edited by Nathan J. Nugent

For more information, address:
press@burningwingsbook.com

A QUICK *Disclaimer*

BURNING MAN DOES NOT ENDORSE THIS book, nor does it in any way represent the views or principles of the establishment. Illegal drugs are not permitted at Burning Man, a legal event held on public land, and are subject to fullest prosecution of the law.

> **Burning Man states:** *The use and possession of illicit drugs and drug paraphernalia are violations of the law. Depending on the violation, you may receive a citation or be arrested and/or evicted from the event. The possession of large quantities or a variety of drugs may be interpreted as evidence of intent to distribute, which is a serious felony offense. Giving illegal substances to someone else could be considered drug trafficking.*

While the event has been dramatized for its overt use of recreational and intentional substances, sobriety is just as common as intoxication. The event itself is a drug of its own. This story is a fictional novel inspired by how Burning Man changed my life. It is one account out of millions of stories and should be regarded as a piece of art. It speaks only for my own interpretation, for no one can dare to dream for anyone else.

I dedicate this book to love in all manifestations.

To every soul who has ever loved.

To the beautiful confusion that defines love.

To the art that love inspires.

To the dust left behind after it burns.

MONDAY
The Long Road Home

TUESDAY
Further Down the Rabbit Hole

WEDNESDAY
Pain is Real. Blood is Real.

THURSDAY
Smoke and Dreams

FRIDAY
The Edge

SATURDAY
Illusion is Just Another Illusion

SUNDAY
The Last Sunrise

People seem to think
drugs and the visions
and realizations they
give us aren't
reality.

They are absolutely
reality.

AUTHOR'S *Note*

N O, THIS BOOK IS NOT ALL TRUE. And I grappled deeply of whether to publish it as fiction or non-fiction. But while it has more truth than fiction, hence the term "mostly true," overall it has become an energy of its own, and is no longer a true account of that fateful week in 2007.

When I began to write this book, it wasn't supposed to be a novel. It was supposed to be a non-fiction fluffy short story about my wings and my first burn. But by the time I finished telling the story of Monday, I had already exceeded my expected word count. I kept going, realizing this was going to be a larger project than I had expected. I paused to develop a timeline of my week, interviewing old campmates and anyone I was still in contact with that had been with me that year. I kept going. Tuesday took me deeper.

When I wrote Wednesday, it was with tears in my eyes. I had no idea I had had so much pain inside me until the words came out. From there I couldn't turn back. While writing, I went back in time and vividly relived each emotion, each hallucination, and each revelation. It was practically a religious experience to time travel back to that point in my life, discover parts of myself I didn't know I had, and turn them into literature.

There are many incidents, conversations, and art pieces that are a culmination of the other years I have spent immersed in Burning Man culture woven into this story. Many of these stories came from deep inside of me, and became my truth as I wrote, allowing my character to develop, and the story to progress as it deserved to.

When these hidden parts came out as monstrous clowns, wise gnomes, rainbow spiders, and fluttering fairies onto the pages of my book, I allowed them. Of course, the drugs didn't help either—or maybe they did? But the drugs are secondary to the experience, the art, and to the people who create both.

Now after experiencing eleven long burns, I can truly say that the story reflects the playa in that it is shrouded in illusion and fantasy. My own fluctuating mindset reflects what a full Burning Man week brings to most: an intense juxtaposition of pain and pleasure, light and darkness, revelation and frivolity.

Why should writing or reading about Burning Man be any different than living it? How do you describe a multi-dimensional experience like Black Rock City for those that haven't experienced it? How do you transcribe hallucinations, religious awakenings, conscious anarchy, and prophetic meetings? How do you placate generations of proudly apathetic, jaded, and volatile burners?

Well, in true burner fashion, you say *fuck you* and do it anyway (write your own damn book).

Does it matter what is real and what isn't? Isn't it all real if you believe it is? Just trust, buckle up, open your heart, and enjoy the ride.

Since my hot mess debut into Burning Man culture I'm proud to say I've become a semi-functioning and contributing member of society. I have run large scale sound camps, crewed art cars, been the first on playa to set up in dust storms, and the last to leave days after everyone else, picking up MOOP and sorting mountains of trash. I've spent months pre-burn creating spreadsheets, info guides, and fundraising for camps. I've written free literature, performed, taught workshops, cooked for crews, taught yoga, led ceremonies and curated sacred spaces.

But none of that really matters. In some ways I'll always be that wide-eyed young girl from 2007, heart broken wide open, and ready for all the lessons the playa had to offer. You can't open your mind without opening your heart, and it is my dream that this book will serve as a catalyst for both closed minds and hearts—that it will offer hope and humanity for anyone who has felt hopelessness and true darkness, for anyone who has been underestimated, for anyone who hasn't believed in their own power.

I hope this book gives a voice to women in this community and paves the way for other female writers to be comfortable in the vulnerability of sharing their experiences in the male-dominated world that is contemporary pop-culture and drug literature.

I want this book to allow the magic of Burning Man to incense the uninitiated to find that essence of hunger for adventure and connection, to know that there is always more, both in this life, and inside yourself—and that every spectrum of human emotion is ubiquitously felt by all.

We are all just mirrors.

LOVE & *acknowledgments*

ON THE SURFACE, THIS BOOK IS ABOUT one mind-bending week of debauchery, but dig a little deeper, and you'll find it's a love story. It's the end of one love story, and the beginning of a thousand more, including one I was able to begin with myself.

Every person I have ever loved is imprinted on my heart, and now also in the pages of this book. I hope each of my lovers will recognize themselves and the lessons they taught me, for better or for worse, speaking through the pages.

Thank you to each of you. You showed me true love, and you showed me true heartbreak. You showed me what my heart was capable of. You showed me, *me*.

Thank you to my campmates for being such vibrant human beings. You made bringing your characters to life in these pages so much fun.

Thank you to all of the hardworking artists who created the backdrop for this journey, as well as the Burning Man Organization itself who plans and produces this insanity year after year. That first year I had no grasp of the amount of work it takes to bring large scale art to a place like the playa. Now that I know I am infinitely more impressed than I was then—if that is even possible.

This book itself wouldn't have been possible without the support of a number of specific individuals, working synergistically to bring this project to its fullest potential.

BURNING WINGS

Thank you to my editor, Nathan J. Nugent, for your infinite support and cutting critiques.

Thank you to Marie Poliak for sharing your incredible art cover and interior art, bringing visuals to my words.

Thank you to Eli Morgan for support in art direction and formatting.

Thank you to Dominique Debucquoy-Dodley for being my Burning Man liaison, and seeing this as my work of art.

Thank you to Alicia Baron for invaluable support in bringing this work to a wider audience (and keeping me on schedule for launch).

Thank you to Chris Flook, both for buying me that fateful ticket (yes, that part is true), and for all your help in bringing awareness to a unique perspective on the event.

Thank you to everyone who has ever believed in me.

Thank you to the infinite dust, for giving me the inspiration to write this book.

-Kyra

Every single person you will love in this

life, or that will love you,

will imprint on your soul, forever.

The love you shared is a tiny seed that

blooms continuously.

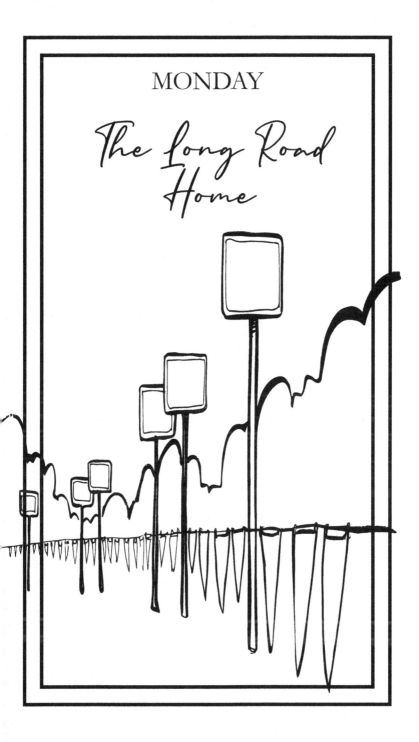

MONDAY

The Long Road Home

Dust below and
stars above, waiting
impatiently for
the sun.

MONDAY: *The Long Road Home*

HALFWAY BETWEEN LOST AND FOUND, that's how the open desert makes me feel. Or perhaps it only brings to light what is already inside of me: that yearning for independence, to push boundaries, to challenge the world, but to still belong to something larger than just myself.

Dust below and stars above, waiting impatiently for the sun.

I'm a strange combination of jaded and optimistic. A wandering fairy with a bleeding heart, looking towards the light, even as it blinds me. It's not so much that I am foolish, although what twenty-one-year old is not?

Rather, my naïveté is rooted in the fact that I am stubborn to a fault. I refuse to accept the darkness I have been shown in the world. I choose, instead, to avoid it at all costs, unaware that it is eating me alive from the inside out. I am too independent to admit that I am hopelessly lost, and, even worse, I have no idea what *found* looks or feels like. I believe that the farther away from home I go, the closer I will come to finding my true self—whatever that means.

The first light of the morning sun softly brightens the dusky sky. It will be the first of many sunrises throughout the week, but the only one I will see sober. I'm sitting in the passenger seat of my friend Spruce Man's old van, in a seemingly endless stalled line of vehicles waiting to enter the gates. I crane my neck out the open passenger's window, making out dusty car after dusty car, weighed down with bikes, trailers, and assorted oddities. Off the sides of the road is Black Rock Desert, an endless sea of dust; in the distance the fuchsia mountains rise, proud and tall.

There is no vegetation here. No life in any traditional sense of the word. No life, except for the droves of us mad pilgrims, that journey here annually to spirit-quest and light things on fire.

I fire up my lighter and ignite the first cigarette of the new day, and hold it in my mouth, so I can grab my ticket out of my purse.

I reread to myself:

THE TICKET PURCHASER OR HOLDER VOLUNTARILY ASSUMES ALL RISK OF PROPERTY LOSS, PER-SONAL INJURY, SERIOUS INJU-RY OR DEATH, WHICH MAY OC-CUR BY ATTENDING **BURNING MAN 2007.** YOU HEREBY FOR-EVER RELEASE, DISCHARGE, AND HOLD BURNING MAN HARMLESS FROM ANY CLAIM ARISING FROM SUCH RISK EVEN IF CAUSED BY THE NEGLIGENT ACT OR OMISSION OF BURNING MAN OR ITS OFFICERS, DIRECTORS, EMPLOYEES, CONTRACTORS, AGENTS OR REPRESENTATIVE You must bring enough food, water, shelter, and first aid to survive one week in a harsh desert environment.

MONDAY: *The Long Road Home*

"Serious injury or death? *Bring it on.*" I mouth the words out loud to Spruce Man, next to me in the driver's seat. Spruce Man doesn't hear me; he has his beanie pulled over his eyes and is asleep—face snugly resting on the steering wheel.

I smile at him, both in acknowledgment as a beloved friend, and the childlike sweetness of a man asleep.

I need more to smile about. Life over the past year has been a whirlwind of lovers, would-be lovers, parties and broken dreams. My young naive heart has been ripped out of my chest, stepped on, spit on, pierced with a thousand pieces of broken glass, and then shoved back into my body, upside down. Yet somehow, against all odds, it still beats. *But for whom?*

I need more men like Spruce Man in my life. Solid, reliable, platonic friends, whom I can trust. Spruce Man is stocky and, while not overweight, round enough that hugging him is a special treat. He is unassuming, physically; it isn't until you know him that you tap into his wisdom and playfulness. He's easy-going, with a heart of gold; yet there is an intellectual edginess with a dash of the nerd—debating for hours about the evolving politics of electronic music and technology. Plus, he can keep up with me when I'm on a rampage; he's a hard hitter too, and good, because raging has been a regular occurrence in my life lately. Admiring his nap, I'm both jealous of his sleep as well as happy to have him as my co-conspirator on this long, strange trip we've chosen to take.

Reaching for my ticket, I embrace my passport to a rite

of passage. I hold the firm and precious stub of painstakingly designed wood pulp to admire it again, its golden hues against green trees reflecting the already harsh morning sun.

While every burner calls every ticket 'the golden ticket,' mine truly came to me as if the universe willed it, or at least that's what I tell myself. A few short months ago in San Francisco's joke of a foggy summer, I was doing what I typically did on every Saturday night since I turned legal: pushing the consumption limit of my tiny body, at some underground club. On this particular night, the club morphed into an all-night afterparty in a *painted lady,* one of those run-down yet still iconic 18th century mansions in Alamo Square. . . Somewhere, after snorting lines of assorted white powders off of a gilded, full-length antique mirror, and doing naked yoga on the roof at sunrise, I lay snuggled up to my new friend, Flook, as he told me about the mythical place known as Burning Man.

I had heard stories before and was still eager for more. Everyone had a different take on that apocalyptic carnival of rainbow dreams. Flook described a dusty utopia, where freedom and self-expression reigned. There, I could be anyone I wanted to be, even myself. I didn't question Flook, I was already there—his reverence and affection for a place I had viewed mostly as wild and ungodly was pulling me in forever. I knew already without a shadow of a doubt that there was nowhere else like it in the world, and it was waiting for me. I was to be initiated into some strange world I could only imagine, and Flook advised me to get ready for a long and winding trip down the rabbit hole. Listening to his voice, I drifted in and out of worlds, my head on his lap, and a giant balloon of nitrous oxide gas in hand.

))☼((

The next morning, Flook dropped me off at my work, a pretentiously zen tea bar in the city's notoriously gay Castro district. It was like working at a wine bar, only with a new age elitism and cult following. My uniform consisted of flowing flower-child skirts, tight black American Apparel tank tops, and studded punk rock jewelry. I served the yoga elite overpriced tea in hand-shaped clay teacups. Lucky for me, everyone always had their eyes down, and anyways, grunge and androgyny were hip, so it wouldn't trigger anyone that I hadn't showered and was wearing a borrowed men's shirt.

I reluctantly climbed out of Flook's car, releasing the wild of the night and getting ready for work, pep talking myself in preparation for the shift. I hugged him deeply in gratitude for the connection, night, and stories, expecting that to be goodbye. But then he took out his wallet and took out a stack of twenty-dollar bills. "What's this for?" I asked, confused.

"I told you." He said, "Every year, I sponsor someone to go to Burning Man. This year you need to go. Experience it yourself." He smiled slowly, showing his deep dimples, and handed the cash to me.

I held the money awkwardly, still baffled. "Ok, so give me a ticket! I don't feel right about accepting cash like this."

He locked eyes with me, held my gaze with power, and asked in a teasing voice, "What are you going to do with the money?"

Without thinking, I answered honestly. "I'm going to buy my ticket," The idea of using his money for anything else seemed preposterous.

That settled that. I accepted the money, hugged him, and began another day of gently infusing white tea buds with spring water, and although I could hardly hold my head up from lack of sleep, I was no stranger to working double shifts after partying all night, and while I took orders and tried not to spill the tea, my hazy head daydreamed of wearing bootie shorts, dancing with unicorns in the desert underneath a day-glow rainbow, while Mad Max men shot guns at the shimmering stars nearby.

In all honesty, even with all the stories, I had no idea what exactly Burning Man was; perhaps some twisted Candyland video game in the desert with no rules and great music? I possessed a natural reverence towards it, some sort of intangible appreciation for it as both a spiritual epicenter, and also a counter-culture cool kids club, a club I now had been invited to participate in. Whatever *it* was, it was calling me home. There was some purpose, some lesson for me there, and I had no choice but to surrender to the path I was on.

The next day I bought my ticket on Haight Street right near the corner of Ashbury, a fitting locus for the marrying of counter-culture revolutions. I walked past the velvet coats and neon colored bikini tops to the counter, where I proudly asked for the ticket that would change my life, a ticket that was the gateway to another dimension, a ticket to Burning Man.

The man behind the counter grinned a knowing sort of smile. He was tall and lanky, wearing a fedora and plaid suit jacket over a skateboard shirt.

"What do you know about Burning Man?" he asked before turning around to find a folder and pull out the ticket.

Absolutely fucking nothing. I'm so excited and so scared. I'm not sure if I'm going to a candy rave orgy or a shoot-out or a meth carnival or a pagan festival.

"Enough. I grew up with the Grateful Dead. I've been to festivals before." I became defensive and stuttered slightly as I responded.

I'll be fine, whatever it is. I'm used to taking care of myself.

He laughs. "This isn't a festival. Make sure you bring enough water and some proper boots. New socks help as well." I smiled and walked out, the ticket that would change my life secured in the inner side pocket of my purse.

I checked it daily afterwards, not trusting that it was real. I somehow expected it to vanish as mysteriously and unexpectedly as it came to me.

☽☼☾

The line of cars moves forward. Spruce Man jolts awake, rubs his eyes, lets out a happy yell, moves his van into gear, and we push on, getting closer to our destination:

BURNING WINGS

Black Rock City, Nevada.

For one week a year, Black Rock City awakens like a phoenix rising from its burnt nest. It is a regular city in many ways. It has roads, a place of worship, an airport, and a unique history and culture. It is a very strange city, in many other ways. Built entirely by its inhabitants, all its dwellings are temporary. The only available forms of transportation are bicycles and 'mutant vehicles' or 'art cars,' elaborately decorated and mutated roaming party vehicles of all shapes and sizes.

Uniqueness and radical self-expression are celebrated. There is said to be no money exchanged—at least not legally. This is a city of freaks, of lovers, and of the fearless ones, a place where all limits are made to be pushed, where rules cease to have meaning, and logic has no foothold, where magic leaves its home in the starry sky to dance with mortals in the dust. And then, when the week is over, the city turns to smoke, and crumbles once again into soft ash.

We inch forward, as the sun peeks over the mountains. Spruce Man switches on the radio. "A Horse with No Name" is playing. Time stands still, and I know that for the rest of my life, this song will remind me of this moment: of the feeling of new beginnings and self-discovery; of uneasy anticipation; of endless dust and possibilities; of rules, just waiting to be broken. I sing softly to myself along with the radio.

I've been through the desert on a horse with no name . . .

MONDAY: *The Long Road Home*

We arrive at the first gate just as the song ends. A red-bearded man, wearing a kilt and platform boots covered with studded metal skulls, pops his head in the car. "Welcome home, children! Tickets? Tickets?" We hand over our tickets to be scanned, before our van is casually searched for stowaways and contraband. There isn't very much not allowed into Burning Man, but unpaid residents, firearms, and illegal drugs are all on the list of prohibited items. We're safe. My stash (meticulously wrapped in saran wrap and placed in my hookah case, which is underneath a pile of tutus and my dreamcatcher wings, inside a large plastic tub) contains mushrooms, marijuana, powdered MDMA, pressed ecstasy pills, LSD, 2CB, and DMT. I hope it will last me through the week.

At the second gate, we are stopped again, this time by a forty-something woman, named Sparkleberry. She is wearing hot pink cowboy boots with four-inch heels, a matching cowgirl hat with goggles attached, a full-length lipstick red fishnet body suit, and a black rhinestone bandana around her neck.

"Give me your virgins," she demands in a southern drawl. In Burning Man lingo, a 'virgin' is a first-year attendee; Spruce Man and I are both virgins. I hop out of the car, happy to stretch my legs. "Come here, Sugar! Welcome home!" I grin like a happy child with a lollipop, and open my arms wide for her. She wraps me up in a giant burrito of a hug. It is the longest and most genuine hug I have had in a long time, and I melt into her embrace, ignoring the erect nipples protruding from her fishnets and smashing into my chin.

"Roll in the dust, Cupcake" is her next command. I drop immediately and roll back and forth on the ground, feeling the soft dust coat every inch of me, surprised to discover silky smoothness like fine dried powdered clay. It sticks to everything it touches, and has a distinct smell that I can't quite identify. Like home, in a strange way . . . which is where I seem to keep being told I am. I ring a giant bell, and everyone around me cheers. Another virgin finishes rolling in the dust next to me. I wrap him in my own giant hug, and whisper to him these magic words: "Welcome home." He grins from ear to ear, mirroring my own smile, before he runs off to ring his bell.

Spruce Man and I hug again and hop back in the van to search for our camp. We drive slowly as to honor the 5 MPH signs posted everywhere. Even with this slow speed we kick up dust around us, it drifts through the open windows, and into our lungs like cigarette smoke.

)☼(

Black Rock City is set up on a semi-circular grid, around the open playa in the center. I was intrigued by the bits of Burning Man lingo dropped with so much casual confidence by those in the know, so I took the time to research a few terms, 'playa' being one of them. In Spanish, *playa* means beach. However, according to my dictionary, it means "an area of flat dried up land, especially a desert basin in which water evaporates from quickly." This definition is suiting literally and logically, and I found solace in that. I found myself thinking about the strength of the earth, and the ways that different parts of it contain their own unique vitality and energy.

The straight, radial roads are named after the numbers on a clock-face and range from 2 o'clock to 10 o'clock (written as 2:00 and 10:00), with 6:00 as the center of town—between the 2:00 and 10:00 extremes, is a road-less open playa. The other set of roads follows the natural curve of the circle. The centermost road on the inside of the city is called Esplanade. Each road after that progresses alphabetically. This year they are named Arctic, Boreal, Coral Reef, Desert, Estuary, Fresh Water, Grassland, Habitat, Intertidal, Jungle, Kelp Forest, and Landfill. We are camped somewhere near Desert and 9:15.

The city is waking up. We drive slowly on the designated road, passing tents, RVs, and makeshift camps. Some camps are haphazardly thrown together with whatever detritus was found, lying around in the garage, but many are complex and even beautiful in an untraditional way. I see rough plywood gazebos, fur-covered log cabins, and welded lotus flower burn barrels.

The city's residents are just as interesting as their dwellings. A naked man wearing a sombrero is pounding a lime-green mailbox into the ground with an oversized mallet—the kind you would use at a carnival to display your strength. Two women, wearing kimonos and pouring Jameson whiskey into their morning coffee, wave to us. Dreadlocked girls in furry thong bikinis whiz by us on matching bicycles, blowing kisses. I bounce up and down in the car, waving back, excited to be a part of this strange new world.

Spruce Man recognizes a hand-painted sacred geometry flag set next to the road, and we find our camp. It is just as colorful as the rest of the city.

First, Rico comes to greet us with full Chinese *yi xing* clay *gaiwan* set in hand. "*Puer?*" he offers, before any introductions are made.

"Oooh! You brought out your *yi xing?* Green or aged puer? Brick or loose? I thought about bringing mine but I didn't want to deal with the clay pots . . ." I inquire and explain all at once. Rico is pleased with my response.

"Oooh! You know your *puer!* Well then, this is a five-year, aged puer from a cake I have been holding onto for a few years. No idea the original age of harvest, I purchased it on a whim from a tea master who didn't speak my tongue after acquiring a large amount of American cash from a transaction I am not at liberty to speak of. . ." He stops to twirl his tiny goatee and look off to the distant mountains as his mind wonders.

"But I have a 1987 that I'm saving for a special occasion. I was thinking that sunrise later in the week would be the perfect time to serve it, perhaps a psytrance sunrise? But who knows what urge will strike? Sometimes the best time is anytime! But I dare say that I hope you are around to appreciate the aromas!" He is thrilled with his thoughts and his bodily mechanics display this as he speaks, without any self-inhibition.

There is no pause in theatrical movement, as Rico

speaks. Like a performer, he pours every drop of his being into whatever character he impersonates. He has many, I will soon discover.

After we officially meet, (he does not, as everyone else has done, welcome me home), I take a step back to observe him. Rico is about 5'6" and thin, with brown eyes that seem too peaceful for his eccentric personality. He is wearing ninja shoes (the large toe separate from the rest), tattered black pants, and a handmade vest, covered in artfully placed tears and studs. He has the kind of trendy asymmetrical mullet favored by Israeli festival heads and vagabonds.

His girlfriend pops out of a tent to greet us. Archinta's face looks like a porcelain doll's, with the largest bright blue eyes I have ever seen. They never seem to blink, holding you in their power and daring you to look away. Her hair is that light blonde, commonly found on toddlers before it turns dark and dirty blonde. Her dreadlocks are not the matted ones you see on grimy hippies, these are the kind done professionally, so that each one is perfectly even, with a delicate curl on the end. Her body is toned, tight, and covered with hours of colorful tattoo work. She tops off the look with a black leather mini skirt, black boots up to her knees, and an Edwardian style crop-top vest.

She acknowledges us like a queen would greet her court—with courtesy, but without any real warmth.

"Welcome home! Respect it and it will respect you!" is her greeting, before she turns her razor eyes on Rico, and they begin that kind of half bickering, instinctive of couples, about how to properly arrange the kitchen.

"The sink and drying area are the most important, and difficult by default parts, and I have already arranged these," she says, gesturing to a bench with a large ornate glass jar of clear water with a spout.

"Yes it looks fabulous, but not yet acid proof my dear." Rico commends her efforts, while at the same time judging them. He sits down to roll a spliff while she glares at him out of the corners of her eyes, arms crossed.

"It's simple enough even for the children of Ken Kesey. You wash your dishes, in the fresh water and bucket, and you leave them to dry on the rack on the tarp next to it. How you can you not fuck that up?"

I almost inquire about the tarp on the ground, *I mean I knew it was "Leave no Trace" but water? Seriously?*

"I'm more concerned with not leaving the gas on," he gestures to a double burner camp stove on the opposite side of the kitchen, on a metal bookshelf, "than being a Nazi about your dry rack."

"I made it child proof. Just wash your fucking dishes. Turn off the damn stove. And be a participating citizen! Leave no trace! Radical self-reliance! Don't be an idiot! Simple!" She says all of this with a deadly calm composure and a deadly glare radiating from her ice blue sapphire eyes.

)☼(

The camp communal area is almost set up at this point, and I appreciate how lucky we are to have a large parachute stretching over most of it. It is held up by zip ties, connected to a few poles, pounded into the ground at seemingly random places. The few small tents already under the shade divide it into a living room area, with an inflatable mattress and camping chairs.

I sneak away to look for a safe and flat spot to set up my own tent. I find a little corner near the parachute but not under it, and begin to haul my dwelling from the van.

I've brought with me a four-person camping tent, twelve-inch tent stakes, a queen-size air mattress, a sleeping bag, and some sage. I set up my little camp quickly—pounding the stakes into the rock-hard ground takes the most effort, but I borrow a giant mallet from Rico to aid me.

To inflate my air mattress I use Spruce Man's air pump, and then, home and bed complete, I begin organizing my clothes. I have enough fishnet stockings to supply a strip club, some crocheted tops, bootie shorts in every color, faux fur goggles, tutus, a miscellaneous collection of cheap lingerie, and my wings. I get lost inside my project, and am interrupted by Rico offering me some sautéed vegetables and rice. Surprisingly, I am hungry, although I eat less than expected in the heat.

Time to transform.

I've never been to Burning Man before, but I want to blend in, yet be unique, and while I have no exact idea of how to do that, I have a tent full of costumes, a childhood of jamband music festivals, and a head full of rainbow dreams.

BURNING WINGS

I tape my nipples with electric tape and throw on some ripped tights, bootie shorts, and my black platform boots.

I'm 5'4", with a scrawny 110-pound body. I have one tiny tattoo of a Capricorn symbol on my right shoulder, and to me it represents ultimate rebellion.

My big eyes change daily between blue, green, and gray. My dirty blond hair is uncut, uncombed, a foot past my shoulders, and woven with colorful ribbons, stones, and bells. A stupid grin covers my face, exposing a gap between my two front teeth. I look sixteen and innocent, but am twenty-one, and ready for a rampage.

The sun is high in the sky. I'm geared for something, I just don't know what, yet.

I want to yell and scream and jump up and down and hug everyone, but I'm not sure how Archinta would like that. . . Unable to sit still, I find my practice staff—a sort of a giant baton made of bamboo—in the car, and begin twirling it, round and around and around. Lost in my own world, I lose track of what's around me.

☽☼☾

"Who the fuck are *you*? What is this?" I look up and see Torque standing with his arms crossed, one hand stroking his chin.

Torque and I have an interesting, strained relationship. He hates me. Of course, since Torque is very pseudo-spiritual, he wouldn't call it hatred; he would describe it as something else, like maybe our energies don't align properly. Not that Torque's energies align, either. Besides being a gay porn star, Torque is also a vegan, a yoga fanatic, and a self-righteous hot mess. At least he's nice to look at, in his trendily couture ripped pants, muscular tattooed chest, and custom leather holsters.

"No seriously . . . I don't know who you are right now . . . but I like this version of you. Very interesting," he mutters, staring at me, before walking away for tea service with Rico.

I roll my eyes and ignore him as Serene, Torque's girlfriend, rolls up on her fur-covered, lowrider bicycle. She is excited to see me, or at the very least has better manners than Torque. "You're here! Hurray!" She wraps me in a hug. Serene and Torque share a meditation practice, an active sex life, and a love for psychedelics; that is where the similarities end. Serene is tiny, and resembles an elven, retro go-go dancer. Her dark hair is cut in a pixie bob, with blue streaks. She is wearing furry boots, black bootie shorts, a bikini top, and giant sunglasses. We hop around in circles, creating tiny dust clouds that hover above the earth like San Francisco fog, before dissipating.

Serene shows me her and Torque's set up, much more intricate than mine. They have two matching four person tents. Serene unzips the first one, just for their queen sized air mattress and new looking bedding. She makes sure to emphasize that it is *organic* cotton. She zips back up the bed tent, and moves to its twin. This one is full of suitcases and packages. She unzips a suitcase and shows me their vacuum sealed outfits, one for each day. I am astonished. I had no idea you could vacuum anything into tiny bags, let alone clothes. Also, I sort of love the dust. It feels real. It humbles me. It makes me feel like I belong.

"If you ever need to open the tent, please make sure to remove your shoes first! We want to keep everything dust free!" She sweetly says before zipping up the closet tent.

Archinta walks by just then. "Good luck with that one!" she says out of the corner of her mouth. "Five burns and I still haven't found a way to master the dust free concept without being a hermit."

Serene and I look around. Yes, it's dusty, but the dust seems content on the earth. I almost want to roll in it again, just to feel its sweet softness coat my skin once more.

Marson appears silently, as he frequently does, unless he's shit-faced drunk. Like a Mad Max version of the white angelic archetype, he actually *won* the Castro's annual "Hunky Jesus" contest, one year.

He makes his way to the center of camp, or at least the place where the edge of the parachute next to our dwelling is, and, as though he was on a soapbox, exclaims:

"Friends! I will show you the land! Come see the sights of this beautiful place! The city that emerges from the dust and returns to the dust! A carnival of wonders! Bring your bikes! We ride together!" he exclaims grandly.

Bikes are necessities for navigating the huge city, and I find mine on the back of Spruce Man's van. I singlehandedly wrestle the bike down and hop on. I'm high on life, and can't stop smiling. Wait! Something is wrong. My feet won't reach the pedals. I quickly realize the obvious: the bike belongs to my roommate who is 6'4" and I am 5'4"!

MONDAY: *The Long Road Home*

I can possibly stay on by scooting my butt off the seat on the front and standing on the pedals. I try this, but fall and lie in the dust in confusion. Serene joins me on the ground and we roll around giggling. Torque, Spruce Man, and Marson stare at us in amusement, before pulling us up by our hands. A suitable bike is located for me to borrow from a neighbor, but I'll have to spend the week scavenging every time I want to ride.

"Wait!" says Marson. "Take one of these first." He hands each of us a small white pill, containing 2CB, a hallucinogenic designer drug, whose effects are semi similar to the psychic effects of LSD, but with more linear ray-like pixelated visuals, with just a touch of ecstasy's euphoric state. We look each other in the eye and swallow.

Bikes are secured, water bottles are filled, and drugs are ingested, but I am missing something important: *my magic wings*.

Shortly after I was gifted my Burning Man ticket, I had a vision of creating wings made from four dreamcatchers. This vision haunted me incessantly. I have always been a little bit obsessed with making dreamcatchers. As a little girl running around the forests of Northern California, I would spend hours enthralled with weaving the unique web pattern that characterizes the Native American talisman. According to the legends told to me, completed dreamcatchers are supposed to be hung over where you sleep, so that they can catch bad dreams and allow the good ones to flow free. Always the altruist, I have made them as gifts for friends and family for as long as I can remember.

BURNING WINGS

To make a dreamcatcher, the first step is to create a loom, onto which the web can be woven. When I lived in the woods, it was easy to find young, pliable branches of trees to cut and dry in a circular shape. Living in San Francisco, I didn't have this organic luxury. Without an easy solution for looms, I put the wings out of my mind, until one day I was walking from work to the subway station at 16th and Mission, and right there in my path, like a sign from the dusty gods above, was a large pile of branches, tied together with a ribbon.

They looked like ornamental sticks from a craft store or florist. They were too perfect to simply have been harvested from the wild. I wish I knew what kind of wood they were, but I still do not. They were at least four feet long and skinny. I picked up the large bundle, threw it over my shoulder, and took them with me on the subway.

Once home I soaked them in my bathtub for five days, until they were pliable enough to be bent into the teardrop shapes I wanted. I tied them in place and let them dry in my window next to the fire escape. The next week, I took a few large rips out of my handblown rainbow glass bong and began my project. I created four dreamcatchers, using rainbow-colored yarn.

On these dreamcatchers, I wove semi-precious stones, glass beads, and bells. I tied the dreamcatchers together, in a four-leaf clover shape, with an old green fabric scarf. I made a sling for them out of the same fabric so they could comfortably sit on my back. I wrapped them delicately in sarongs before placing them on top of my tutus, on top of my drugs, in my large tub of playa clothing. And now, I will wear them proudly, comfortable and empowered, after far too many years of insecurity and fearfulness in my own skin.

Now, *finally*, I pull my homemade dreamcatcher wings out of my tent and put them on for the first time, feeling invincible. Something shifts with this sacred object in place. They have come so far, and represent *everything*. They are a sacred object symbolizing freedom, beauty, and strength. When I move, they jingle. When light shines on them, they sparkle, and I know, without a doubt, that they are magic. They belong to me as completely as I belong to them, and we empower each other to be so much more together than we were apart. On my back they gain dimension, becoming a living breathing object, deserving of respect and reverence. In turn they offer me confidence, radiance, and meaning. Together we give one another purpose.

With all as it should be, our strange new family heads out, searching for something, but unable to definitively describe what, exactly. Distraction, adventure, fun . . . ? Yes, all of these, and something deeper. Some way to push boundaries, to ignite something inside us. Something to counteract the numbness that is necessary to survive in the outside world of false promises and shattered hearts. Something to make us feel *alive*. After all, isn't that the ultimate revolt against the polite puritanical ideals thrust upon us? To play without apology?

The drugs help.

The edges of the white clouds, scattered across the pale

blue sky above us, swirl around in circular patterns, creating a moving painting. We ride through the city streets until we get to the edge of the road, cheering and singing as we go, the hot midday air whipping our faces and the sun beating down brutally on our backs and heads. Once on the playa for the first time, I can't keep the corners of my mouth from curling up. Marson leads us fearlessly, riding erratically as he yells.

"Follow me! Behold our glorious city! A city built with the calloused hands of carpenters, the hearts of lovers, the eyes of visionaries, and the souls of sages." He rides in circles around us, almost taking out Torque, and continues:

"A city where we, the people, are truly the driving force of our own destinies. We are not a democracy, but we each have a voice in our society. We are not a dictatorship, but we are all the masters of our own lives. We are not a communist society, but we all contribute to the community!" He speeds off, taking us past singing steel flower gardens, ten-foot-tall glaring monsters, and a forest of ribbon.

"The treehouse is this way!" The ground churns below me, like the top of a geometric lake rippling in the wind. I skillfully navigate around the pulsating ground, maintaining my balance on my bicycle as we approach a treehouse. The tree is about forty feet high and made of twisted, welded metal. Atop it sits a house, complete with windows and a chimney. We stop to stare at the phenomenon that is a tree in the middle of the desert. The house breathes in and out, just like a person, calling me.

I hop off my bike to walk closer to it. I hoist myself

up onto the tree, and climb a ladder until I'm inside the tiny house, where there are a few people resting and meditating. The rest of my band follows me, and we cuddle up together in the corner, interrupting the silence, laughing at the patterns spiraling on the wall in front of us, that only we seem to be able to see.

Soon, we have the whole treehouse in sync, tapping into our visuals, or perhaps just imagining the intricate designs that seem so real to us. Then the house begins to float, as if with a thousand helium balloons tied to the top. I peek out the window and watch, as the ground gets farther and farther away.

I see The Man, as he sits in the very center of the open playa. He rises tall above everything else around, commanding attention. Below him are green waving hills. Each year, The Man stands guard over his city and its inhabitants, before being sacrificed in flames on Saturday night, while thousands look on and cheer. I've heard this year the population will top forty thousand, a record population, and my heart races at being a part of something of such magnitude. Soon The Man is tiny, and our little house is floating in the swirling clouds, a part of the moving painting that before I could only watch from afar.

Marson pulls out a bottle of Jack Daniels, and the sounds turn to stories as the bottle is passed. The conversation naturally flows and the words of strangers turning into friends dance around like butterflies on flowers, taking turns with each petal. They begin about vices; alcohol, drugs, at home and at past burns, but they progress, each person excitedly expanding on one another's experiences, and then adding on their own interpretations.

It strikes me that this is what people do when they are together. We tell stories. We share pieces of ourselves with one another. Stories about being human, about the things that unite us, and remind us that every emotion and experience possible can be ubiquitous even if on the surface, they appear to be separate. No matter that we all came from varied places and circumstances, in this moment in time we all ended up here together in this mad place, where age, ethnicity, and social status seem to no longer divide us.

I'm still grinning like the Cheshire cat.

This is my life. It's so weird. And it's so beautiful. There is hope.

In our floating house is a man named Gerald. Gerald is a logger from Canada. He and his buddies use their vacation weeks every year to take a road trip down to Burning Man. They haul their own wood to build log cabins to camp in for the week.

Gerald is a force. His large body is dressed head to toe in various plaid garments, and his coarse gray beard is divided into three braids tied with ribbons around the ends. He is sitting in a perfect lotus pose, cross legged with each foot on top of the opposite leg. His kilt is demurely tucked between his legs, and he acknowledges this along with the fact he never wears underwear.

As Gerald talks, I try to imitate his lotus pose, lifting my right leg up and attempting to place it on my left knee, but the right knee hovers a good nine inches above the ground. Torque watches me, amused, and gracefully pulls his long muscular legs into the pose.

"Padmasana," he says with a smirk.

"Open hips means emotional opening and release," Serene says as she mimics the men with her own legs. She looks like a goddess, a goddess of contemporary revelry.

I recross my legs so my feet are back under my knees with as much grace as I can muster and giggle. I am not sure what I am a goddess of. *Maybe I'm a giggle goddess!*

I look up from my silly legs and notice the boy I am sitting next to—Jonmone, he calls himself— staring at me. It's not a threatening leer, nor the dazed zoning out of the immensely stoned. It's a polite curious flattering stare.

"Do you know how beautiful you are?" he says softly. At least I think that's what he said.

"What?" I'm high still, of course.

"Do you know how beautiful you are? Not the surface, I mean, yes of course, but . . ." Now he breaks eye contact for a moment to recenter, then he looks back with his dark sensitive eyes and continues: "Your energy is beautiful. I appreciate beauty. Thank you."

"Thank you." I'm blushing a little. He hands me a woven fan, and his fingers are long, caked with a few days of playa around the nail beds.

I smile and see his aura glowing around him. It's purple around his body, but turns yellow as it fades out into the oxygenated dusty air, and shoots rays like a sunbeam.

I blink and the aura disintegrates, but now I am blinded by his clothing. He's wearing a long orange and gold robe that shines when he moves, although he does move slowly, so it is a graceful shimmer. On his head is a plastic crown with multicolored feathers attached meticulously with copper wire. Under the robe hangs a single carved bone pendant on a hemp cord. His face is dark and wise with a wide nose and a large lower lip, calm and collected, but his young age is exposed by his smooth hairless chest, with a light layer of sweat on it.

All of a sudden his aura comes back on, brighter this time, and a lightbulb hovers above his head, blinking on and off.

"Wait! Take a look around for a moment . . . I want to take us in. An image of us right this second, in this moment. Take it! You see it?" We all look around.

"No." His soft voice commands attention. "Really look at each other, in the eyes, make contact; see the soul in the body." I gaze around the room, locking eyes with each soul, and after the initial urge to look away, I feel my vulnerability pass and I understand. *Each body is a soul. Each soul occupies a body.*

Jonmone speaks again. "I'm going to take this image and turn it into a puzzle. A thousand piece puzzle. And then I'm going to break it up, and then put it back together." For some reason this makes sense.

"We are all like pieces of a puzzle and we all connect to each other."

I can see the puzzle, tiny pieces of cardboard imprinted with the memory and image of this exact moment in time. Hands begin to pick up the pieces and join them together, so that we can see that each piece has a perfect home within the others.

"It's a metaphor for all human connection." Gerald speaks again in his deep voice.

"It's not even a metaphor, it's just reality." Jonmone corrects. "This is the catalyst. It's already here."

We sit in silence pondering this magical puzzle that is not symbolic, it just is. It already exists because we can all see it.

"Burning Man is just a giant puzzle." I giggle again as I speak. "I hope I don't lose any pieces!"

"Burning Man is an evolution. More of a three-dimensional model if anything. . ." Joy Luck speaks clearly and with elegance.

Joy Luck is Chinese, with two long braids of blue-tinted hair, and has that mystical aura around her: she looks young, but seems old, at the same time. She has been to Burning Man ten times and tells us the unique story of the city.

"Twenty years ago, or wait . . . twenty-one years ago, my friend built a man on Baker Beach in San Francisco. It was just a thought. One of those little ideas that we get in our head, but he followed his instinct. He built a man and lit him on fire. A few friends came to watch and drink beer and whatnot. No big deal. And then he did it again, the next year. And again. Each year the man got a little bit bigger, and more people came. It's hard to say when it began to have more meaning. When did this man, become a beacon? I don't know." She pauses to smile and straightens her vintage cotton jumper.

"So, how did it get moved to Nevada?" I ask. I'm trying to imagine this experience in cold and foggy San Francisco, and just cannot equate the two.

"After a few years of this, the cops came and wouldn't let them light it. It became too big and outgrew the beach. So, they began to search for somewhere they could go to build a bigger man. They found the desert. There is no one here to bother, and nothing else to burn."

"And deserts are famous for spirit quests," Torque interjects self-importantly, "I've always been called to the desert to commune with the spirits."

"Well," continues Joy, taking a sip of the Jack Daniels before passing it on, "Yes that is true, but that just came by itself. No one was looking for a spirit journey. Back then, they just wanted somewhere to go to burn shit, without pissing off the Law. You look out and see a city out there, but this used to be a bunch of punks and hippies, shooting guns and drinking beer. There were no roads, there was no order, there was just The Man. And as these things happen, it grew and it grew and it grew, and it became a city. The government (as well as practicalities) forced it to grow up. To become a place where we provide for ourselves, with what we call *Radical Self Reliance,* but also a place where we support each other and form a community. Everyone is here according to free will." She pauses, and a thoughtful look comes over her face before she continues, "We must respect the land, as well as our neighbors. We push limits, but we also support each other. In all my Zen meditation practice, I have never found peace like I do here at sunrise, at the end of the playa. This power was not planned. It just happened."

"You may just see chaos here, but if you look closer, you will see so much beauty and order that is formed, not in spite of the chaos, *but because of it.* Society likes to teach us that if we are given true freedom, all hell will break loose, but perhaps we will learn to love and support each other, not because we *have* to, but because we *want* to." She smiles.

I smile too. I have hardly spoken, because I am entranced and content to simply absorb and witness. This. This simple scene right here, and the depth of philosophy feels like the answers to a million questions I didn't even have the awareness to ask.

If I came all the way here just for these precious moments in this floating treehouse, then it's already worth it.

As the bottle of Jack Daniels nears its end, another visitor pokes his head into the little house. He is wearing a jester hat with tiny bells on it and a tie-dyed sarong, wrapped around his waist.

How did he float up here?

But the little house has landed gently, back on the tree, without anyone's noticing. We hug Joy and Gerald goodbye, before climbing back down the little ladder, onto the pulsating dust, and riding off again, this time towards The Man.

)☼(

I ride hard and fast towards him, with such intensity, I hardly notice that I have lost my companions. When I get within a few hundred feet of him, I stop and allow my bike to drop to the ground next to me. I walk towards The Man, as if drawn by a magnet, entranced by the effigy that inspired this mythical place. Unicorn bicycles, frog golf carts, and schools of glowing fish whiz by me. I walk to his outer circle, but do not cross the line in the dust. I can't explain why, but I know I am not ready yet. I simply gaze in appreciation at him, and the work that must have gone into his creation, but I have no desire to get closer.

Somewhere a subwoofer wails, and familiar vibrations spread across the playa. I realize it is getting darker. The sun has disappeared behind the mountains in the distance, turning them lavender. Survival skills kick in, and I begin the ride back to camp.

Blood covered zombies roam the open road, with *papier mâché* axes, attacking everyone who is foolish enough to be caught. They drag away laughing fairies, and force feed them tequila, until they agree to join the movement. I swerve off the road to avoid the chaos, although (come to think of it), there will be a blood red moon tonight . . . *Perhaps I will join them . . . No. That's silly. What do I want with zombies and blood? I would rather play with fairies and dance all night!* I shake my head and laugh to myself. *What am I thinking joining the darkness?*

Just then, from a distance, I can see a procession: men and women in white robes, walking with lamps, placing them, one at a time, onto tall posts that line the paths cutting through the playa, to guide the city dwellers from the Esplanade to The Man. They mesmerize me, moving slowly and deliberately, as they bring fire and light to the otherwise unmarked paths. They bring a new energy to the desolate landscape, a sense of reverence and peace. I feel protected and safe.

Even the zombies give them space, aware of the sacred bubble that surrounds them. I recall what Joy said about finding order amidst the chaos, and I'm delighted to not only witness that symbolism so clearly, but to actually feel that energy shift in myself, and my body tingles with the power that is omnipresent here. I swear the dust settles before them as they walk, bowing down to them like devotees offering prayers to priests.

)☼(

Sunset and sunrise are the best times to re-unite with campmates, and everyone seems to be at camp then, gearing up for the long night (or day) ahead. The changing of the sun and the moon mark new cycles every day, with new requirements for human comfort. The desert is harsh. The days are hot and the nights are cold. I replace my fishnet stockings with leggings, add a green see-through crocheted shirt, and a blue Chinese silk jacket, lined with white faux fur.

I eat three goji berries, drink a large can of coconut water, then an avocado and a pressed ecstasy pill for dinner. The ecstasy will soon flood my brain with serotonin, norepinephrine, and dopamine, stimulating my senses to turn the simplest touch into a religious experience. I fill up my flask with Fernet Branca, and hide it in my right boot pocket. In my left boot pocket go my organic cigarettes and a lighter. I ignite a handful of glow sticks and stick them in my messy bun, adding to the stones and bells and ribbons already woven into my half dreadlocks.

The stars are bright. They dance above me, suspended by invisible threads from the dark blue sky. The rising red moon is brighter than the stars. So bright, I think I can see the individual craters on the surface, waiting for the full eclipse, hours later.

With my wings on my back, I know I am safe. They make me invincible. I take off alone and on foot, leaving behind the competitive story-telling theatrics of Rico, Archinta, and Torque. No one notices my leaving and so, no one says goodbye.

)☼(

Alone without Marson to guide me, the roads confound me. I get lost a few times before I find Esplanade, but once there I can use The Man as my guide as I set off through the center playa, passing on the north side of him, aiming for 2:00, where I have friends camping at a sound camp called Cy-Top.

Again, I do not stop at The Man, choosing instead to admire him from the distance. During the day, he loomed tall, as a wooden colossus, with a backdrop of open desert and mountains. Now at night, he is brilliantly lit with green light. Behind him are stars and the moving city. Like The Man, the city has drastically changed for the night.

Lights of all colors have taken over the horizon; lasers shine at all angles, trying to reach the stars above, getting caught in the dark matter that separates earth from heaven, fantasy from reality. In front of the cityscape are more lights: lights from the art cars roaming free, and lights from individual commuters on bikes or small vehicles. Just like in a real city, everyone is on their own schedule, anxious to get somewhere.

)☼(

It must take me over an hour, but finally I find Cy-Top and my friend and sometimes lover, North, who is doing sound-checks. North is tall and skinny, with bright green eyes; his hands, musician's hands, deft and wise; his pale sun-bleached blonde Southern California surfer hair, loose and sloppy dreadlocks. He's perfect for right now. I watch him work, through my dilating eyes, as his aura grows blue and then green. When he sees me, he hugs me tightly and whispers into my ear, "Welcome home."

His home, Cy-Top is a real, organized community camp, with planned conscious hip-hop and world music parties slated for later in the week. Although it's already been building for days, it's not completely set up. There are two large domes: one a personal backstage lounge area, made of giant PVC pipes, and another to house the dance floor, next to the street, made of metal pipes. There are boxes upon boxes of fabric, hardware, speaker cables, and who-knows-what else. I love watching everyone work together, running about immersed in mini projects, stopping to chat and laugh. Again I am struck by the same deep human connection I experienced earlier sitting together and telling stories, but here it is evidenced instead by working side-by-side.

))☼((

When North is free, we adventure off together into uncharted territories, hitching a ride on a giant purple double decker bus. We climb up, not sure what to expect, and discover a fur covered interior with couples and groups engrossed in the beauty of one another; a psychedelic play party rages inside.

Between sips of Fernet, we steal kisses and giggle about the absurdity and beauty of life and of love. Each of us has had our hearts broken this year, by people we loved and trusted. Through mutual heartache, we find solace in each other's arms.

There are no plans to fall in love, but isn't every moment love anyway? It feels good to love each other, especially while covered in pixie dust, tripping, in a moving purple palace, wearing magic wings.

Our connection is different from what I thought love was supposed to be, the deep soul yearning, the fairy-princess dreams of happily-ever-after juxtaposed with long nights crying in pain alone, my own identity so wrapped up in another that I no longer had any room for myself. But here, with this kind man whom I love but am not in love with, I am myself, and I begin to recognize the many forms that love may enter. Maybe love is just a breath, a moment, a blink of the eye in the present. Maybe love really can exist without jealousy, without ownership, without pain.

I lose myself in his green jade eyes, just as I lost myself hours ago, in the moon, memorizing every detail I can before I am forced to blink. We climb up to the top of the car, to watch the world roll by. Flames shoot out in the distance. I pull an ecstasy tablet from my belt, bite it in two halves and feed North one, saving the other for myself. We use the last of my Fernet to swallow them.

The car winds its way to the 10:00 side of the playa, and we hop off, making our way back to my camp.

)☼(

The moon is high overhead and glowing luminescent bright, so bright that we use its light to see our way down the streets. When we get to camp, no one is home. I raid the kitchen and my drug box, find more Fernet, and more ecstasy, and we climb up on top of the van to moon-gaze.

"Isn't there supposed to be an eclipse tonight?" asks North.

"Yes! There is! What a perfect clear night for it!" I agree snuggling up to him and feeding him another pill, a full one this time. The natural energy is already so intense, that it overpowers the chemicals; it's hard to separate sensations.

We stare at the moon, and have no idea whether the eclipse is happening. I'm not sure I know what an eclipse is. . . North tries to explain it to me, and gets lost in the spinning stars. We begin to kiss again, deeper this time, bodies pulsing against each other. The still night air begins to pulse with us.

Up until this point there hasn't been any wind; now it begins, as if a part of the music. I push away for a moment to catch my breath.

My vision begins to blur with the serotonin rush to my brain, as I come up on the second pill.

Or is it my third?

"I want to make love in the middle of a storm, while we come up on ecstasy," I slowly announce, drawing each syllable out, not so much for emphasis, but because speaking is suddenly a new sensation. Each word, each breath has new depth, as it rolls through the corners of my mouth and escapes between my lips, into the universe.

We move into my tent and I get my wish. The wind blows harder, shaking the sides of the tiny, flimsy structure. My carefully organized piles of clothes are undone; my mattress, completely deflated. Dust blows in under the rain flap, coating us and my possessions. None of this matters, compared to the sensations of human touch, release, and bodily worship.

We finish, intertwined, on top of the crumbled plastic mattress and tangled tutus. Words no longer have meaning, as we lie in our nylon bubble of post-coital, chemically-enhanced ecstasy.

Each speck of dust in the tent glows like a firefly.

I watch them dance with each other in awe, until I slowly come back into my body.

I am camped near the road and soon become aware of voices on it, telling jokes, telling stories.

MONDAY: *The Long Road Home*

"It's on fire!"

". . . my friend saw it, they're trying to put it out now."

"I heard it was someone from Thunderdome."

"The Man! Burn, baby, burn!"

"North . . . are you awake?" I nudge him. "Are you listening to this?"

"No way . . . Can't be true. It's only Monday. They burn The Man on Saturday."

And then Spruce Man knocks on the tent (not that you can really knock on a tent so much as shake it).

"They burned The Man! You guys in there?"

"Yes! Hold on!" I jump up, pulling on shorts. "No fucking way!?" I say as I unzip the tent and hop out, barefoot and topless, to hear what has happened.

"Yo, Spruce Man!" says North, joining me, wearing just his pants, and giving his long-lost brother a hug. Our camp is home again and quickly we reconnect.

They, along with Rico, Archinta, and Serene congregate in our living room, drinking *puer* and whiskey, and debating the politics of The Man's burn. The parachute has collapsed in the small storm, so navigating the living area requires punching it up, as you go. After verifying that the rumors are true, I head back to my tent to gear up for another adventure. I find my boots, socks, and something to cover my bare chest. I locate my cigarettes, refill my flask, chug some water, stash sunglasses and mushrooms in my pockets, grab my magic wings, and I'm ready.

We head out towards The Man, or what is left of him. Even from the Esplanade, I can see flashing lights and the blockade set up around his remains. Spruce Man saw the whole thing, and tells us about the spectacle of the early burn: how the fire trucks couldn't get close enough to the fire to put it out because the shaded oasis under The Man blocked them. The trucks spewed out gallons of precious water aimed at the flames, but by the time they hit their target, the water pressure wasn't strong enough to extinguish it.

Up close, we see that The Man is now black. There are no more radiant green lights on him, rather there are spotlights set up, facing him, so that the crews can access the damage and initiate a repair plan. This is the first time in Burning Man's twenty-one years that The Man has burned early. We are witnessing counter-culture history in the making. For years, there will be stories traded about this night. I eat another pill.

The night has taken on a new energy, an escalation of unchecked hedonism, stimulated by the full blood moon and blatant disrespect for the community's sacred symbol. There are no rules anymore, and yet, even in the chaos, I am surrounded by community and I feel safe. I know that when I need water, it is there. I know if I need a hand to hold, any stranger would oblige. The vandalism of The Man has taken us farther away from the outside world; it has united us.

)☼(

We find ourselves in a large outdoor dance club; the speakers pump out sound and energy, while fire shoots out in bursts from invisible cauldrons. The faces of my friends change from red and luminous to dark and subdued as they move to the infinite beat. We shed our jackets, leaving them in a pile on the ground as the crowd moves us, first this way, and then the other. The music is magic, uniting strangers and making them fast friends. I dance until my feet can't move anymore and then I find North.

The two of us leave the lights and the music. We don't speak as we walk, hands clasped. The dark sky has begun to brighten slightly as we walk to The End of the World. I shiver in the desert air, coldest now in this hour before dawn.

The End of the World is marked by an orange trash fence. The playa here is different from the one I have begun to know. I am now used to the omnipresent dust, but here, it is condensed, hard and cracked, extending far into the horizon in non-symmetrical geometric shapes.

At the End of the World, we find a lone structure. It is a metal geometric shelter, a dark blue-gray, almost exactly the same as the sky. We duck through the entry and find a secret world. The ground is lined with Astro turf. In the center is another metal structure, painted the same color as the outside. Three others are in here: two asleep on the ground; the third, in a trance, leaning up against something in the middle. I approach, and it feels like walking towards a speaker, although I don't hear anything. When I reach out to touch it, the vibration pulses through me like an electrical current, yet it is soothing and calming, like a cat's purring.

A pair of eyes, just below me, refocuses to make contact with mine. Someone smiles. "Welcome home," he says softly.

I remove my wings and sit down next to him, resting my back on the vibrating healing machine. Unzipping his dusty backpack, he pulls out a whipped cream canister, silently unscrews the top, pops in a nitrous oxide cartridge, and re-screws it until the familiar scratchy sound of the gas releasing fills the tiny structure. Inhaling the whole load in one breath, he then hands me the canister and two cartridges, before his eyes glaze over again and he enters another dimension.

I hand one cartridge to North and repeat the process of releasing the mildly anesthetic gas into the canister, and close my eyes, retreating into my own dimension of consciousness. I dance and swirl to a melody that has flown through the desert to me:

> *Welcome home… welcome home… welcome home… this is your home… you are home… you can never go home again… home… home is where the heart is… fly away home… use your wings… your wings will take you home…*

My eyes blink open before I realize I have fallen asleep. My body had found its way to the ground, using a backpack as a pillow. North is curled up nearby, in fetal position. It is brighter now, if not warmer. I grab my wings and leave the structure, walking alone to the trash fence, just in time to see the sun rise over the mountains.

I have survived my first full day at Burning Man.

MONDAY: *The Long Road Home*

TUESDAY

Further Down the Rabbit Hole

The choice is yours,
conform,
or live your life
as if your life
depended on it.

CHOKING SLIGHTLY, I FORCE MYSELF TO eat some hippie oat pellets in warm organic soy milk for breakfast. "Human maintenance" is what Rico calls it. The necessary things we must do for our bodies, to keep them not only functioning, but in a fit enough state to stay up all night in the desert, dancing and drinking. My human maintenance also includes brushing my teeth, chugging a half gallon of water, and changing into a crocheted bikini.

I collapse into a bean bag chair in our living room, while Torque lectures me on the importance of purchasing goji berries organic, not noticing the irony of how his dogmatic health quest contradicts the first aid kit full of synthetic drugs he holds in his hand. I politely nod my head when necessary; holding it upright is hard. I've had about an hour of sleep, if my estimate of the time I spent at the installation in the deep playa is at all correct.

I could try to rest, but the very thought of it seems like admitting defeat. Sleep is for quitters, and I have nowhere to go. My tent feels like a sauna, and looks like an explosion in a brothel. I've tried to make friends with Archinta, but she seems utterly confused at my interest and niceties. I have a hard time with pessimists like her and Torque; I don't get how they can be so negative, and they don't seem to trust my bubbly optimism. I'm not sure why I am so socially bubbly and infatuated with altruism. I have this childlike belief that if I treat others with kindness, then they will treat me the same. I haven't quite proven this theory yet, but I'm still committed to testing it, against all odds.

As I yawn excessively, one of my neighbors interrupts Torque's organic tirade to offer me an upper. "Hey Alice, want the yellow pill or the blue pill?" I choose the blue, without asking what it is, and within fifteen minutes, I perk up and begin pacing spastically.

I need to get out of here. There's so much to do! Time to play!

)☼(

I take Spruce Man to barhop. There is no official barter system nor money exchanged at Burning Man (except, I recently learned, for a coffee bar at Center Camp, and ice distributors the organization offers); rather, there is a "gift economy." Gifts are given freely without any expectation of reciprocation. Gifts vary from lip-balms, to outdoor nightclub admissions, to tickets. Alcohol is, and will always be, one of the most popular gifts. I have brought many of my own gifts to dispense—hand-sewn leather pouches, dream catchers, crystals, and tea.

I didn't realize I was supposed to bring my own cup for the bars—apparently, it's a common courtesy in this society that I'm still learning the rules of—and when we arrive at the first bar, a lavender oasis underneath a few tapestries, the bartender, Loveless, gifts me a cup. She is in her forties, and is wearing a lavender dress and a bright orange cowboy hat.

"Okay," she says, "I'm going to give you this pink princess cup, but you have to promise to carry it with you all week. Most bartenders won't be as nice as me. My name might be Loveless, but no one can say I don't have any love."

"I promise." I cross my heart. "What should I drink?" I ask.

She takes my cup and fills it with lavender liquid. "Lavender vodka lemonade, of course." She smiles at me as she hands me the cup. "How's your vacation going?"

"Vacation?" asks Spruce Man. "Is this a vacation?"

She laughs and points to a sticker above the bar. It reads:

MY VACATION IS YOUR WORST NIGHTMARE)'(

I laugh out loud, as well. "This is not a vacation. This is an adventure." When I think vacation, I think of a place where there are no responsibilities, where whims are catered to, where it's clean. Here, doing anything is a glorious struggle. Going to the bathroom requires a bike ride and a nose plug. A thin layer of dust covers everything in sight.

She smiles again. "I agree. This is only a vacation in the sense that it is an escape from the mundane. Typical vacations are founded on caste systems and roleplaying. The only way to take care of our needs is to pay for it. Why work all year to spend two weeks paying someone else to make our beds, cook our food, serve us drinks, drive us around . . . ? Where is the fulfillment in that?" I don't have an answer, so I just shrug.

She continues: "So here's the thing . . . Who are we really? In the default world, we size one another up, based on our clothing and careers. We go through life, being taught how to conform, how to fit into a box. We learn to base our worth on credentials, false images, and a bank account. Some people fall into this trap, and begin to see themselves as nothing more than these material things. So, what happens when we remove these things? What happens when we enter a world where limits are pushed, and we can be anyone we want to? This concept can be incredibly liberating, or frightening. Who are we without these social defaults? In this world where pushing the limits is celebrated and uniqueness is favored, we have the chance to reinvent ourselves."

"So," I wonder out loud in response: "Who am I?"

Spruce Man easily answers, "You're our Fun Fairy!"

"Oooh, I like that! Can that be my playa name?" Some people choose to go by their given names, and others instead use special names just for Burning Man. "But, that still doesn't answer my question. Who am I?"

Loveless laughs again. I'm enjoying her laugh; it's radiant and unashamed. "Only you, my darling, can answer that question. All I can tell you is that you're on the right track. Never stop searching, and never stop blessing the world with that gorgeous smile of yours." She moves on to make drinks for a tie-dye-wearing couple, settling in next to us.

I finish my drink, grab Spruce Man, and head out, questions still swirling in my head.

Are we our clothing? Are we our actions? Are we our thoughts?

TUESDAY: *Further Down the Rabbit Hole*

Are we the people we touch? What is under all that? What should I drink next?

"I feel like it's a trick question," says Spruce Man, reading my mind. "I mean there can't just be one single answer to 'who am I?' It's way more complicated than that."

"I feel like I'm more than one person, sometimes. Just by playing dress up, I can be whomever I wish. But I don't think that's what she meant, did she? She meant something deeper?"

"I think she did," answers Spruce Man, "But luckily, we have five more days here to figure it out, and something tells me another drink will help."

We are outside a hodgepodge island-themed bar. A blue reflective sheet stretches from an RV to tall poles, staked into the playa. Underneath the makeshift shade is a tiki bar, AstroTurf, and an eclectic collection of dusty couches.

The tiki bar specializes in mojitos, so that is what we order. The thought of drinking muddled mint and ice-cold rum in the middle of the desert, while wearing magic wings, feels incredibly indulgent and unreal.

"Doesn't it feel like everything is here just for us? Like this is a dream that we created to give us exactly what we want? Like it's all just synchronicity?" I ask Spruce Man.

"Synchronicity?" a man next to me interrupts our conversation. He's slim, wearing simple ankle-high boots made of scratched leather, ragged jean shorts that look expensive, a cut-off black t-shirt with the arms fully exposed, and Gucci ski goggles, shoved up on his head like a headband. In one hand is a lit cigarette and in the other a martini glass.

"Why yes, perhaps you've heard of it? It seems to be everywhere!" I giggle and wave my glass, spilling a tiny bit of my mojito in the process.

He laughs a cultured laugh like he's at a gala at the country club, and then makes a soft bird sound. "Birds do it seamlessly. We can too. It's very simple."

I imagine him as a pretentious quail. "As are most simple things . . ." I counter.

"Yes, simple things tend to be simple." Spruce Man agrees.

"Fucking exactly! If you understand simple synchronicity, then you understand it all. When you create a bubble of people, all here for the same reason, we create a magic realm, where anything is possible." He laughs again, making that quail coo.

"You don't seem simple." I laugh an awkward laugh and take another drink out of my princess cup.

"Ha ha! Well I'm not simple, but synchronicity is. It's this: we are just the portals for magic. We are just the portals for information, flowing through us. When we tap into this fully, when we are in places like this, radiating with spectrums of energy. . ." He trails off and laughs again. The bartender tops off his drink. "Can I have some olives too?" he asks flirtatiously, and of course she obliges (only they are not olives she places in his glass, they are pickles, but this detail doesn't seem important to anyone but me).

"Wait, so why are we here? The playa is about contribution, right? What can I do to help orchestrate this?"

"Get the fuck out of the way," he says, deadpan. He

sees my face fall, and he softens again. "It's just information, and we are just the holders. YOU are the holder. You are the question and you are the answer. Stop trying to analyze and understand it. Just accept and release and enjoy. Have a martini, laugh at the bullshit, accept and release."

I must look confused, as I ponder this new knowledge, and he tries to explain: "Just accept you are in between the truth and the vessel. Stop thinking and just be."

I furrow my brow, trying to think about how *not* to think, and it's very difficult.

"STOP! You're overthinking not thinking! Just drink your mojito, and jingle your wings, and get the fuck out of the way. Now, if you'll excuse me, I have a shibari workshop to attend." He kisses both of us on the cheek, opens a torn lace parasol, and struts off into the dust.

I'm still thinking about how not to think, and this process seems to contradict itself by nature. I can't imagine a world inside of my head devoid of words, although I think that would be peaceful. The words never cease, chattering and narrating my life at every waking moment, even conversing between themselves, until I have no idea what I really think, or who I truly am. *Which voice is the holder? Which voice is the key? Which knows the correct answer to the puzzle that is my life?*

"So, tell me about these wings of yours, Fun Fairy!" says Spruce Man, who seems as taken aback from the conversation as I am. I come out of my head and back to the bar, happy to lighten up and change the conversation back to frivolity.

BURNING WINGS

"I thought I did! They're magic, in case you were wondering. They keep away the darkness, and make people smile. Look at all the pretty things on them." I take them off, so Spruce Man can look at them up close, and I can point out all the details: the rose quartz for love, the amethyst for calming, the tiger eye for power. . . .

I feel a hand on my shoulder, and turn around, it's Flook! I squeal in excitement, jump off my chair, and almost spill my drink.

"Flook! I'm so happy you're here! Spruce Man! This is Flook who bought me my ticket! Flook! Everything you said about this place is right. It's everything and yet there aren't enough words to describe it all!"

Flook has the darkest and kindest eyes I've ever seen. He is dressed simply, in Carhartts, a tattered bleach stained T-shirt with a skull, and huge dusty boots. His dark and thick hair is almost shoulder length and pushed back behind his big ears. His smile is still large and contagious and seems to stretch to the edges of his already wide and round face.

He envelopes me in a large bear hug, and I find my breath calming with my cheek pressed into his chest, listening to his heart beat like a steady drum. When my heart has slowed to match his own, he senses it, and gently pulls away, placing his hands on my shoulders so we can lock eyes.

"I told you, you were supposed to be here. I'm glad this is medicine for you too." There's a twinkle in his eyes, mischief combined with wisdom. One hand reaches around me to touch my wings. "Did you make these?" He asks, to which I nod. "They're beautiful. I'm glad to see you put in the time and intention with your own hands. I'm sick of seeing native crafts made in China and sold to unsuspecting hippies. Did you know that most crafts sold as 'native' are actually made in China or overseas? Fucking drives me crazy. It's like Burning Man's gifting principle, all these people coming with these generic plastic mass-produced toys made overseas. Gifts should be authentic, useful, handmade, or if you can't make them yourself, at least support local artists."

"I love the gifting, and giving gifts. I didn't bring much, but I brought art supplies and tea."

"Speaking of a drink . . ." He unclips his dented metal camping cup, and when our bartender comes back over, she smiles with nostalgia and reaches over the bar to hug him, shorter but even deeper than how he hugged me.

"It's good to see you. Ready for some moonshine?" Without waiting for a reply, from an unmarked plastic bottle, she pours who-knows-what into his cup and into a shot glass of her own. She nods to him and watches with amusement as he swigs it without flinching.

"Nicely done Flook. Not your first rodeo. Here's to 1997!" She raises her glass to him, and then gulps it down herself, shaking her head as it goes down her throat before ducking away to serve a naked man a few stools down.

Flook grins. "Ha, that was back in the day!"

"What was your first year?" Asks Spruce Man.

"1995. Different world. Less than three thousand people, no tickets, no roads, a small center camp. It was like coming across a band of desert nomads."

"Wow. I can't imagine. What a different world. I think

64

the first time I heard about Burning Man was when my father was trying to get rid of an old couch in our garage. It must have been around 1995 as well. . . . About the same time I went to my first Rainbow Gathering. It was nothing like this though! Anyway, he said he wished he knew someone going to Burning Man so he could give them the couch to use and then burn. Then he told me a little about having to bring in all your supplies to the desert. That's so funny I just remembered that." I smile, lost in memories of me as a little girl, with no idea how prophetic that small interaction would turn out to be.

"How are your supplies?" Asks Flook. "Did you bring enough food and water?"

"I think so. I hope so." Now I'm calculating my goji berry and granola stash. I have two gallons of water a day at least.

"The playa provides!" Says Spruce Man, raising his drink.

Flook laughs, not cruelly but with irony.

"I really dislike 'the playa provides'—the playa provides one thing, *playa*. If you want something, bring it, and be prepared to share. But don't come into this community, or any community, expecting to be provided for. It's not about what the playa provides, it's about what you can provide. *You are the playa.*"

Spruce Man takes a sip of his drink, slightly abashed. "I didn't mean that I expect anything, it's just a thing that people say. It's rough here."

"Ha, yes, the playa is literally trying to kill you, or at least test you, to see if you can handle it. It's not an easy thing to go to, and it shouldn't be. That's one of the things that is so amazing about it. We come in to this insane desolate place and help one another."

Again I think of Joy Luck and her words, *what if humanity helped each other because we want to, not because we have to.*

I share this sentiment with Flook, and he smiles. "Yes! That's all it is! That's true communism, not that red state propaganda bullshit. True communism is true community. You give when you have extra, and you accept when you don't, but you don't expect any handouts."

"You helped me. I wouldn't be here if it weren't for you."

"You needed it. And it wasn't a handout. I fully expect that you will contribute."

"I want to! Is this land connected to your ancestors? I remember you mentioning you were Native American in San Francisco. I know that Pyramid Lake, the one we passed on the way in, is sacred land, right?" I lean in towards Flook, excited to discover that this magical man who gifted me my ticket has energetic ties to the magical wings I felt called to create.

"So, and I say this with love, there is a lot of ignorance from the white man about Native tribes." I blush a little, feeling silly and dumb for daring to think that the tribes are all connected, but he is not judging, just stating facts. "The local tribe here is the Paiute. There once were over five hundred unique tribes and communities in what we now consider America. My tribe is Yaqui, from Mexico, but

I was adopted. I can't claim a native upbringing, I grew up a privileged life in California, more privileged than yours from what you told me of your own childhood, without any connection to reservations or of any native struggle. All I know now about that I taught myself."

Spruce Man and I are entranced, his academic brain for the history, and mine for the stories of connection, *more stories of the things that make us human,* and I ask for more: "So how did you find yourself here? What was the draw? And how did you find your way to your ancestors? I wish I had a connection to my own, this place is the closest I've come to feeling like I belong to something larger than myself."

Flook nods. "I understand that. Something large was missing from my life, and I left that clean existence at fifteen to find more. I guess you can say the rave circus called me!"

Spruce Man raises his glass again, "To the rave circus!" And this time Flook matches his with his empty cup. I can tell that Spruce Man wants to start trading rave stories but he knows to wait, to allow this unique story to continue uninterrupted.

Flook obliges, "I worked every job I could that interested me; I became a part of rave culture, dance music culture, and Burning Man. I made it a mission to study and learn from native leaders. The connecting factor through all of this is the tribal principles of communism."

I nod. "I feel the spiritual connection here. It's deeper than anything I was ever taught in church, I want to soak it all up."

"Soak it up, but without service and activism, spiritual

quests are just self-absorbed. The metaphorical white man loves to think you can do anything with money, but you can't buy or sell spirituality. You can purchase spiritual experiences or emblems, but true spirituality is interwoven with reciprocal energy. It's like the way that the earth cannot be bought or sold. I think one of the biggest issues with Burning Man and 'civilization' alike, is a vast majority of people live ON the earth, rather than with it. Humans are the only animals who choose to not live in harmony with our mother, and not giving back to her will be our biggest downfall as a species."

Again, I nod in agreement. "Everything that touches me I yearn to share so I can give back. I brought supplies to share the art of making dreamcatchers because it brought me so much joy to make my own."

"I'm happy to see that you took the time to make these wings yourself instead of mass-ordering them. First gold playa star for you! Do you know about the legends of them?" We shift subjects naturally.

"Well, I always thought they were to catch the nightmares and let the good dreams through, but I found another story that I like even better."

"I would love to hear it."

"So, this is what I remember, and I'm sorry if I get it wrong." I pause, gulp another sip of my mojito, close my eyes, take a deep breath, and then I begin:

"A long time ago an old man lived on a mountain, high above the clouds. He was a shaman, a spiritual leader,

and visions came to him that he shared with his people. One day, a spider walked up to discuss the great mysteries of the world. As they spoke, the spider kept his hands busy, weaving a web onto the old man's sacred willow hoop.

"The spider just picked it up, without asking, and began to weave his web on it. The old man either didn't notice or didn't mind. I don't remember. What I do remember and can almost imagine, is how they spoke of the great cycles of life: of birth and death and all that comes between. Of how each end is just a new beginning, and how all beginnings come from endings. Of how amidst each stage, there is good and evil lurking, and of how each man or woman must decide for himself or herself which to worship.

"When the spider finished speaking, he passed his web to the wise man and said, 'This is my gift to you. This web is a perfect circle with a hole in the center. Use it wisely, inspire your people to follow in the harmony of nature, trusting and acting on their dreams and visions. The Great Spirit will filter the forces of good; trapping the bad forces in the web and allowing the good to grow.'"

Flook nods. "I like your interpretation of it, and happy you took the time to do some research. But it's never just good or evil, or darkness or light." He smacks his hand on the bar and grins. "Yes! You just reminded me of one of my favorite quotes by John Lee. That thing will always remain in my brain: 'Light is incomplete without darkness. One cannot exist without the other . . . Ride the dragon.' Darkness and light aren't necessarily opposing forces. Darkness wouldn't exist without light. It wouldn't be darkness. Just wait until you visit The Temple, you'll understand it all."

"I can't wait."

"Can I look at your wings?" A girl about my age with a blue mohawk and rust colored skin interrupts. "I love dreamcatchers."

"Of course." I remove them, and happily hand them over for her to try on. She is wearing shorts, tinier than my bikini bottoms, as well as a push-up bra, covered with plastic rhinestones of various sizes. "I like your sparkle bra. What's your name?"

"I'm Pony! We can bedazzle you, too!" She gestures over to an RV, where a group of girls play with hot-glue guns. From gallon zip-lock bags, full of beads and stones, set up on the top of an ironing board, they glue sparkly things onto the bra of a sleeping companion on a lawn chair, as they happily chatter.

"Can you please?" I ask gleefully, and then glance over at Flook. He laughs, "Go have fun! I have to get back to camp. There's always work to do."

I'm both happy and a little sad I have no work to get to, but perhaps bedazzling bras is work of its own. Spruce Man leaves to find a bathroom, and I follow Pony as she takes me over to introduce me to her companions, and soon the ribbons in my hair and the looms of my wings are covered with more beads than before. They admire my wings, and I tell them the story of their genesis.

I finish the last of my mojito before I have a burst of inspiration.

BURNING WINGS

"Hey! Does anyone want to make dreamcatchers? I'm camped a few blocks away, and I brought enough supplies for you all to make your own!" For one of my playa gifts, I have brought extra looms and supplies, so I can teach a class. I stub my cigarette out into an old Altoids tin. Littering on the playa is an extreme *faux pas*—this is a *Leave No Trace* event. There are no trash receptacles and each camp is responsible for removing its own rubbish, recycling, and even gray water. The playa must remain untouched. For months after the event, volunteers patrol the miles of desert the city builds on to locate every last stray cigarette, feather, beer top, and accidental offering left behind and covered under the dust.

Pony and one of her friends eagerly agree. We load up on mojitos before departing. Spruce Man is back and only too happy to leave with a trio of sparkly, giggling girls. We skip down the streets in unison, until we arrive back at our shanty home. Someone has thankfully repaired the fallen parachute, although it still hangs low in places.

After rummaging through my destroyed tent, I find my art supplies and create a studio of sorts on a miraculously inflated air mattress, underneath the sagging parachute shade cover. I tell the story of how the sticks came to me that dark and rainy night in San Francisco, and of how I took that treasure and made the looms. I take out my piles of colored yarn and embroidery thread, and begin a sample dreamcatcher for them. I show them how to keep the string taut with their fingers, and keep each stitch evenly spaced with the last, always striving to find balance, even amidst challenge. I spread my jewels and treasures over the air mattress, for them to personalize their own creations. My new friends begin the process of making their own designs and weaves. I set my own dreamcatcher down so I can lie down. The long day is catching up to me.

How am I so tired?

I curl up on the air mattress, listening to the giddy sounds of their chatter. In my short time here, I have already been given so much, I am happy to be able to return the favor.

I am home. I am exactly where I am supposed to be.

I'll just shut my eyes for a moment . . .

)☼(

I jolt awake. It is dark. Someone has covered me with a blanket. My students are long gone. A green fairy sits next to me.

"You're awake! I was hoping you would wake up! I had the most lovely day. I found a camp that does crystal healing and sound meditation. You should come with me tomorrow. Your friends said to say thank you for the dreamcatchers. We tried to wake you up but you were so tired, you didn't budge. I'm glad you're safe and home. How are you?" Serene is dressed head to toe in gauzy layers of green, and has green wings made of fake leaves. She is the exact embodiment of a classic wood fairy.

"I fell asleep." I state the obvious, disappointed in myself.

"Yes . . . human maintenance is necessary. I took acid so I doubt I'll sleep anytime soon. Torque took four hits. I'll have to find him soon, I imagine. . . . Would you like to go back to sleep or come play?"

"I want to play!" I respond, without having to think about it. I rummage through my tent, finding layers of ripped fishnet, the top stockings secured with a garter belt, a tutu, and a bottle of vodka, and I'm ready for more. By that time, Serene has disappeared, but Spruce Man is home.

What would I do without Spruce Man?

"I'm so happy you're here! Serene got me awake and riled up, but I guess she flitted away. Kind of rude, but how do you get mad at a fairy?" I realize then one major difference about Serene and myself is how confident she is in her own needs, and in the present. I decide she must have less voices in her head, or else she listened to the one that lives fully in the moment. *Maybe she's into shibari too like that guy today? They're both so unattached to obligation. I should find out what shibari is, maybe it's a Taoist thing?*

"Yeah, sounds like her. She'll turn back up when she's ready. Do you have any mushrooms easy? Mine are lost in one of my toolboxes," Spruce Man asks.

"For sure! Let me find them! Hey what's shibari?

I think I want to learn more about living in the moment."

Spruce Man laughs. "Oh I bet there's a few camps who would love to tie you up and teach you their ways. But tonight I want some bass!"

My faithful companion and I dip into my stash of

psilocybin mushrooms, choking down a few of the bitter and earthy dried fungi before we set off, making our way towards the sound camps on 10:00. The dried mushrooms, used for hundreds—or even thousands—of years for their hallucinogenic powers, have been a favorite of mine since high school, when I used to take them in the redwood forests I grew up in, playing in the trees with imaginary beings. Here it is different. Once again, the darkness has changed the city into nothing but light and sound. A giant lime green goldfish vibrates my chest bones with its subwoofers. A heart, shooting red lasers, practically blinds me.

"Fuck yes. I think Basshoney's playing! I want dirty. I want grimy. I want glitchy. I want hip-hop. And I want my face melted off by his bass. Let's go!" Spruce Man gets a dark twinkle in his eye, and I follow him across the street, where we are quickly lost in a giant dome on the corner of Esplanade. It's the biggest dome I've ever seen, at least fifty feet high in the center. Inside is an orgy of sensation. Lights, lasers, deep bass, cages, and scaffolding. Pulsating bodies are everywhere, and there is no way to get straight across. So instead, I dance through.

I flash back to a pearl of wisdom that my father passed on to me: "*You can never walk through a crowded dance floor; you have to dance through it.*" I think of his words often, when I'm packed in a tight nightclub, in a sea of beat and bass worshipers. There is a magic that happens sometimes on the dance floor, when everyone is on the same rhythm, and moves individually but simultaneously. Sweaty bodies brush up against one another, so synchronously, that there is always room for everyone's full expression in the close-knit crowd, and their bodies move without strain or restriction from their neighbors, everyone guided by a musical conductivity. And then someone will walk, push, or stumble through this perfect pulsating rhythmic groove, pop that bubble, and bring me back to the life I was trying to escape.

Speaking from experience, it's much more conducive, not to mention enjoyable to all involved, to dance through the dance floor. As in the default world, there is rarely a straight path. It is better to dodge and weave through, find the path of least resistance and minimal impact, to reach the final destination. It took me a long time to understand this kind of magic, to really learn how to let go of my insecurities and inhibitions, and feel peace on the dance floor.

Now I tap into this. The music takes over, and the lights cut into my eyeballs, whether my lids are closed or open. There is no escape, and I don't want one. My senses are obliterated by stimuli. My thoughts and the endless words that take over my head are pushed out into the void, replaced with pounding music and the unshakeable urge to move my body. The other people in the dome enhance this feeling, as they are of the same mindset. I dance and I dance and I dance. I dance inside. I dance outside. I dance on scaffolding. I dance in cages. I dance with strangers. I dance until I can't dance anymore.

Music is the driving force for so much openness and acceptance. Why would anyone want to fight anything, when acceptance and love will go so much further? What does a straight line serve, when it is thwarted with resistance and contention? Why would any smart, sane, or intuitive human being, want to make life more difficult, when there is a simpler and better way? Why would anyone shove through the dance floor, and not just dance through it?

The dance floor is a metaphor for life, a place where time can only exist in the present.

After minutes or hours, I need water, a bathroom, and a cigarette, in that exact order, and after finding Spruce Man in the crowd, we make our way out of the dome, tripping over the piles of bikes piled out front, and then down the now familiar city streets, dodging the multitudes of scintillating creatures that float by us.

The plastic bathrooms are at the corner, marked by a high blue light, and once inside, I feel more confused than I did in the club itself. The scratches, stickers, and writing on the walls seems like they must be messages placed there by the gods just for me, but I can't quite figure out what language everything is in, nor will any of it hold still. Finally I decide some things are better left unknown, but when I get up I can't remember if I should pull up my panties, fishnets, or tutu first, and figuring out the complexities of my costume without allowing my tutu to touch the walls, seems like a ridiculous task, so I open up the door and walk out with my tutu around my waist and everything else on my ankles. The cold air rushes against my face and bare legs, and I stand on the dust, laughing hysterically.

Here, finally, I get all the layers up in the right order, without twisting any of the garter straps. *This is my great accomplishment of the night.*

BURNING WINGS

Spruce Man is on the corner waiting, oblivious to the struggle I just overcame, and since it's too complicated to describe to him, I just cling to his arm for support, for my vision is blurred and the lights seem to have taken on new expressions. Away from the crowded dance floor, the night has grown colder, so we stop to warm ourselves by a communal fire pit.

A large metal trash bucket has been welded into a round shadowbox where cut-outs of birds and flowers expose burning embers and wood. It is surrounded by people, hovering and sharing the cozy heat the fire radiates. As the flames light up their faces, everyone looks very old. Something about the angle of the light, highlighting every possible wrinkle, the wrinkles seeming to deepen and osculate into each other.

Spruce Man begins a monologue about trance music, and how dubstep is trying to take over. I'm distracted by the fire, and the mutating rainbow wrinkles, so I just smile and nod. No matter how many DJs and producer friends I collect, I can never seem to keep track of the various micro genres going on. Dubstep, at least, is distinct, and if I can't decide if dubstep is dubstep, I think of octopuses farting, and then I get my answer.

"Who wants to listen to octopuses fart all night?" he asks, I'm not sure if he's talking to me or himself. I giggle. *He read my mind.*

"It's better than psytrance at least," I manage to respond. Psytrance is all that our campmates listen to, and I just can't figure out its allure. "It sounds like drunken aliens trying to beatbox."

"Fucking dubstep. It will never catch on, you watch. Give me breaks, all day every day, please." A girl, standing next to us, overhears and laughs, as she turns to us. "How's your burn going?"

"Amazing! Just danced our asses off in the Seizure Dome and now we're exploring. How about yours?" Spruce responds.

"Pretty badass, so far. My friends and I built a giant sunflower windmill we're going to install in the deep playa tomorrow." I notice she is wearing sunflowers all over her garden hat, and her cargo pants are also decorated with sunflowers, made of puff paint.

"More breaks! I love breaks!" I try to enter the conversation, but my contribution is now about two interactions irrelevant (mushrooms always seem to destroy my conversational skills), so I decide not to try anymore; the fire and the rainbows are more entertaining, anyway.

"Where about in the deep playa? It's endless out there. I feel like I could get lost, away from the city." Spruce Man picks a fallen sunflower up from the ground and hands it to her. When she reacts, her smile-lines distort even more, and I watch in amazement as they slither away from her face. "I bet there are lost hippies that live in the mountains year-round!" Spruce Man continues.

The Sunflower woman looks at me, and her eyes are yellow like sunflowers, with tiny black speckles in them. "Funny you should say that. . . On our drive in we picked up a hitchhiker in Reno. Young hippie boy, he had a backpack and a few gallons of water. No ticket. The shit you do when you're young!" She shakes her head. "When we got to Gerlach, he told us to stop and he hopped out of the car. Said he was called to walk from there."

"Gerlach? That small town we drove through with the last gas station? Isn't that miles away?" The fire is alive. The sparks reverse cascade into the sky and turn into stars.

"Yep. People are a special kind of crazy here. I wouldn't put it past that little hobbit boy to make it here safe and sound, I've been praying for him."

She lights up a joint and offers it to us.

"It's so desolate, though. Nothing grows here," Spruce Man says, as I take a giant puff of the joint (holding back my cough) and pass it along. "I mean how could anyone survive here?"

"Nope. Nothing grows. That's a fact. You know about the playa? Its pH?" she says. I stop to touch the ground, pick up a bit of the loose dust, and watch it float away, as I sprinkle it back on the ground. I have a sudden urge to build giant sandcastles, and to crawl inside of them, *inside* of the playa. I laugh thinking about this, about how people like to live on the earth, when really they should be living inside of it, or at least with it.

"Alkaline, right? The opposite of acidic?" I studied this in school, and can't remember anything about its specifics. I wish I could speak; luckily, Spruce Man seems to be saying what I would say, if I could.

"Yeah, it's not only super alkaline, it's also got crazy mineral properties. The rain falls down all those mountains, taking minerals with it, and then it pools on the playa. When the sun dries it, the water evaporates and the minerals remain." I nod my head in agreement, even though I'm still thinking about my sandcastles. "The playa is magic. It's electromagnetic, alkaline and mineral dense. There isn't anywhere else like this on earth. No fucking wonder everything is so weird here."

"It's definitely weird. And I'm ready to get weirder," says Spruce Man.

"Oh, you want to get weird, do you?" asks Sunflower Lady. "Try the absinthe bar, down the street. They'll take good care of you." Tiny, gently glowing fireflies swarm her sunflower hat. I'm hoping they will follow us as we leave, but they don't.

)☼(

We find the green absinthe bar; it's about a block away next to a giant red tire-swing. There is a multi-page menu of the many flavors available, and it lists everything from fruity strawberry-watermelon, to soothing licorice-mint, to the more obscure jalapeño-thyme-apple.

Absinthe is a distilled, robust alcoholic spirit, made from various herbs, including wormwood, fennel, and anise. It has mild hallucinogenic effects, and was favored by late Parisian artists, writers, and revolutionaries, thus creating a bohemian allure that extends to this day. It is referred to as *la fée verte* in French, or *the green fairy*. Legend says that after drinking enough absinthe, a green fairy will appear to guide you deeper into enlightenment. Strange to think that I've already seen one green fairy guide today, but rather than guiding me, she left me for an acid binge.

We find seats at the long green bar, under a green light. The bar is covered with green tapestries and green Christmas lights. When we finally get the bartender's attention, his teeth glow green, as he grins. His name is The Wiz, and he, along with his camp, has spent the last year making this endless selection of absinthe, just so he can serve it to us now. The Wiz is large and lumberjack-like, with broad shoulders, a protruding belly, and a full beard. He moves methodically, as he expertly prepares our drinks. He scans the back bar (each of the bottles is a recycled liquor or wine bottle, labeled with masking tape), grabs two, and then takes our glasses to rinse. He places my princess cup and Spruce Man's metal coffee mug on the bar, pours an ounce or two of green liquid into each one. He places a small antique slotted spoon across my cup and sets a sugar cube on it. He takes a metal pitcher from under the bar and drizzles a clear liquid slowly over the spoon, causing the sugar to melt. He gives it a quick stir, and then passes it to me, while he repeats the same process on Spruce Man's.

It tastes like springtime debauchery. The flavors are rich and fresh inside my mouth; they gently warm me as I swallow my first sip. We finish our drinks quickly, order more, then more again. Somewhere around our fourth glass, after a few more mushroom caps, the green takes over, and Spruce Man's green skin grows scales and shimmers in the twinkling green light. I look down at my own hand and am astonished to see that it, too, has grown its own iridescent scales, although mine are smaller and smoother than Spruce Man's, like the underside of a tropical fish. I touch my rainbow-scaled arm and it is smooth and cold.

"Spruce Man . . ." I whisper, "Do you see the green scales?" I present my forearm, and he takes it in his hand.

"You're tripping, and your skin is looking a bit mermaid-like. Check out this vein," he replies, as he traces the tiny vein paths on my hand, amidst the scales.

"No! I mean! Do you see it?" I don't know how to fully communicate my own thoughts, nor alert him to the fact that his eyes have now turned yellow and reptilian.

The Wiz returns to us. His jade scales are larger and rougher than ours and remind me of an alligator's. When he opens his mouth to speak, his long, forked tongue unrolls like a carpet.

"So, sillies. I hope you appreciate the green here. It is apparently—I did not know this a year ago— very difficult to consistently procure anytime, except for December. So, all of the green lights here and the green decor, we got by staking out Christmas sales and garage sales." He loses his train of thought, and stares longingly off into the distance. Then he remembers we are here and continues: "I know this is not the most brilliant conversation in the world, but it's late and shit's weird and why not? I wanted to share with you this piece of this camp you have become fond of." I have no idea what he is talking about, but there is quite a lot of green in the bar, and I can appreciate that. "There's so much more than meets the eye here. Every camp you see, you have no idea of the effort it took for them to come. Even the shittiest rundown camp still took days of organizing, transporting, and set-up. It's amazing what people will do for the chance to live in the fucking dust for a week. Like spend a small fortune on green Christmas lights."

I feel as though I am inside one of my favorite childhood books, *The Wonderful Wizard of Oz.*

"You know how in Emerald City, in *Wizard of Oz*, everything is green? Well, in the real book, before the movie, when Dorothy and the Lion and the whole gang make it to Emerald City, it's not really green. . . See, they have these glasses that they attach permanently to everyone's heads. The glasses have green lenses. So, it's just an illusion. Understand? It's not real. It's just an illusion. But it feels so real. It feels so green." As I say this, I realize that the green here and the scales may not be real.

Maybe this is just an illusion. But, it has to be real!

I reach over to touch The Wiz's rough forearm, and sure enough, his tough scales vibrate my fingers as I run them down the length of his arm towards his hand. He catches my rainbow hand in his, looks me in the eye, suddenly completely coherent, and says, "Illusion and reality are just two sides of the same coin. Sometimes reality is real to one person, but an illusion to another. We all exist in our own realities, our own illusions. Who are we to tell someone else that their pain, their love, their experience isn't real? We can only control our own realities, our own minds. And perhaps, all that prayer and manifestation is is the creation of a web of illusion so thick, that it blinds us permanently. We are all just stuck in a beautiful dream. Enjoy it. Fuck whoever says it isn't real. Fuck whoever wants you to conform."

A tiny green fairy levitates just over his right shoulder. I wish I could make out her features, but every time I focus on her, she vanishes.

"Who is to say who is correct? Are you virgins?" Spruce Man and I nod. "Just wait until you get back to the default world. Then you'll begin to see real illusion. It's on the television, in the news, on every piece of concrete. They will tell you that this place is just an illusion. They'll tell you we're the crazy ones for wanting more, for daring to dream. The choice is yours, conform, or live your life as if your life depended on it. Welcome down the rabbit hole, kiddos. It's only Tuesday, and it only gets weirder from here."

WEDNESDAY

Pain is Real.
Blood is Real.

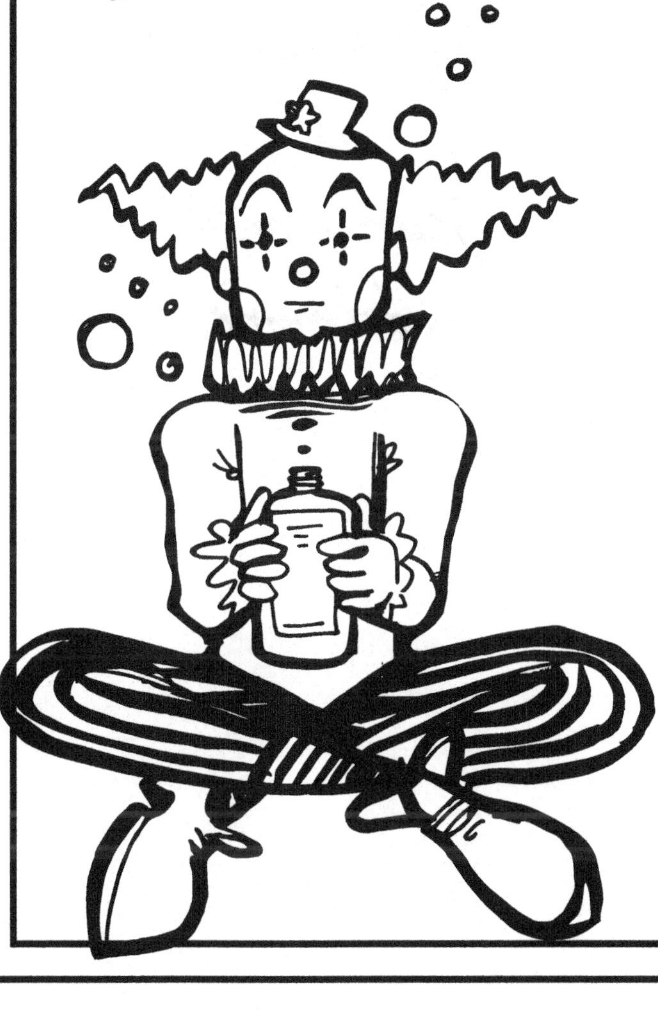

My vacation
is
your worst
nightmare.

DANCING WITH FIRE FEELS LIKE dancing with the devil: it's a rush like no other, a delicious dismantling of the illusion of fear, and a transcendence into the resulting world of ego-filled complacency. The first time I saw anyone spin fire, I was entranced. I couldn't believe that anything could be so beautiful, so dangerous, and so sensual all at once. There are many mediums used to spin fire—balls on strings, hula hoops, fans—but I always have and always will love the staff the most. After being first introduced to it, I wasn't sure how to go about getting my own fire staff, but then an old dreadlocked man gave me one at a drum circle at Hippie Hill in San Francisco's Golden Gate Park. It was just a piece of bamboo, about five feet long, with torn up fabric tied to either end; but it was enough for me to teach myself on. I taped non-slip webbing I got at a dollar store to the center for grip, and duct taped the ends to weight it.

I practiced every chance I got, making up tricks and sequences as I went along to compliment the few that an old lover left with me. I used to borrow his "real" fire staff, and it was with his that I first lit up using fuel and fire; now I am ready for my own fire. I have brought a five-foot hollow aluminum pole and eight feet of Kevlar wick with me, trusting that someone will help me build it. Burning Man is the quintessential place to find people to help you build fire toys, and in perfect synchronicity, just a few blocks away is a staff building workshop, where the guide book given to me upon entry promises supplies and construction support.

I have slept two hours, eaten a half a piece of quesadilla, and drunk a few cups of *sencha* (grassy and super green Japanese tea), for breakfast. I'm wearing a white knit tank dress with nothing underneath but white panties. Like always, I have my wings and platform boots on.

Within an hour, I am the proud owner of a brand new handmade fire staff. On each end, rather than duct tape, are two tightly wrapped rolls of Kevlar. I have pounded the nails into the Kevlar myself, attaching them to the wooden dowel inside the hollow aluminum. The middle of the staff is carefully covered with blue bicycle grip tape and secured with black electrical tape. It's beautiful. I stay for an hour or so to spin her and meet the other fire spinners at the camp. She is weighted perfectly and she seems to know my body already. I can tell we will be friends for a very long time.

Rejuvenated by the art of creation, I head into the open playa, walking past The Man and the many people working on repairing him so he can be burned again on Saturday. I don't want The Man, anyway. I want *her*. I am ready for The Temple.

The Temple lies on the open playa where 12:00 and Esplanade would be if Esplanade extended in a full circle.

The Temple is the yin to The Man's yang, the Shakti to Shiva, the moon to the sun.

They exist together in balance and contrast, as much as they complement each other.

WEDNESDAY: *Pain is Real, Blood is Real*

The Temple has only been a part of Burning Man since 2000, but it feels to me as though she has always been in the city. Each year she is different, but I am sure this must be the most beautiful temple to ever grace this land. She is over sixty feet tall, with three stories erected in an almost Japanese pagoda style. The spaces between her main beams are inlaid with a million, tiny laser-cut scrap wood pieces, giving her walls a delicate lace effect that reminds me of a cathedral. If viewed from above she would be symmetrical, with four ground level open entrances. The second inaccessible level has four large circular cut-outs between the wooden lattices, one for each side. The top level is simply open so the blue sky tinged with clouds shows through it.

Looking at her, I envision her first level as an Earth element as it connects to the dust, her second with its round openings as Water, and her third open level as Air. Fire will come on Sunday.

I walk towards her slowly, entranced by both the physical structure and by the energy shift I can feel, the closer I get to her. I know I am not the only one. The Temple has her own aura of calm and grace that can be difficult to find elsewhere on the playa, or the world for that matter. She commands respect and reverence in the same way as a procession of monks or an elderly grandmother would. There are no words needed to remind all who enter to shut their mouths, take a few deep breaths, and be prepared to bow down to something older and wiser than them.

Around The Temple clumps of bikes create a barrier between her and the chaos of the rest of the city. I walk around the bikes until I am standing directly in front of The Temple, with her in front of me and The Man directly behind me. It is high noon and the sun is overhead. I am sweaty from my walk and looking forward to shade, but I pause in the open to simply admire. My breath slows and sticks in my throat at the closeness of such power. I suck in another mouthful of hot air, draw it through my entire body beginning at the stomach, moving into my ribs, and up into my chest. I hold it there before releasing it and stepping towards her.

The people in The Temple all have the same look in their eyes, of surrender, as if after fighting a war they thought they believed in, they have now accepted every-thing they thought of as wrong. It is a look of resignation, but also of hope for the future. A look of understanding that they now have the wisdom and power to ensure that no one else will make the same mistakes they did. It is an acceptance of the darkness that exists next to the light. That we will all burn someday in our own way, and only then will we be truly free.

The walls have writings and offerings on them. I see photos, old letters, art, clothing, and stuffed animals. I pause to read some of the writing.

Mom, WHY? I was just a little girl. No on should have to experience that. I want to forgive u. I want to. I try. I try. But how can I forgive the mess you have left me inside my own head? Fuck you forever so I can un-fuck myself. —Dot

WEDNESDAY: *Pain is Real, Blood is Real*

The vulnerability displayed here cuts to my soul and almost makes me look away out of respect. It's so personal, like watching strangers make love through a one-way mirror. What right do I have to intrude? And yet I can't avert my eyes.

> Charles, I love you. Now and forever I will never forget you. You never paid softly but I know you were. I forgive you.

Fragments of others' thoughts and lives wrap around me. Suicides, rape, abuse, love, hope, dreams, *forgiveness.*

> Miri, my baby, my darling,
> I stare into your eyes and I know there is hope for the world. You are so pure and untouched. It frightens me to think of the ways I will corrupt you. I didn't expect to be a parent this young, but here we are together. I swear to you I will do my best. I hope you will forgive me for the times I will lose my temper, for the times I am too tired, for the times I will cry, for the times I will yell. I am sorry. I want to give you what I never had, but I am so afraid I will only pass my pain along to you. Forgive me.

Over and over forgiveness is mentioned. I walk slowly through The Temple, my eyes taking it all in.

BE HERE NOW.
ITS VERY SIMPLE
YOU FUCKFACE
I LOVE YOU

Every inch of The Temple has a new story, a tiny peek inside the head of another being's life.

FUCK THIS LIFE WHY WOULD ANYONE LOVE
ME I DONT DESERVE YOUR FORGIVNESS FOR THE
MONSTER YOU HAVE MADE ME. MONSTER, YOU
HAVE MADE ME MONSTER YOU HAVE MADE ME
ME ME LOVE IS A FUCKING LIE JUST LIKE I AM

I don't even notice the tears slowly running down my face. When I finally do, it's too late, the once silent tears have evolved into full-fledged sobs.

I love you. Yes YOU. I love you. Whoever you are. You are worthy of love. You are love.

I sob openly. I cry harder than I have in years, and don't know who or what I am crying for. A pink-haired man in tiny rainbow shorts hugs me and moves on. A paper that looks like it's been ripped from a journal catches my eye next:

If I can share anything that I've learned in this short life, let it be this: IT'S NOT ABOUT YOU. All that drama and suffering and shit that you think your parents, your lovers, your friends, and even strangers put you through? All the shit that you cling on to that you use to define your life, your suffering, your progression? IT'S NOT YOURS. Yes, even the abuse, the cheating, the lies, the gossip... All that. All that crap. It's just fluff. It's just the remnants of someone else living this human existence with toxicity. Whatever was done to you, your family, your ancestors, what you hold is yours alone, your experience that you choose to carry. I found this peace by imagining being stuck in a room with another human I've never met who is having a negative experience. I am there, I am witnessing, I can empathize, I can offer comfort and wisdom, but I know it's not my work. It's just someone else going through their experience and dropping their dark energy bullshit balls in your area. Why would you pick them up? Why would you carry them with you? It won't help them. It won't help you. It will just damage you and cause you to carry more dark energy balls along with your own, more to carry, more to drop, more to obsess over, more to distract YOU from being your divine self. You can hold space for others without taking on their shit. Your ego wants you to believe that everything revolves around you, but IT DOESN'T Let that shit go man. IT'S NOT YOU.

BURNING WINGS

I recoil from that last one, *how can it not be about me?* I cry still. A dreadlocked goddess in a flowing skirt and tie-dye crop top grabs my hand and walks with me for a few minutes before releasing me. Still, I soak in the stories offered, the emotions are like a new drug. I need more. *Just one more, then I'll stop.*

> *I am not the things that have happened to me. I forgive but I will never forget. Here I am free, but is it just an illusion?*

The sobs engulf my whole body, until it is convulsing with their power. Snot clumps out of my nose and drips down onto the dust. A man with a tattooed face hands me a tissue and I blow my nose. Still I can't look away. *Just one more.*

> Ahmed—
>
> You were too young to die, but you were an old soul. You took me to my first burn, you kept me alive physically and mentally. Even when you were drunk you had an aura around you that made me feel safe. I felt so safe with you. I always thought I would be the one to go. I always thought someday you would stand here and write to me. I was the stupid one. How am I still here? How are you dead? May you find your true peace.

WEDNESDAY: *Pain is Real, Blood is Real*

One more. The tears blur my vision, but I can still make out the scrawl.

> i have experienced more love and openness in a
> single day here than i have in my whole life. i
> walk now with an open heart.   nally seeing what
> humans are capable of when they love. i beg of you
> who reads this, do not let this gift go in vain. you
> are the doorway and you are the key. you don't
> know the pain i have inside of me. if i can love
> again then so can you. if i can forgive then we can
> forgive together.

Finally, I can't read anymore. My head swirls, little stars crowd my vision, and I crumble. An elderly woman, in hiking boots and a Hawaiian print shirt, catches me and wraps me in her embrace. She looks like a tourist, and she is my angel. She walks me to the center of the Temple and rests me on a blanket, next to an old African man in a white robe playing crystal singing bowls. I remove my wings and lie down on my back, staring up at the blue sky, showing through the ceiling above. She holds me and strokes my hair until I can breathe again, and then she kisses my forehead and leaves me with my little fairy. The bowls calm me, their vibration reminds me of my sunrise.

Was that only this morning? No, it had to have been yesterday.

Time no longer exists.

The silent tears won't stop. I cry for these strangers that are now my family, my tribe. I cry for Dot, Miri, Ahmed, and all the unnamed. I cry for the stories told and the millions that will never be shared, that will burn holes inside of minds until they destroy. I cry for my own untold stories. I cry for my the many trespasses against me over my short existence. I cry for my own broken heart. I cry for the mistakes I have made. I cry for my parents, for their broken dreams. I cry for the pain that is life. I cry because, even with all this pain, love still peeks through the cracks. I cry because we have the power to forgive. I cry because it feels so pure to release.

I cry because I finally see the darkness inside of myself, and inside of everyone else alive. I have spent my life trying to push out the darkness, flirting with it, but ducking away just in time, or so I thought. Now I see how mistaken I have been. It has been inside me all along. *I haven't escaped anything*, all I've done is push it farther and farther inside of me, until now it erupts completely and encompasses me.

With these thoughts, I get myself up and make the decision to leave The Temple. Somehow, I remember my wings. Somehow, I find my staff.

My talisman. My magic tools.

Black fog seeps out of my pores and surrounds me.

I am the darkness.

I don't have to pretend anymore. I am invincible. Slowly, I make the journey back to camp on foot, without water, and before the sun sets.

WEDNESDAY: *Pain is Real, Blood is Real*

I choke down two bites of vegan boxed macaroni and cheese for dinner. The noodles are shaped like little bunny rabbits and that makes it more palatable. Somehow, I dress myself for another night.

It feels like I'm getting ready for war. There is no way but forward. Rest is not an option. Rest is failure. I've cried out all my pain. I am invincible.

Bring it on. I can handle it.

I am in circus-striped tights, black bootie shorts, a black long-sleeved shirt, a black vest, a black fedora, a black vampire cape, and black boots. My wings are the only color I have on. I take another pressed ecstasy pill and stash a bag of MDMA in my sock. I have a flask of bourbon, my wings, and my fire staff. I am invincible.

I set off alone.

On Esplanade, I find a fire-dancing performance in progress, on a stage. I stand off to the side observing the performers. I am at least as good as half of them. I can do this.

I am invincible.

I remove my cape, hat, and wings. I soak the wicks at each end of my fire staff in an open container of white gasoline set up to the back of the performance area. Slowly, I count to ten as I twirl each end, drenching my virgin wicks in the gas. I find a safe place nearby to shake off the excess gas, as I have been taught, so that the loose flames won't spin onto the audience and myself.

When it's my turn, I walk slowly and sultrily onto the stage, the poi performer before me lights each end of my staff with his fireballs hanging from chains. Immediately, they burst into flames, just a few feet from my face. I begin to dance, slowly at first, and then faster and faster. The fireballs on my staff make a loud swoosh-y sound as they move through the air. I spin and spin and spin until the flames are long gone. The crowd cheers.

I want more.

Again and again, I soak my staff and re-ignite it. The ecstasy is dull but present, gently coaxing what little serotonin I have left into my brain. The fire brushes my skin; it doesn't burn me.

I am invincible.

After what feels like a hundred spins (but probably is only four or five), the gas runs out, and the universe decides I have had enough fire. I move on, walking through the playa, waiting for something worthy to distract me. My expectation is a challenge to the playa gods; any bar or club won't do right now. I want depth. I want darkness. I want to go as deep as possible, until I am completely consumed. Only then in pure shadow will I find the meaning of light.

I march quickly and with purpose, each footstep taking me farther away from safety. I don't waste my time smiling at the people I pass like I usually would, instead I walk by without acknowledgement, avoiding eye contact. Everywhere I look, it's the same shit: lights and lasers and speakers.

Finally, something grabs my attention. It is a giant uncovered dome set up on the inner playa next to Esplanade. It is covered with people who have climbed up on all sides of it and are cheering with emotion and rage. It looks like a cage fight is going on inside. I make my way forward to this temple of aggression and release. I leave my staff to hoist myself up on the dome, climbing carefully up a few levels, until I have a perfect view of the fight underneath. Two participants battle each other with foam bats. Each is attached to a harness which is suspended from the top of the dome.

The crowd is rowdy, yelling, screaming, banging on the steel bars of the dome. Someone passes me a bottle of whiskey and I chug it before passing it along. Despite a few years as a cheerleader in high school, I've never understood the pull of competitive sports, but watching the fights rage below, I feel myself attach emotionally to the contenders, feeling each of their victories and failures. I begin to sweat just watching them. I scream along with the other spectators, happy to release my emotion and pain in a new way. I don't even think I understood how much pain I carried inside of me every minute of every day, until earlier in the Temple.

I am love. I am pain. Love is pain. Pain is dark. Love is dark. I am dark.

I scream until my voice is hoarse. I am considering climbing down and moving on—I must pee—but then the next set of new fighters walk in and I can tell they will be worth staying for. They are Amazonian warriors of men; each is well over six feet tall and bulging with pure, burly muscle. The Man in Black is dressed from head to toe in black leather, from his leather knee-high platform boots covered with crossing straps, to shorts strapped on with a black studded belt. Even his black dreadlocks are wrapped with black leather bands. His arms and chest are covered with tattoos that I can't quite make out, but I imagine they are of demons and bloody babies.

His challenger, the Man in Pink, wears pink furry leg warmers, a pink pleated miniskirt, pink bracelets, and has pink yarn dreadlocks that extend down to his butt. He has a Hello Kitty tattoo I can make out on the back of his arm. He glares through the slits of his pink eyes at the Man in Black and spits right in front of him, without losing eye contact.

They are strapped in, given their weapons, and a horn blares, signaling the start of the fight. They slowly circle each other, for what seems like ages, before the Man in Black makes the first move, lunging towards the Man in Pink before he hops away. They repeat this same sequence a few times through before the Man in Black is able to pin the Man in Pink, forcing him to retaliate. I can't tell what is going on, they are lost in a whirl of bruises and dreadlocks, before they are pulled off each other. The horn blows again and they lunge at each other once more, there is no strategy now, just instinct and rage. Again and again, they meet in battle. Again and again, there is no winner. The Man in Pink has a bloody cut on his cheek. The Man in Black is limping. Still they fight. Finally, in a show of superhuman strength, the Man in Pink crushes the Man in Black underneath him.

The crowd goes wild. I can't tell where my own screams end, and the others' begin. I am one with everyone in our animal rage. I discover that for all I preach about love, a fighter is in my nature, just as surely as a nurturer. I embrace this realization and allow the feeling to encompass me whole, with no regard for what it means for me, for everything pure that I preach and stand for.

Fire is real. Tears are real. Blood is real.

The Man in Black is carried out of the dome, on a stretcher. The fight is over and the Man in Pink is the undisputed winner. He is paraded around the ring while the crowd chants "Two men enter, one man leaves! Two men enter, one man leaves! Two men enter, one man leaves!"

My throat is hoarse and I can't imagine any fight comparing to that one, so I climb down from the dome. When my boots make contact with the playa, I move with a new swagger, a new attitude.

Don't fuck with me.

Staff in hand, I strut back into the open playa, ducking into a porta potty to pee and take more drugs. I find another vial on the ground, full of a white powder. I snort some without knowing what it is.

Does it really matter?

My nose is burning and my head is on fire, but it doesn't matter, since I am invincible. I stomp down Esplanade, daring anyone to get in my way. A day glow cat with an evil grin and twitching tail picks me up. I hop onto its back and light up a cigarette, watching the city float by. Another of the cat's passengers cozies up to me, melting my shell. She looks like she is sixteen, in the midst of her Hot Topic rebel stage, complete with a double-pierced lip, bleached-blonde hair with pink tips, and so many studs she seems untouchable, just like I feel. I share my cigarette with her and she gives me my first)'(necklace. It is a triangle mood necklace with the signature man inside of it. It is such a dark blue that it looks black. *"Perfect,"* I think as I put it on.

I hop off at a giant red circus tent. Inside a full freak show is in progress. Clowns rule the tent, with grotesque white faces and striped clothing. Contortionists hang from the ceiling and walls. Lasers and lights blind from all sides. I dance through the crowd, and when I hop onstage I realize that the DJ is my friend Coco. It was at his mansion months ago, that my ticket to this insanity manifested. I have come full circle. I dance fast, fighting the music to see who can move harder. I am a spinning whirl of stomping feet, gyrating hips, and waving body parts.

An unshaven heathen of a man, wearing leather and black eye liner, eyes me as he dances beside me. Soon, he is behind me, still dancing, and I begin to feel his body move into sync with mine. Then, he is rubbing against me seductively. I spin around to glare daggers at him in challenge, daring him to continue. He smiles at this, and moves even closer to me, face-to-face this time. His hands are on my hips. The lasers are in my eyes. His mouth is on my neck. My head is dizzy, and still I dance, pulling away just enough to pretend I am in control, but allowing him to think that he is.

I'm fourteen again and I want him to stop kissing me. I want him to stop but I'm so drunk, I can't move. I scream silently but all that comes out is a whisper . . . "No . . ." I say again and again but he doesn't listen. I am powerless. I am weak. My body is not my own.

"What the fuck! You crazy bitch!" He screams like I shot him, but it was just a bite. He got too close. He backs away from me, holding his bleeding neck. I smile and keep on dancing. I'm almost there, I'm almost back in control. The light is no more.

One of my wings is broken, no wonder the darkness is consuming me. It hangs limply and off center, but I can't bring myself to remove it. Instead I eat more MDMA. I don't have any water. I grope the flask of whiskey in my boot. It's empty. The playa has eaten my whiskey, and a grinning evil clown gives me a bottle of gin. His face is white, and painted on it is a huge smeared red mouth that extends down to the base of his chin. His eyes are bloodshot and as red as his mouth.

The smell of the gin makes me gag; I drink it anyway, trying not to vomit at the wretched combination of cheap liquor and bitter drugs in my mouth. I dance it off. Harder and faster.

Break on through . . .

The music is inside of me.

Break on through . . .

Coco is playing a Doors remix, and I lose myself in Jim Morrison's hypnotic voice, mixed together with dark bass and circus funk.

Break on through . . .

I dance as if possessed.

Break on through . . .

The dancing turns to convulsions.

BURNING WINGS

Break on through to the other side!

The bass drops and my head explodes.

Chunks of my brain and skull splatter over the crowd. Coco wipes off a piece of my scalp from his forehead and keeps on playing.

The clown stares at me disapprovingly and takes a sip of his gin. He is the only one who seems to understand that I have a gaping hole where my face used to be.

I watch all of this in horror, helpless to stop the warm river of blood that pools from my body and begins to cover the stage.

The nausea is rising. I might have to vomit now.

Not here. Not here. Not here.

I shove my way through the crowd, out the front of the tent, then follow it around to the back, where no one can see me, on my hands and knees, retching behind a huge generator. Since I've hardly eaten any solid food in the last few days, all I can release is liquid. When there is nothing left, I crawl on the playa back to the front of the tent. About three feet from the ground there is a slight overhang that connects to the tent's stake ropes. It is here I curl up. I can't move.

The clown watches me from the darkness, ten feet away. He sits cross-legged on the ground with his gin. Thankfully, he doesn't come any closer; I'm not sure I could handle that smell again.

My head is spinning. The drugs have finally caught up to me. I lie in agony for what feels like hours, praying that no one will find me and try to help me. I am beyond help.

WEDNESDAY: *Pain is Real, Blood is Real*

I asked for this and I will deal with my pain alone. I stare back at the clown but I have a hard time focusing my eyes on anything, so I finally close them. My little fairy curls up in the crook of my neck.

I am no longer invincible.

)☼(

Eventually I come back to life. When my eyes open, the clown is gone. I pull myself up and make the trip back home, getting lost more times than I can count; the streets have turned into labyrinths, without any clear direction and the bright lights that once guided me, now confuse me.

Finally, I find my street corner and locate my camp, or what remains of it.

Home is fucked.

The parachute has fallen again, and I cannot walk without ducking underneath it. I find my campmates in the living room. I chug some water, light a cigarette, and curl up in a giant beanbag to watch the drama unfold. They are in worse shape than I am, if that is possible.

Torque is pacing spastically around the kitchen, as he mutters to himself (or anyone who is listening): "Motherfucker shouldn't have let me borrow his jacket if it was that big of a deal! Lets me borrow his priceless, full-length leather jacket, and takes me to the Seizure Dome. Shouldn't go in there anyway . . . Cops everywhere! You don't know who they are, anymore! They're everywhere, here! Like taking candy from a fucking baby!"

"I told you not to wear leather, it's hypocritical. We're *vegan*," Serene says softly, from her camping chair. She is huddled up with her crystals. I want to hug her, but I can't move.

"Torque! Calm the fuck down!" Archinta yells at him from her tent.

"Calm the fuck down? Calm the fuck down? Tell that mother fucker Marson to calm the fuck down! Did he have to punch me because his jacket got stolen? Did he have to drink a bottle of rum in an hour? Did he have to dump a fucking plate of fucking spaghetti on my head?" Torque is getting louder.

"Did you have to take six hits of acid and snort half a vial of ketamine?" Serene retaliates. "Do you know how much we're going to have to sage you, before you're allowed in our tent? I can see your aura darkening! It's dark, Torque! It's so dark!" She holds up a large white quartz crystal, in front of her face (presumably, to ward off his aura).

"Don't you understand?" he wails, "The drugs are the only things that make sense, anymore! Everything is fucked! Camp is fucked! It's all fucked! 'Camp It's All Fucked' we shall call it!" Torque paces and vents, knocking over some loose bottles in the kitchen.

"When it happens, it's over. And, when nothing makes sense, what can you do? Shall we ask the speed freaks with the missing fingers? Perhaps a cup of anti-freeze tea?" He curtseys, mimicking a lady, pouring tea into a cup. A giggle erupts from my mouth, before I can help myself.

Torque turns to me, now. "No, fuck that! Sometimes

the only thing that makes sense is to put your dick in a cup! How about that?"

Torque unzips his pants, drops them to his ankles, pulls out his limp, porn star penis, grabs a white porcelain tea cup, and places his dick delicately in the cup. He rests the cup on the table, so that it can sit there without his holding it up. He lifts his arms above his head in triumph.

"Now my dick is in a cup. Thank fucking God, something makes sense again."

BURNING WINGS

THURSDAY
Smoke and Dreams

Dreams are serious
business!

Unless, of course, they're
not!

THURSDAY: *Smoke and Dreams*

SKIPPING DOWN THE STREET IN BLISS, I feel my wings jingle and my scarves flow in the wind. I have repaired my damaged wings by weaving glow stick bracelets into the looms to act as a cast for the broken wood. It is a new perfect day, and I'm on an important gnome-adopting mission with my friend, Taylor Starshine. The sun is shining, and the darkness of the night before has dissipated from my memory.

I have spent my morning serving tea at Center Camp, a large public open tent, the size of a city block, in the city center at 6:00. The structure is kept open in the center area for curated and impromptu performances. Around this hub are places for lounging, art displays, and small stages. Center Camp is also the place to purchase the only two items I now know are legally sold on the playa: coffee and ice. By default, this space turns into the neighborhood coffee shop. It's family friendly and safe from the debauchery that characterizes much else of the city, such as evil clowns, feuding men in skirts, and dicks in cups.

To bring my serving supplies over, I borrow a large tricycle from a neighbor, and haul a vat of hot water, and my own tea set. I make a little picnic area, decorated with crystals and tapestries. I curl up into a small ball next to my tea altar, and float away into dreamland, until a passerby queries about my set-up. Then, I jump up, all smiles and love, to brew them my special Chinese leaves.

I had brought with me the two opposites of tea land: white tea and aged dark *puer*. White tea is made of the first tea buds of early spring, which are gently dried without any processing. They are brewed delicately, with low temperature water, as not to damage the leaves, coaxing nothing but the purest flavor from them. White tea is soft and velvety, with light floral undertones. Everyone likes white tea. Taylor Starshine and Serene are white teas. Aged *puer* is at the other side of the spectrum. Torque and Rico are aged *puers*. Aged *puers* are dark and earthy. They are brewed, with hot water, from fully oxidized, aged, and fermented tea leaves. They are an acquired taste: dark, mysterious, deep, and with the dash of fresh dirt or the bark from a tree. They are not for beginners.

Spending my time napping and serving, in a bright and public place, has allowed me to overcome the previous night. I've spent the morning alternating between reliving its terrors and lessons, and trying to shut them out.

I meet a man dressed as the devil. He sits next to me and grins stupidly, in pure joy. On his lap, is his one-year-old daughter, dressed as a tiny angel. Her name is Angel, and she was the driving force behind turning his life around. He happily drinks my tea, as he regales me with stories of motorcycles, crystal meth, and depression. Now he is radiant and sober; he has an angel to guide him. I don't quite have an angel, but I have a tiny fairy, and, as a surefire defense mechanism, I have reverted to my own fairy mode. I'm wearing multiple silk and cotton scarves, wrapped around my head, waist, and chest. They keep on falling off, and every time I stop to rewrap them, they end up tied in different placements and knots. I have turned in my black platform boots, and replaced them with a knee-high, brown vintage leather pair. I have a wicker basket, full of treasures. The sun is shining, and life is beautiful. I wave to everyone, as we skip, blowing kisses. My fairy trails behind me, a tiny glowing green light, hard to make out in the sunshine.

How could I ever have believed that the universe was anything less than perfect?

Taylor is petite and blonde, with long hair that cascades down her back. She is wearing a long silk skirt that blows in the wind, a translucent lace tank top, and *bindis*. We are on our way to a Gnome Adoption Camp, so Taylor can adopt a gnome.

"I don't know very much about gnomes, besides that they are small, and seem to enjoy wearing pointy, red hats. They might be friendly; I guess it depends on the gnome. Gnomes are complex and sacred beings, and I want to respect each one as an individual, and yet I honor the community that they exemplify." She skips as she speaks.

"They all seem to be old. I don't believe I've ever seen or heard anything about baby gnomes." I answer her back with a gleeful laugh, imaging baby gnomes, and how cute they would be.

"So, what sacred dwelling or womb do they birth from? I mean, if there are no babies that manifest? There must be a seedling process of growth!"

"Maybe they hardly have babies, but they live a long

time. Like turtles."

"Turtles are also such sacred creatures on this earth! I feel like gnomes and turtles would dance so well together and be best friends."

"And then the gnomes could ride the turtles!"

As we skip, I feel a presence behind me. I ignore it for a full block, until the feeling grows; I am being followed. The next time I stop to retie my scarves, I peak behind me, just in time to see him duck behind a U-Haul.

Sneaky clown. I knew it.

The Gnome Adoption Camp has a line out the Gnome Dome. A ceremony is in full swing, as we arrive.

"Adopting a gnome is a great responsibility, and one that should not be taken lightly. Gnomes live long lives . . . This is not a goldfish!" Someone in the line snickers, and the officiant stops to glare. He is dressed like a purple alligator, and his tail makes patterns in the dust as he moves. When he is satisfied that order has been restored, he continues: "Do you solemnly swear to protect, nourish, and love your gnome, for as long as your gnome may have you?" The couple about to adopt a gnome holds hands, smiles, and nods, eagerly. They are dressed in matching striped sailor outfits. Taylor and I simultaneously hold hands, in celebration of what is to come. They have decided to name their gnome, Blossom. Blossom is about eight inches tall, slightly overweight, and smirking. She has a blue dress on, so she matches her new parents.

Taylor is giddy with glee about having her own gnome, to love and cherish. I am sure she will be a very good gnome mommy. She is very happy and nurturing. She makes me feel as though there is no such thing as rain—only rainbows, and that every problem can be solved with some sage and a hug, and I wish that I still too had that optimism. She is practically bouncing up and down, as we wait at the end of the long line.

After signing the proper paperwork, the sailor couple collects the gnome and a disposable camera—as part of the adoption agreement, they must take photos of the gnome in various places on the playa, before returning the camera on Sunday. Taylor taps on the officiant's shoulder to ask about putting her name on the adoption list. The list is long, and he isn't sure if they have enough gnomes. Her bright smile grows tense, and a tiny bit of light goes out from her big blue eyes. Taylor is not used to being told *no*. It's not that she is demanding, or entitled (like Archinta), it's that she is so earnest, saying yes to her is a special treat, accompanied by watching her face light up.

A single fat tear falls from her left eye and cascades down her rose-colored cheek. She wipes it and stutters, "I . . . I . . . I just really wanted a gnome to love and cherish. I read about this camp in that tiny book and, since that moment, I had a vision of having my own gnome, to carry with me, next to my heart, and to share this magical experience." I hug her close, wishing I had a gnome to offer her, but all I have is a grinning clown and a green fairy, neither of whom will hold still long enough for me to fully verify their existence.

We leave the Gnome Dome, empty-handed, walking

slowly down the road, holding hands. The wind has begun to gently blow, rippling tents and hanging tapestries. The sun is high and bright; as the wind picks up even more, its light begins to slightly dim. I can't remember if I'm on drugs or not. Being here is a drug, all on its own. My vodka and cranberry is almost gone.

We find a red furry bar for shelter. The bar itself is painted in zebra stripes. The bartender is a Scotsman, named Uncle Sam, wearing zebra leggings and a cowboy hat. He is possibly the hairiest man I have ever seen. We politely ask for vodka cranberries.

"What? You can't order a homo drink here! Whiskey or whiskey it is." We order whiskey.

"Good choice," says Sam. Sam is . . . gay. He takes three shots for every one we do, and analyzes the pros and cons of gnome adoption.

"Don't cry, little fairy love! You were not meant to adopt a gnome, today. Gnome children are big commitments. You have to carry them all the time, since their legs are so tiny. Thankless bastards, they are. Often, we think we are ready for a huge life step, but it's not our time. You have to trust, whether it's in the universe, God, or whatever truth you believe. Ultimately, we have to believe that there is some order to the madness, and trust, trust, trust. Someday, you will be a wonderful gnome mama, but today isn't your day. Here, have another shot. It will make the dust less noticeable."

Trust? Trust what? Nothing is tangible. Nothing is permanent. Everything is fleeting. And my feet hurt almost as much as my pounding head does.

THURSDAY: *Smoke and Dreams*

Speaking of the intangible, I realize how much the dust has picked up. I had thought the tiny storm on Monday was as bad as I could expect, but already the wind is blowing stronger than it was then, and I can tell this is just the beginning. The tarp covering the bar is banging against its posts. Sam has a thin layer of dust covering his face, except for the small area directly under the brim of his hat. Each line of his face and every long hair on his chest and arms is now accentuated by the dust.

"Where are we?" I ask. "Will it get dustier?"

"You, my little darlings, are at 7:00 and Arctic. And, yes . . . It's going to get a lot dustier."

"I appreciate this human experience of intensity and dust, but I feel as though rejuvenation would benefit us, and we could best recharge energetically if we were able to get back to my oasis at Cy-Top," says Taylor.

I take another shot and weigh my options. I live much closer at 9:15, but Camp It's All Fucked was torn to shreds when I left this morning (after waking up on a beanbag chair, cradling an open bottle of red wine), and I'm not sure I want to sit out a dust storm there. I could barhop alone, and see where the universe takes me. Or . . . I could make the long trip to Taylor's camp, Cy-Top at 2:00. Cy-Top would be the best place to wait out the storm, in one of its two large domes. It also has North.

"I'll go with you," I decide. I've survived the nightmare of the previous night. If I could handle that much cataclysmic turmoil, how bad could a little dust be?

We leave Sam and his bar to walk down Arctic towards

7:00, and then down to Esplanade. We have two choices now, we can either take the Esplanade the full circle from, 7:00 to 2:00, or we can cut across the open playa, to the right of The Man. Across is more direct, but the Esplanade will offer us a road to follow.

"Straight across is faster." So, we begin our journey.

I realize now why we were told to bring goggles and dust masks; the dusty wind is beginning to blind me. I stop to grab the cheap swimming goggles I have in my wicker basket, and then cover my head and face completely with the pale green gauzy scarf that used to be my shirt. I find another scarf for Taylor. The dust is steadily growing thicker.

The Man is just barely visible through the dust, as we stare out into the open playa. There are no other landmarks large enough to show through the thick haze.

"You ready?" I ask. My little green fairy shakes her head at me in disbelief, astounded at my resolve to traverse the open sea of dust in conditions like this, before the wind blows her away like a stray flower.

Taylor takes a deep breath in. "Yep. Let's do it. I accept all the challenges of the universe. I am whole. I am complete. I accept this journey, in all of its extremes."

We clasp hands, and begin walking towards The Man. The wind blows from what seems like all sides, pulling at us, trying to dislodge us from our path. We are not fazed. Onwards we walk, one foot in front of the other. After ten minutes of careful walking, we pause to turn around. We can see nothing of Esplanade or the city. We turn forward again, and The Man has vanished.

The wind is relentless, the playa pelts us like a plague of miniature locusts. It surrounds us, making me wonder how the wind could possibly be blowing from every angle at once. It is in my mouth, my ears, my eyes, and every crevice on my body. It consumes me. It is so thick, that when I hold out my hand in front of me, it appears transparent, as the dust in front of it camouflages with the dust behind it. I can't see my feet anymore. There is nothing but dust. Taylor is no longer recognizable; the only way I know she is still there is that her hand is tightly clasped in mine. There is nothing but the dust. Dust below and dust above, with no end in sight. We walk on, slowly, but soon we are no match for the storm.

Continuing is futile, since we are now completely blind. We crumble down into the dust, sitting on the earth, holding each other like twins in the womb, a tapestry wrapped around us to cover our bodies and our heads, so we can attempt to breathe. We laugh uncontrollably because there is nothing else to do. There is no more oxygen, there is just dust.

We suck the dust through our nostrils, where it travels down our respiratory system, until it fills our lungs with the fine alkaline powder that is Black Rock City. From our lungs, the dust makes it into our bloodstream, moving through the vessels, filling our hearts, and then, once again, traveling outwards. Now, there is not just dust around us, it is also inside our skin. Our skin dissolves, as the dust eats us from within, and soon we are just particles, reflecting what little light still shines through the storm.

Higher and higher we climb, swirling, traveling with the wind, somersaulting in circular patterns, over the city. We work our way into every single available crevice, into the cracks of RV windows not properly latched, under rain flaps on tents, into coolers and domes and yurts; trying to level them, to knock over every piece of carefully construct-ed standing structure. They are temporary. Dust is forever.

I feel a strange sense of ownership over this land, and a rage at those who dared to enter it, and tried to build on it. How dare they use this sacred space for their debauchery? I vow to destroy their hard work. This is our land. This is dust country.

I'm back in the city and roaring drunk. I've been drinking all night, and a good part of the day before. I walk down the street, furious at some slight. That's not really why I'm upset. It's him. It's still him. It's always him. I'm crying, but I'm so angry I don't notice. It's everything he represented, both in our love and in his betrayal. I knock down a trash can in front of me. I tried so hard, and it was all for nothing. Nothing. Nothing. I knock down another trash can. And then another. And another. Fuck him. Fuck life. Someone opens a window to yell at me. Who the fuck cares about you? I yell back. Who the fuck cares about anything. It's all for nothing. There is nothing but pain, nothing but broken dreams, nothing but dust. Dust every-where. From dust, we came, and unto dust, we shall return.

THURSDAY: *Smoke and Dreams*

)☼(

The wind calms slightly. I open my eyes, and cautiously inhale. I hadn't realized I was holding my breath, until now. Taylor's bright eyes stare back into mine, through dusty eyelashes and goggles I can still see her dark pupils. The tapestry is still whipping violently around us, but at least we can breathe. My fairy is back; she cowers with us, still just a dull green light. I try to focus on her, she is trying to tell me something.

"*Watch out!*" I hear a voice in my head say.

I push the tapestry off us. Although the wind still whips hard all around me, I can see twenty feet or so. As I look around in confusion, in all directions, I see giant sails, with a skull and cross-bones, rise proud and tall, magically appearing through the dust storm. The sails are attached to a ship; a large pirate ship is coming straight towards us. It would have run us over, if we had stayed under cover in our tapestry. I jump up, shouting at Taylor, "A ship! Pirates!"

The ship spots us and I hear voices: "Fairies ahead! Stop!" The ship brakes to a standstill, about five feet in front of us. I have no idea what direction it came from, or where it is going. Everywhere is dust. By now, we are on our feet, and ecstatic to be rescued. Our rescuers are not quite so charmed by us. We get hauled up onto the deck, and meet Captain Jack. His face is covered completely in snowboarding goggles and a skull dust-mask.

He pulls down his mask to sneer at us, "Let me guess . . . First year, first dust storm?" he asks with disdain. "You're lucky I found you. You would have blown away, like pieces of MOOP, or some other jackass would have hit you. Go sit down, before you fall off. You think this is your fucking playground?" Then he laughs a deep hearty belly laugh. "This is *my* fucking playground. Now let's go." He flips a switch and Queen floods the speakers.

"Another one bites the dust!" He yells in time with the lyrics.

We run away from him, as the music pierces us, and make our way to the back of the ship, to giggle and watch the dust roll by. Screech, part of Captain Jack's camp, tells us the ship is called the Munchkin and plays exclusively hard metal and Top 40 hits from the eighties. Screech is lean and skinny, his dark hair standing upright at impossible angles, usually only achieved by hair gel. The incredible, life-giving playa dust seems to have accomplished this alone. The dust is so intense, I can hardly make out his other features; he takes a single finger and wipes off my goggles. The world is clear again, and I can make out his three-day dust-covered stubble and skull neck tattoo. I laugh out loud at my newly returned vision.

"You think that's awesome? Want to see something even cooler?" he asks with a mischievous smile.

"Uh, sure," I answer, hesitantly. He reaches his right pointer finger into his right nostril, scrapes it around, and then pulls it back out. On it is the largest booger I have ever seen. It is black and lumpy, with tinges of classic green and blood red, in parts. I stare for a few seconds in amazement, before remembering to be revolted and look away. He flicks it over the side of the moving art car, and laughs at me.

"Your turn," he challenges. "You never know what's inside of you until you take the time to dig. Go deep, little fairy; there's more to you than meets the eye."

"You have no idea." I take my pointer finger and test out my own nostril. My nail scrapes around, detaching a large mass connected to my nasal cavity. I gently file at the sides of it so I can keep it intact. When it finally slides out it is almost as massive as Screech's. We both ogle it, with the appreciation of pre-teen boys. I lift my finger up higher, so we can see it from all sides. Taylor shrieks when she sees my booger. I flick it at her, and she screams even louder, trying to brush it off. I dissolve into giggles, laughing harder when Captain Jack glares at us again.

We cuddle back up, and I wipe off her sunglasses so she can see again as well. The dust is still moving rapidly in patterns, with slices of blue in between. The Man suddenly looms large, to our right. I can feel the dust's anger at his existence. I imagine The Temple, and all the writing inside of her, covered now in dust. The Munchkin continues to crawl through the open playa at a snail's pace. Here and there, we see other vehicles, sculptures, and bikers, but, for once, the playa is mostly empty. The dust is battling the playa's usual perpetual movement. For now, at least, the dust is winning.

As the dust resettles, I feel my body rejuvenate, and Taylor also perks up. Suddenly, the edge of the city is before us. Finally! Esplanade! I now understand what sailors feel, when they catch their first glimpse of land, after months at sea. I never felt so much relief. The large camps along our city's main street are some of the more extravagant and well-organized communities, and they seem even more beautiful to me, at this moment. They represent civilization and safety. The Munchkin inches along so slowly, that a giant snail literally passes us. Finally, it is close enough to the city for us to depart.

We thank Captain Jack for rescuing us. He removes his mask and goggles; his eyes twinkle emerald green. "You dumb fairies were somewhere between lost and found, but mostly lost. I'm happy we got you found, at least this time." We nod and hug him, and miraculously, he hugs us back. "Don't do stupid shit!" are his last words to us as we carefully hop off the Munchkin and back down onto the dusty ground. We wave, until it disappears into the brown clouds, as mystically as it came. With goggles and makeshift masks on again, we head towards Cy-Top, slowly and carefully.

At camp, expecting safety and shelter, we encounter more chaos. The center of the main dome has completely collapsed. It wilts sadly into itself, the metal warped and bent, as if it were made of paperclips, instead of steel. The wind has stopped blowing, and the dust begins to settle a bit. The camp has been building these structures for seven days now, readying themselves for the opening party. Tonight was supposed to be the night that they finally turned on their sound system, and enjoyed the benefits of all their labor. Now their hard work is ruined, crushed by the relentless dust.

My vacation is your worst nightmare.

Taylor flits off to check on her tent and the kitchen,

and I wander through the shattered camp and find North, near his tent. Like all the others, it's covered by a thick layer of the fine beige dust. He is staring, in dismay, at the camp's other dome, their "backstage" communal dome, constructed of PVC pipe, also collapsed.

"Can you believe this?" he asks as he gestures at it. "The heart of the storm slammed into our camp. It tried to destroy us. This sounds crazy, but it almost felt personal, like the dust had a vendetta against us."

"That doesn't sound crazy at all," I respond slowly.

We cuddle on an outdoor couch, oblivious to the dust, again swirling around us. It is gentler than before, and feels familiar now. I tell him about Taylor, and our journey across the dust, of cowering under the tapestry, and of our rescue by Captain Jack and his crew. I don't tell him about my fairy, or how *I turned into the same dust that tried to destroy his camp.*

"Are you ok?" he asks, as he pulls out two pressed white tablets of MDA, and offers me one.

"Yes. . . We shouldn't have tried to make it straight across. I had no idea of how intense the storm would be. Actually, I could be talking about anything here: the emotions, the rushes, the highs, the lows; everything takes on new energy. It's so charged, it's incredible. *It's the most beautiful nightmare I've ever had.*" I swallow the pill, and wash it down with a warm beer. MDA is fun: it's similar chemically to MDMA, but slightly more psychedelic. I hope for rainbows, as I swallow it.

We sit in silence for a short eternity, once again a part of the dust, before North speaks again: "You saw the dome that collapsed? Our dance dome? There was a girl meditating in the center of it. She was on her back, on the center platform, in the middle of the storm, having this spiritual experience." He pauses and looks off into the distance. I clasp his hand and hold it as he continues. "She felt the storm, and thought about the dome. She watched it bend and wrap around her, as she lay in her own fantasies. Just when she imagined the dome collapsing, it did. The center point fell almost fifteen feet, and held itself together, a foot above her head. When she opened her eyes again it was hovering above her. She could have been killed."

"Show me the dome?" I ask.

"Fuck! I should check on the equipment, too." He stands up, and I follow.

The wind and dust have picked up again; it is wild and hazy, but nowhere near as intense as when we were trapped on the playa. We walk back through camp, as he tells me about the metal used in the construction of the dome, about the weight it can withstand, and how the heart of the dust storm whipped across the open playa, crossed The End of the World, and then wreaked havoc, directly on their camp. We stop in front of the fallen structure. It looks like an art sculpture: a testament to the impermanence of this place, and of how, in the eternal struggle of man vs. nature, nature will always eventually win.

As I stand next to the carnage, in awe of the storm's power, North checks the intricacies of his sound system. When I hear the speakers fire up, I smile. It must have survived the storm. I turn to smile at him, and he raises a fist in triumph, yelling "If we have music, we have hope!"

I am feeling the drugs. My vision blurs, my head spins, and a familiar feeling overtakes me: a combination of heightened stimulation and numbness. Without thinking, I walk into the collapsed dome. The walls have fallen apart, to make a center opening, around the stage. I release the scarf that is my shirt, so my breasts are bare. I remove my boots and socks, and then I climb onstage. I begin to dance a dance I didn't realize that I knew. It is a dance of worship, to the destroyer, to trusting in the process, and to the order that exists within chaos. I dance to release my boundaries and inhibitions, and to celebrate the beauty that is found in mayhem.

When we are stripped down completely, what is left?

Someone begins to pound a bongo drum. My hair whips around wildly, as the music moves me in perfect time to the invisible wind. I dance. I dance like I have a thousand times before, yet, this dance is different; there is a gentle urgency in it that I can't explain. I am more than just myself, and my dance has a purpose. It is an ode to the wind, the stars, the fire, and to life, itself.

What is life?

The wind stops. So, do I.

I lie on the stage alone and half naked, in the exact spot where a woman could have died a few hours ago. Above me, is the rippling sky, finally blue again. The dust has now settled completely. It is late afternoon; I can tell time by the angle of the shadows the sun casts.

What is life? Life is a test.

BURNING WINGS

The shadows of the collapsed dome are contorted spider web patterns, covering my body. The rainbow spiders are coming. Their brightly colored legs seem ridiculously long for their tiny bodies. They are all over the dome, crawling on the bent poles. Now they begin to make their way down the fallen sides, using the shadows as an extension of their web. I'm not afraid of insects. Still, I rise up before they can use their shadow web to get to me.

The few people that remain in the common area are unconcerned with the spiders. Instead, they are focused on repairing the lighting and the collapsed infrastructure. I slowly dance my way out of the dome and towards the open playa. I set my tapestry on the ground and release down onto it. This seems like the ending to a story, and yet I wish for Taylor, and her soothing energy.

Taylor appears behind, and lowers herself down, as if she heard my spirit speak. We sit on the edge of civilization, staring out into the vast openness. I am astounded at the sheer amount of space that exists. I can see a giant oil rig, a mile out, and the tiny people who have climbed atop it. Again, I find Taylor's soft hand in mine, as we watch this dream, in silence. Large gods and goddesses cry and sob in front of the rig, expressing their unbridled emotion at the end of the storm, and the reappearance of the structure. A tiny house floats in the sky, miles away.

"In the dust, it was impossible to measure distance and space," I say, slowly, "and now I remember how big it is out there, and how small I am."

"Our souls are immortal, and yet we, as human beings,

in these bodies, are so small. I felt that fragility when we were out there together. In just one afternoon here, I felt all the emotions of human life: Hope, disappointment, fear, love, danger, safety . . . And yet, amidst the frantic race for survival, we are always protected." Before, I saw Taylor as a carefree nymph, and now she speaks with a new wisdom. "In a single day here, I feel as though I have lived a full life."

"Yes!" I exclaim. "That's exactly how I felt here, my first twenty-four hours, as though I had lived a full lifetime: as though, if I had left after that first morning, all the effort and time I spent preparing and getting here, had been worth it. Only, it didn't end; it has become more and more intense. Every time I think I've hit a pivotal point, I find a way to reach beyond it."

"I hear you and I feel your perception. Looking back, I should have been scared out of my mind in that storm, but I was still wrapped in my heartache about the gnome. And now, the gnome sounds so silly! During the storm, I was anxious and uncomfortable, and yet I had to laugh at the unbridled intensity of it all. I was so unprepared! I had only my sunglasses and Tibetan scarf to shield myself!" She laughs her adorable laugh, and again she becomes a child, reveling in her first scabbed knee. "I had heard stories, and I knew about the dust, but experiencing it firsthand was so intense! It took over! Did you feel its power? Did you get swept away too?"

"I *was* the dust. And when I was the dust, nothing else existed. It makes you think about life, outside this place. About how wherever you are, can consume you, can make you forget about everything else that exists. And yet, there are a million worlds that co-exist, side by side at all times—"

"We are each our own world, and sometimes, our worlds intersect."

"And how many storms have we been caught in . . . that I didn't even notice?"

"Until it's over?" A man interrupts us, from behind. We stare at him in confusion.

"Excuse me," he says, "I didn't mean to intrude, I couldn't help but overhear. I'll leave you be, but can I take your photo?"

We nod our consent, and he takes a single shot of us, from behind. We are topless, sitting on a purple tapestry, at the end of the world, looking out at the infinite. When we turn back, he is gone.

"But perhaps that's how life is. . . . We become stuck in a fog, and can see only what is right in front of our faces—" Taylor continues hesitantly.

"If we take the time, we will realize that the world, and our consciousness, are vaster than we can imagine.

"We are just mortals stuck in a dust storm, seeing only what is in front of our eyes, not realizing how much is behind the dust. . . ."

"Or maybe . . ." my fairy whispers softly in my ear, "We are all just dust. . . ."

)☼(

Green bikes are community bikes. If you find one, it's

yours until you park it, then it's fair game, once again. I find one of these magic bikes at Cy-Top, attach my basket to the handlebars, kiss North goodbye, and set off into the openness, pedaling slowly. I ride leisurely. Having the bike below me allows me so much more freedom, that I enjoy the pleasure of riding, rather than walking. Instead of cutting straight through the center, I decide to go the longer way home, taking a large loop through the deep playa. I pass art cars, playing their music, shrines made of skulls, and my magic treehouse. Instead of going towards any of these things, I am called towards the void, to the darkness.

Suddenly the dust overtakes me. At first it is just a haze, and I feel as though I am riding through a thick fog, except dry. Then the wind picks up again. I slow down, and pedal as slowly as I possibly can, but I hit a patch of loose playa. These dust patches are like booby traps. The ground is so smooth and hard, and then you roll over a giant sand trap and riding is suddenly impossible. During the day, they are easy to spot and dodge; at night and during storms, they are a constant reminder that this city is not just about celebration, it is also about survival.

I land on the playa floor on my side, my bike half on top of me. Staying here seems to be the safest option, at least until I can see (or a pirate ship rescues me). So, I cower on the dust, hugging my bike against me, wondering where my fairy is. I hope she is okay. The dust is trying to eat me again, but it is not as strong as before, and I can keep it out of my body with minimal effort.

The wind stops, as mysteriously as it began, and the

whipping dust calms back down into a haze. I stand up without dusting myself off, *that would be useless,* and I wheel my green bike in what I believe is the direction I was going. There is nothing but dust in all directions. The world is gray. I think the sun has set, but I can't be sure. A pink light in the distance isn't expansive enough to be the sun. Or perhaps it is. It's all I can see, in any direction, so I begin to wheel myself towards it, as if in a trance.

When I get closer to the light, I can see it is not one light, but a few, on top of a strange structure: a large gray fenced-in area, about thirty feet across and six feet tall. In the center front is a huge, bright pink skull cutout, made of pale pink squiggles. Its eyes are barred windows, and its mouth is a doorway. It sneers at me.

As I stand in front of it, intrigued and confused, a man walks out of the mouth. He is wearing a pale pink military style uniform, complete with helmet.

"You're late," he states sternly.

"I am?" I ask, confused. "I don't remember making an appointment."

"Of course, you did! You're here, aren't you?"

"I suppose you're right."

"Come on. We've been expecting you. There is a lot of work to be done." He turns and walks purposefully into the mouth, and I follow him. Inside is an open waiting room with benches. Everything is a dull gray color. There is a long countertop, and a woman wearing a matching pink uniform is behind it.

Another man, wearing a striped one-piece suit, is in

front of the counter, arguing with her. "I just don't understand why you have to be so bureaucratic! I just want to be in control of my own dreams! How can you people do this?"

"Sir, sir, I'm going to need you to calm down, sir. You think I want to be here? I'm doing you a favor! Now sit back down and fill out the paperwork correctly! I couldn't possibly process your passport without form 56217.43A. Don't get mad at me! You didn't even have an appointment, after all."

The man turns around in a huff and sits down next to me, while holding his stack of papers and a pink crayon. "Have fun," he says to me, before scribbling something I can't read on his documents.

"Miss! Yes, you! We can see you now." I jump up and walk over to the counter. "You're late," she tells me.

"Yes, I must have forgotten about my appointment. I apologize. It's easy to lose track of the time here. There were gnomes and spiders and dust and pirates . . ."

"Yes, yes, I've met the pirates. Dreadful, just dreadful. Well, you're here now and we have lots of work to do." She looks deeply into my eyes. "Why do you want to enter The Land of Dreams?"

"The Land of Dreams? I thought I was already dreaming?"

"Oh, dear no! To enter The Land of Dreams legally, you must have a passport!" She pulls out a blue-covered passport book and opens it. "See, it says right here:

. . . and though your Dreamworld does not necessarily have to have any connection with the real world, as we know it, and with the systems imposed upon us, (un)fortunately you'll have to live it inside that same real world."

"I don't understand what this has to do with my passport."

She sighs. "Just fill out the paperwork and then we can talk more." She hands me an obscenely large stack of papers and a blue crayon. I return to the bench, next to the man in the striped coat, who is still scribbling away.

I look down at my papers. They begin simply enough:

Physical Date of Birth

_____

Mental Date of Birth

_____

Home Telephone Number

_____

Business Telephone Number

_____

THURSDAY: *Smoke and Dreams*

Number Where You Can Be Reached While Dreaming

_____

Forever Young? ☐yes ☐no

But then they move on to more complex questions:

List of Personal Heroes

_____

What Would You Want to Be If You Ever Grew Up?

_____

Where Do You Intend to Go In Your Dreams?

_____

Who Will Join You in Your Dreams?

_____

Describe Your Utopia

_____

What Do You Intend To Do While Living in Your Dream?

_____

BURNING WINGS

I begin by filling out the simpler questions. I decide that I can be reached, while dreaming, through my childhood phone number, which miraculously I remember still. What would I want to be if I ever grew up? *Happy,* I finally decide. Where would I go in my dreams? *Everywhere.* My Utopia?

This is my Utopia, but with less dust and more fluffy things. Kittens would be nice, too. And bubbles.

It's hard to write coherently, in the tiny boxes while on drugs, with a tiny crayon, but I do my best. The man in the striped suit has finally filled out his paperwork correctly. He is given a passport and ushered out another door, at the back of the waiting room. I look longingly at the door, but my paperwork must be processed, before I can join him.

I go back up to the counter. The woman sticks out her hand expectantly and I hand over my documents. She shuffles through them, then takes out a red permanent marker and circles a few answers. "Ma'am, you clearly did not understand section 823.55A, nor did you properly fill out section 823.58B, specifically questions 8 and 12." She hands the papers back to me.

"Are you serious?" I ask in amazement.

"Dreams are serious business! Unless, of course, they're not! Now fill out your documents properly and we will proceed from there."

I reluctantly return to the bench, and do my best to complete the rest of the paperwork. It is getting cold and I want a drink. Finally, I walk back up to the counter, and she approves my documents with an oversized stamp. She summons the man I met outside, and he takes me to the next counter.

THURSDAY: *Smoke and Dreams*

"Place your right hand on the bible." I place my right hand on an old copy of *Hitchhiker's Guide to the Galaxy.* "Now, repeat after me: 'I am entering the Land of Dreams, by my own will and at my own risk.'"

"I am entering the Land of Dreams, by my own will and at my own risk." I dutifully begin to repeat each line, one at a time:

"I will abide by all laws set forth by the overseers of the Land of Dreams, or else I will abide by its own laws, as determined by each individual dream."

"I will abide by all laws set forth by the overseers of the Land of Dreams, or else I will abide by its own laws, as determined by each individual dream."

"I acknowledge that though my Dreamworld does not necessarily have to have any connection with the real world as we know it, and with the systems imposed upon us, I will have to live it inside that same real world."

"I acknowledge that though my Dreamworld does not necessarily have to have any connection with the real world as we know it, and with the systems imposed upon us, I will have to live it inside that same real world."

"I understand that I am responsible for my own dreams, and that no one else can dream for me."

"I understand that I am responsible for my own dreams, and that no one else can dream for me."

"I do hereby state my intention to enter the Land of Dreams, and do release the bureaucracy from any and all accountability, resulting from injuries incurred, as I dream."

"I do hereby state my intention to enter the Land of

Dreams, and do release the bureaucracy from any and all accountability, resulting from injuries incurred, as I dream."

He hands me a shiny new passport with a blue cover. It says in large letters PASSPORT TO THE LAND OF DREAMS, and then in a smaller font in the artwork: *All people are equal, but some dream more than others.*

He stamps the first page, and then escorts me to the rear of the room, to a single door. He opens the door slowly, and then holds it open, as I walk through it. On the other side of the door is the open playa. It is now night time, and the dust has subsided. About twenty feet back, is a small structure; it looks like an old western saloon, only the size of a closet. I turn back around to ask about it, and the door has closed behind me.

I am responsible for my own dreams. No one else can dream for me.

I walk slowly towards the structure, alone. As soon as I arrive, a man pops out from behind it. He is wearing a black and white striped suit, and looks exactly like the man I saw before, in the waiting room, except now he is living his dream. His giant smile makes him look like a new person. Without speaking, he takes two bottles from under the bar; one is bourbon, the other vodka. With the grace and presence of a mime, he presents each one to me with a flourish, before pouring two shots.

"Would you like the dark or the light?" he asks me.

"Do I have to choose?" I respond.

He shrugs. "It's your dream after all. In my experience, they contradict themselves, the light and the darkness."

"But why do I have to choose? Isn't life light and dark?"

THURSDAY: *Smoke and Dreams*

"You always have a choice. You might not like your choice, but you still have it."

I ignore him and drink them both. It's my dream, after all.

FRIDAY
The Edge

With a head full of
acid, madness seems
reasonable, and sanity,
certainly negotiable.

FRIDAY: *The Edge*

STARS AND STRIPES GENERALLY CONJURE up images of all-American patriotism, Christian ideals, shiny cars, and fake smiles. Not here. A man, wearing a tiny t-shirt, dances in circles, waving a large American flag. "Welcome to the American Dream!" he yells, as he swings his penis from side to side. "This is the American Dream! CAN YOU TASTE THE PIE?"

"What the hell is the American Dream, anyway?" says Spruce Man. "I think of men in ties, and white picket fences, and the suburbs; but that doesn't sound like a dream to me, that sounds like a special kind of hell, for people with no imagination."

"The American Dream is dead," says Torque.

"The American Dream is just that . . . a dream. A dream in a dream land." The words come out of my mouth before I realize what I'm saying, as if someone else is speaking for me: "That shirt-cocker is right, *this* is the American Dream, at least the real one. Where else can you come from nothing and be whoever you want to be? When's the last time you went to a bar and no one asked you 'what you do'? Like that's all that fucking matters? Like our worth is supposed to be defined by how we make money? There's so much more!" I'm getting heated now, and my arms wave around for emphasis. "Isn't the dream to control your own life? Not to be pigeonholed into living the life you were doomed or blessed to be born into?"

Torque laughs. "We are the fucking American Dream, because we are the freaks and we aren't afraid to celebrate it."

The sky is clear and bright as we hit the open playa, walking into the void. This time we are prepared, with water, dust masks, and goggles. More importantly, we have dosed ourselves with liquid LSD, before leaving camp.

"Lysergic acid diethylamide takes one to other dimensions!" Rico explained earlier, "It has been the drug of choice for artists and visionaries since the 1960's. Its effects are intense, long lasting, and varied for everyone who ingests it. For some, come full-on delusions, for others only rainbows. In my humble opinion, if you're going to worship those gods, go deep, go all the way."

We took his advice. We can handle it. We are no strangers to it; we are now seasoned burners with four days of experience behind us. We are home. I am wearing a very short, lime-green pair of 1970s-style track shorts, nipple tape, furry boots, and my magic wings. A large cow lumbers down the street, overtaking us on our right. Two riders on top wave to us, as they struggle to steer it. The air behind the cow ripples with rainbow tracers, flowing behind her like streamers in the wind.

The clown follows me, but he keeps at least ten paces back. We have an understanding now. I have accepted his presence, and he gives me my space.

We are walking on the moon. Every motion becomes slower and slower, so that I can embrace the microscopic details of it all. The rainbows follow us.

Open spaces can feel like freedom, reminding us of the infiniteness we embody; or they can feel overwhelming in their immenseness, reminding us of our minuscule role in the infinity that is life. To me here, the playa is both at the same time. I am incredibly aware of each step I take, as I walk farther and farther away from my little home.

A large, blue shark, snakes across the playa, zigzagging at a turtle's pace. We run to intersect its route, but if it is a turtle, then we must be moving at the pace of snails. The shark lumbers on as we run, awkwardly chasing it. We are a sight. . . . Torque and Serene dressed as steampunk kittens; Spruce Man in a spiked collar, old t-shirt, and pageboy hat, and me in my jingling wings and furry boots.

Who am I? Who am I? Who are these people? Where are we? Is this real life?

The shark slows, so we can catch up to it, and one by one we are pulled into the hole between its fins. Inside is a blue tunnel, lined with small fish, swimming up and down the walls. We sit on the bench to watch the fish in wonderment, as they dance, gracefully, this way and that.

Following a stray fish, we climb a ladder at the rear of the shark, so we can scale up onto its top fin and watch the playa float by. The other fish come with us, and escape through the hatch at the top of the shark. The still air begins to dance, as they swim up from the shark's belly, free at last to paddle out into the open sky. They glisten softly in the sunshine, as they dance up, up, and away.

The playa is clear now, up to its edge, where the mountains loom, miles away. I've heard it is so vast, that you can see the curvature of the earth, there. I try to test this theory, but the horizon won't stop undulating, and I get confused. After blinking to reset my vision, I see a dust cloud forming in the distance, turning a patch of the clear sky into a contorted mess of brown cotton candy splotches; my head cocks in incredulous amusement. It feels like I could just bend over and take the swirling treat into my hands to eat it. I can practically taste the sugar melting in my mouth.

Yet. Brown sugar melting in my parched mouth? Who would want brown cotton candy? Whose idea was this?

Someone at carnival headquarters didn't realize that chocolate cotton candy may not be the most marketable item in the food court.

Best to stick to bubblegum flavors. Better for business.

"It looks like it's picking up," Spruce Man says, as he leans up next to me. "I hope it doesn't get as bad as yesterday." *Me too.* I'm not sure if I'm invincible right now. I'm thinking . . . not.

But there's something about acid, a kind of possibility for supremely justified recklessness; shit, think of the Manson family. Right after we took the liquid drop, one of our neighbors told us about a suicide the day before, just a few blocks away from us. A man hung himself in the center of a famous community camp. Supposedly, he wasn't noticed for hours, even as he hung in plain sight. The obscene becomes the ordinary here; everyone who passed by him thought he was just another art exhibit.

This piece of information hardly rattled me, and I now

stop a moment to wonder why. *When did I become so apathetic?* How could the news of a man's purposeful death in this dream place hardly move me? Am I now fully jaded? Have the drugs rendered me unflappable to anything not directly impacting me? Where has my empathy and altruism gone? Or is this just a dark validation that I'm finally living in the moment, engrossed in my own journey, and this faceless nameless man who I don't know commands no energy expenditure from me, as I've already given so much of myself to a myriad of other seemingly preposterous energetic internal discourse?

My lack of empathy for this, proves, beyond measure, that there is no normal here, just illusions, heaped on top of more illusions. It is as if someone placed us inside of a snow globe, removed the fake snow, replaced it with glitter, shook it up, and then dropped us into a fish tank in a penthouse suite of a brothel in Las Vegas; there are far too many layers of chaos to even begin to make sense of it all, much less understand how to get out unscathed. With a head full of acid, madness seems reasonable, and sanity, certainly negotiable.

)☼(

I'm still on the shark.

Spruce Man points at my necklace. It's bright green. "What does that mean?"

I snap back, shrug and smile. *Just be here now, isn't that what they try to teach me?* "Green means I'm alive! Also, maybe that it's time for a shot? A hug? An adventure? All of the above!" I jump on top of Spruce Man, wrapping him in a giant hug, as the shark lurches to the left. He holds on to me, so we don't fall over or off the side, and safely returns me to the ground.

"Careful, Fun Fairy. I'm not sure if your wings will save you if you fall off this guy."

The meandering shark switches directions again, thankfully this time towards 10:00. The fish trail faithfully behind the shark, trying to get back inside the belly that, only moments ago, they were so excited to escape. Perhaps, they exemplify the self- imposed prisons humans seem to crave—relationships, jobs, homes . . . The subtle addictions of conformity that we create out of habit, too afraid to really live.

Who knows how long the tiny fish lay trapped inside the shark? Now, only minutes after finding freedom, they are frantically trying to return to their captor. *"That will never be me,"* I promise myself.

The chocolate cotton candy cloud expands, again and again. Every time I blink, it doubles in size. The wind blows, whipping the beads in my hair and making my wings jingle. Then, as I blink again, the dust surrounds us. I activate my magic bubble aura (a trick from a fortune teller I met earlier) so that the dust cannot rape my pores and take me away again. Today it dances on top of me, tickling the hairs on my body, but unable to penetrate into my soul.

The shark slows down and makes its way to Esplanade and 8:00, just as the heart of the dust storm catches up to us. We hop off, back out through the fins, and make our way to our camp on foot, walking fearlessly in our masks and goggles. Particles of dust blow every which way once again, blinding us and confusing our sense of direction. Luckily, the streets allow us to follow the rough rows of camps that line them, and each corner is marked with a signpost. We can still hear life in the camps: laughter, music, and the occasional megaphone, screaming obscenities and bad jokes to all who will listen.

Upon our return to camp, the wind escalates even more. Loose tents flutter, chairs overturn, and half the parachute is ripped off, flapping in the wind: a repeat of yesterday's intensity, which does not entice me to explore amidst the storm.

)☼(

Camp It's All Fucked is still a wreck. Where would I begin to repair the damage? The once pristine kitchen features playa and bacon grease-encrusted pans, now full of what looks like mud. Bottles of Jameson and cans of coconut water litter every surface, cigarette butts overflowing from them. At least one camping chair is destroyed, a hole where the seat used to be. The parachute cover now comes completely off, and we band together to wrestle it to the ground. Marson is still missing. No one has seen him since two days ago, when he dumped a plate of spaghetti on Torque's head.

The only logical thing to do seems to be to bring a pile

of pillows, a bottle of tequila, and fifty nitrous oxide cartridges inside of a U-Haul trailer, and wait out the storm.

I suck down balloon after balloon of the sweet gas, getting lost inside the beautiful chaos that is my mind. Once again, I am inside the floating house, only outside is a thunderstorm. Lightning flashes over and over, each time illuminating new parts of the house.

> *Flash! The clown sits in the corner with his gin, glaring at me.*
>
> *Flash! The rainbow spiders crawl at me from their secret web, high above.*
>
> *Flash! My fairy flies in the center, emitting a green, aural glow.*
>
> *Flash! My wings are burning, but the fire doesn't burn me.*
>
> *Flash! An alligator with a long forked tongue pushes the clown out the door.*
>
> *Flash! The little fish swim in through the open windows and flood the tiny structure.*
>
> *Flash! The fairy uses the fire from my wings to ignite the fish, one by one.*
>
> *Flash! The fishes explode with loud pops.*

Flash! I open my eyes and I'm in the trailer, drooling on a dusty pillow. My legs are up the side of the wall. The back of the trailer is wide open, and I can see that the sky is clear, once again. I push myself up, take a shot of tequila, and head out to investigate.

Torque and Archinta are having a tea service, while Rico

juggles. I trade in my tequila for *Keemun* tea and ketamine.

Rico's left eye is swollen completely shut. He arrived on the playa with a mild bacterial infection and the dust has made it worse. Even though he hardly leaves camp, he keeps himself busy, cooking for everyone and playing with his toys. Rico is a master fire dancer, juggler, story-teller, and tea-maker.

While Rico entertains himself with juggling, Torque tries to shove as much ketamine into a small vial as is possible.

Archinta pours a cup of tea for me, into a small white porcelain cup. *Keemun* is a famous Chinese black tea, with toasted, dark chocolate aromas. Ketamine, on the other hand, I don't think I've ever tried. I won't say it never worked its way into my system, as part of some drug cocktail or another, but I've never intentionally taken it. It's an animal tranquilizer, categorized by the government as a "dissociative anesthetic." It is used medically, in liquid form, to be injected directly into the blood stream, but it can also be dehydrated, until it makes a soft white powder, giving a false impression of innocence. It is not a uniter like MDMA and MDA, but rather a dissociative, taking its users down a different kind of rabbit hole.

Torque seems to be at peace with life and with me. He is whistling, as he happily spills more ketamine onto his pants, than he gets into the vial. I zone out, staring at his strong hands. His fingers are long and competent; I trust them more than his overpowering eyes.

"Would you like to lose yourself or find yourself?" he

asks, breaking my spell, before he snorts from a tiny vial in his hand.

"I'm not sure. I'm honestly not sure anymore if I take the drugs to lose myself in myself so I can find myself . . . Wait, does that even make sense? What I mean, I guess, is that . . . I mean . . ."

I stop, take a deep breath, re-center, and begin again: "What I mean is that some people take the drugs to lose themselves, and they end up finding themselves in the process; and others just as readily, take the drugs with every intention of finding themselves, and end up losing themselves."

Rico comes closer, still juggling, to join the conversation. "It's the same thing. Or at least one can lead to the other. Whenever we leave the known for the unknown—be it in mind or body—we always take a gamble. We may lose it all, but we might find it all!" He drops a ball, does a spin, and a moment later it is back in the air as if it never touched the earth.

"You think we're the first ones to use mind-altering substances to cross into other dimensions? The Aztecs had *ayahuasca*. The native Mexican people had *peyote*. The so-called witches of Europe used hallucinogenic herbs and flowers, like belladonna. Shit, the south African bushmen slice open their scalps, and rub hallucinogens into the open wound!"

Torque nods his agreement. "Plants are medicine. Stupid fucking conservative dickwads trying to control everything and telling us what religion or drugs are allowed in polite society. Americans think, 'this is what I know and what everyone else thinks is wrong,' but it's all just subjective, right? Burning Man is medicine! Plants are medicine! Drugs are medicine! Some are medicine for the mind. Some are medicine for the body. Sometimes, same thing. But, how did we learn which heal and which ones fuck you the hell up? Trial and error. Trust. Don't die, hopefully. That's all I say, every day." He laughs for an uncomfortably long time.

Archinta pours herself another cup of tea, ignoring him. "It's the game. How far can you go, without going over the edge? Those are the people I want to meet. The ones who have gone all the way into the darkness, but come back to choose the light. There aren't very many anymore: most of them are lost children, phony shamans, or certifiably batshit crazy. 'The Edge . . . there is no honest way to explain it because the only people who really know where it is are the ones who have gone over.'"

"Tom Wolfe?" asks Torque.

"Hunter S. Thompson, of course," responds Archinta. "I keep on thinking I've found the edge, but then I find another, and another, and another." She laughs. "I must be really good at holding on! Or else I'm more fucked up than anyone knows."

"Archinta, you're the hottest mess I know," Torque says sweetly to her, before turning to glare at me: "You going to snort that or what?" I bring the small vial to my nose and inhale the white powder into my right nostril, where it burns slightly.

"Rainbow!" yells Archinta, as she stands up from her

camping chair. Sure enough, there is a perfect rainbow forming across the pale blue sky, above the dusty city. I shakily push myself up as well, and make my way across our destroyed camp to Spruce Man's van, zigzagging as I walk. I seem to have lost partial control of my limbs. I somehow manage to hoist myself clumsily on top of the roof to see the rainbow stretch from one end of the playa to the other. Each color is more vibrant and unique than I ever thought possible. I had no idea that purple could be so *purple*. I still have the vial in my hand, so I take another snort, into my left nostril this time.

I try to tell Archinta and Torque about the colors in the rainbow; the words get stuck. I try again, and all that happens, when I open my mouth, is a tiny stuttering sound that I am sure cannot belong to me. I can see the words so clearly in my mind. *The colors are so vibrant!* But they won't leave the opening that is my mouth. I try again and again; they don't come out. By now, I have repeated them in my head so many times that I am confused.

Did I actually say anything? Have I spoken? No one has answered. So maybe they haven't heard me. Should I try again?

I can no longer stand up, so I melt onto the van's roof.

It's not the most comfortable place in the world; it will do until I can relearn how to speak or move my legs. In the meantime, I watch the rainbow grow brighter and brighter and brighter, until it splits open and each color transforms from solid to pixelated blocks, that swim out of the arc and double and double and double again. When I blink, there is not one rainbow, but two.

FRIDAY: *The Edge*

Again, I try to share this. *Double rainbow! Double rainbow!* But again, my mouth has ceased functioning, and I am left with nothing but mindlessly repeating words that are unable to escape from my body. I feel trapped and helpless.

The rainbow wraps around my face, as if someone tied a blindfold over my eyes. As my vision blurs, the vibrant colors turn darker and darker, until all there is, is blackness. Slowly, a light blinks in the distance. I follow the light. At first, it appears to be white. As I get closer, I realize that it is not white, it is pale blue.

The light is high up above me. I climb up a ladder to find it. Higher and higher I climb, the wind whips against my hair, trying to push me off the ladder, but I am too strong. I continue up the rungs, until I come to a platform. I can see the city pulsate and sway, hundreds of feet below me. It is so close and yet so far away. I climb higher. I climb, still chasing the light. The light is not blue anymore, it is gray.

The light comes from a single glowing screen inside of a gray box. The walls are gray, the carpet is gray, and the ceiling is low, covered with artificial light. It's like an awful holding cell. The walls bleed pain and sadness.

There is a gray clown in the corner, staring at me, laughing at me. His nose is red, and so are his eyes. I try to yell for help, but I can't control my mouth. I try again, and finally I let out a scream. I am covered in blood and I am alone.

I am alone and I am in hell. I need my wings. I need my wings, and all I have is a useless gray clown, who stares without blinking. This is a nightmare, and my wings are supposed to stop the nightmares.

Where are my wings? Where are my wings? Where are my wings?

"Where are my wings? Where are my wings! WHERE ARE MY WINGS!" I am screaming at the top of my lungs, as I lie in a fetal position on top of the van.

"Chill the fuck out. Your wings are around somewhere. I just saw them," Archinta yells, as she climbs up with me.

"What happened? Where was I? My mouth stopped working . . . and the rainbow blinded me . . . and my mouth stopped working . . . and there was blood . . . it was awful. I lost myself."

"Or did you find yourself?" she asks with a wink. "Sometimes we need to bleed to release what we hold onto."

"I'm . . . I'm . . . I'm pretty sure that was me, lost. I don't think I like ketamine."

"Ha hah! Well, first of all, congratulations: you officially survived your first K-hole. Second, you and me both, babe." She is sitting cross-legged on the roof, while expertly rolling up a spliff. "My last trip, a family of rabbits surrounded me. They were those really cute, tiny rabbits you see in pet stores, except they were pastel-colored, like the Easter Bunny. They surrounded me, so I had to listen to them while they told me not to eat them. I haven't touched rabbit meat since."

"I couldn't move my legs or mouth, and I lost the rainbow world to a place with no color. No color and no love. Everything was gray. It was awful. I wanted to scream but no one would pay attention, even if I could. It hurt so bad. They told me it wouldn't hurt, but I felt it. Every single second I remember."

"That is exactly why I stay down the rainbow rabbit hole. No matter how bright the colors become, they're still safer than gray. Better to always be so alive and intense that there might not be any room for rest or quiet, then to be so complacent that you forget that each and every color has its own smell, or that you can have earth-shattering sex with only your eyes, or that . . ." She trails off, and her gaze rests on the distant mountains.

This is the most vulnerable I've seen Archinta. Until now she has seemed impenetrable. Now, I can see that she, too, is just made of tiny particles of matter, forged together with gold fairy dust, fine aged scotch, and far too many years of taking care of herself. She sighs and it sounds like a prayer. . . .

"What the rain feels like on my naked skin."

"Being blindfolded by a rainbow," I whisper back.

"Breaking mirrors for no reason than that you want to make art with the pieces."

"Drinking a bottle of whiskey on a rooftop at sunrise."

"Jumping off cliffs, without knowing how deep the water is."

"Lighting your possessions on fire, just to watch them burn."

"Falling in love, as if you've never had your heart broken."

I stop. That one gets me. I'm not sure if I can ever

love again. Not like *that*. I block *him* out. It still hurts. "But, numbness is safer."

"Eventually, you have to deal with your stuff. Better to face it head on, than to wait for the unknown. Trust me, I've been through my share of shit, and no one can save you, but *you*. Make the drugs a tool, not a vice. Anything can be a crutch or an instrument, it's all in how you enter the experience. Try it. Next time someone offers you a substance, instead of taking it blindly, stop. Meditate. Ask yourself what you are trying to accomplish with the experience. Identify the spirits. Honor them and ask for guidance."

"I've never thought about it that way. I've always looked for the experience first and the lesson second." Although the rainbows have long since faded, we stay put to watch the sun set. I guess I feel obligated to embrace the dream I am in since I dreamed into existence.

"Take control of your own destiny. Give it a try. Seriously, take five minutes before you ingest anything and see what happens." She stands up. "Now pull yourself together. This camp doesn't need any more hot messes. The men seem to be taking care of that just fine." She takes the tiny vial of evil, still clutched in my hand, and climbs down from the van.

After a few steps, she turns back to look at me with her blazing eyes. "Can I ask you something? This 'nice girl' thing you do? It's not an act, is it?"

"Me? An act? No. But I'm used to people thinking that it is." I slowly answer.

"Yeah, I'm not used to people like you. Keep your

purity. It's rare." She turns around again, without a look behind, before I can try to explain to her that *I'm not that pure.*

And then from the distance I hear, "Fun Fairy! Are we still going on our date?"

My date with Serene. I had forgotten about it. We are going to go art car hopping. The master plan was to ride various cars across the playa and see what adventures we find along the way. It seems exhausting, but I need to escape from my mind.

The only way out is through.

Slowly, I pull myself together. Sometimes when your world is falling apart, all you can do is pretend. I dress up for the occasion, wearing fishnet tights, fishnet thigh highs, a garter belt, a fishnet dress, and a long black jacket. Serene is dressed like a feline, with tiger-striped leggings, a short bomber jacket, and a light-up brown-striped fedora hat with pointy cat ears on top, and a long fluffy tail. We make a large thermos of *genmaicha*—Japanese steamed green tea with puffed rice. It tastes like popcorn. Perfect for our carnival.

My wings are in the U-Haul, right where I left them. I take the wings, but leave the nitrous oxide. I don't take any drugs with me. I'm probably still coming down from the acid, although the ketamine must be long gone by now, thank goodness.

We load up on glow sticks, clasp hands, and walk out into the busy, pulsating streets of our city. Every night it grows more and more crowded. New glowing sculptures, RVs, and people are everywhere. That's one of the funny things about this place: as soon as you get used to anything, it changes.

Out in the open playa, we can see even more clearly how the city has grown. Yes, it was always a chaotic mess out here, but there were once gaps between the lasers and twinkling lights. Now, there are no cracks, just layers of life. The lights do seem to be condensed around one area, somewhere out in the deep playa, perhaps a mile away, *although distance is an illusion of course,* and we intuitively begin to walk towards them. Energetic synergy is easier to understand, here. Again and again, I am aware of the magnetic energy funnels, created by so many beings, traveling to the same place at the same time.

On our way we see a house made of stained glass glowing in the desolate desert. Lights hang from its ceiling under a tin roof and illuminate the hundreds of panels that form the walls. The house hums and lightly vibrates. I'm not sure how I can feel it from twenty feet away, but I can. Serene and I walk slowly towards it, in awe of its obvious magic. The closer we get to the house, the louder the hum becomes, like a swarm of bees. As I try to remember what drugs I have taken so I can remember this combination to replicate this feeling, Serene squeezes my hand and says: "It's a sound bath, can we go in?" I nod and we make our way over the humans lying on the playa floor, to the welded iron door of the structure, ducking under prayer flags, and enter carefully.

The carpeted floor is covered with people laying peacefully against each other, reminding me of leaves in the fall on the park ground. They have the same look as The Temple worshipers do: peace and reverence. In one corner a man and a woman wear white and gently stoke giant crystal bowls. Serene and I find an unoccupied space and cuddle up, her back against the wall, and my head on her lap. She strokes my hair gently as I shut my eyes. "Try to let go." She says as she attempts to run her fingers, partially clad in fingerless gloves, through my tangled hair.

I sigh, and I try to. But I wish I knew what I wanted to let go of. The drive for meaning and purpose that constantly holds me hostage is so intense! And yet it's like a beacon for me to keep on going, to keep on surviving, against all odds. . .

The colors of the stained glass cut through my eyelids, and while I can no longer see the designs the panels make, I can see the colors dance together in large patches. First the fire colors come out, the yellows and oranges and reds, big blotches of them, as if someone was hurling watercolors against the absorbent paper that are my eyes. The music, if you can call this pure expression of sound "music" is inside of me, not just my eye lids, but my chest and my head as well.

Isn't all sound music? Does it need a beat? Or does it just need a purpose?

Serene has succeeded in combing out a small section of hair between my right temple and the place above my right eyebrow. Still she strokes it gently. Now the earth colors dance, the greens and blues and purples, taking over the fire and calming my breath.

I wonder what color my necklace is.

BURNING WINGS

But I do not open my eyes to check, instead I watch the painting inside my lids, and try to slow my breath to match the music.

Enormous glowing trees with wide arcing branches covered with leaves made of multicolored lights dance gracefully, and then begin to burn from a fire that seems to begin in their core, spreading quickly until their branches disintegrate into flaming bumblebees. The bees buzz loudly and swarm together in search of the floating flying saucer flowers that hover in the sky, and elegant giant butterflies fly up into a starlit sky and form rainbows. The rainbows burn too, but their ashes arc up higher and higher and birth clouds. My fairy dances among the clouds, and as she flies through them, she leaves little tunnels. The clouds dance and grow, filling the tunnels, expanding, until finally they burst and they rain down bright drops of metallic liquid. I focus on one particular drop, and it descends towards me, in slow motion, until it lands right on my third eye with a wet plop.

I jerk up. "Shhhhhh," says Serene, "You fell asleep. Let's rest a little longer."

How did I fall asleep? I've only been here for a few minutes.

But I don't argue. I haven't moved my head more than an inch, but I release it back down to her lap and hug my knees closer in towards my chest, finding an awkward fetal position. She continues to stroke my hair, her nimble fairy hands have untangled another few inches, moving farther away from my hairline and higher up on my head towards my crown. She gently massages the highest point of my head with one hand, and the other is on my third eye, in the center of my forehead above my brows.

The earth colors are back, especially purple and blue. I breath into them and into Serene's touch, so light and yet so deep at the same time. I truly relax now, and release out a long slow exhale. I turn over so I am on my back, my knees bent up as to not kick the people near me with my giant boots.

When I open my eyes I see a pirate on my other side. His hat is ragged and dusty, his eyes blue, bold, and rimmed with black eyeliner. He smiles at me, then at Serene, and then he shuts his eyes and journeys to another place entirely. The colors around him glow bright, a myriad of glowing specks. He speaks calmly and slowly, somehow completely in synchronicity to the music, which has no beat, and yet his words rise and fall in a steady hum.

> *"Everything is real inside the illusion of time, anything that can make you feel genuine.*
> *"Now inside your head is an endless garden, an amusement park, or perhaps an ark!*
> *"Not an arc like a rainbow, with one center and a hundred golden ends, but an ark like a boat, ready to transcend.*
> *"Now listen closely to me, as I guide you through this particular uncharted sea.*
> *"For your mind is an open book, a skeleton key, full of mystery."*

BURNING WINGS

My eyes close and I journey back into my head. It's a huge room full of giant shelves full of bound books. The ceiling is glass and rays of light pour into the room, illuminating every inch of it with its warmth.

> *"Imagine clearly, as balloons fill this vast place, expanding*
> *and multiplying, taking up space.*
> *"Each balloon, you see, is simply a puzzle piece, of which*
> *you have the power to hold or to release.*
> *"Do you see the balloons? Yes? Now make them small, so*
> *that you can touch and sort them all.*
> *"Some are colorful and some are stark, some are bright and*
> *some are dark."*

The books have turned into balls and they fall off the shelves, making endless piles on the ground. It's overwhelming and I'm a bit irritated it's so messy in my library, and that when I try to put the balls back on the shelves they just roll off. My clown is there too, and he begins to pick up the dark balls from the ground, and juggles them, first beginning with three, and then picking up more and more while the others are in the air, until the whole disheveled library is swarming with dark balls. They don't glow exactly, but they radiate power, almost like a negative light. He smirks at me and my frustration as he plays with my darkest memories and thoughts.

> *"Use your power, use your mind, and begin to sort them, to*
> *make them align.*

FRIDAY: *The Edge*

"The dark ones are heavy, yes I know, but they have served
their purpose, let them go!"

My fairy is back next to me, and she flaps her wings, creating ripples in the air, and the black balls begin to deviate from their neat arcs and hit the shelves. The clown can't keep them all in the air, and as they fall onto the ground, they roll into a corner of the room where they fall down a little hole.

"Now you should be left with only the light, now breathe into
them—make them bright!"

The remaining balls glow like lightbulbs, and I am able to pick them up and place them on the shelf next to me, where there are stands for them. I display each one proudly, like a crystal ball.

"The choice is yours, can't you see? I am only a pirate, don't
listen to me!
"But if you do, I'll tell you true. Darkness has its purpose,
release it, allow it through.
"Keep the lessons but release the pain, for what's the point of
carrying a chain?
"It's all just an illusion, fluid and intangible smoke, and yet
it still will make you choke.
"It's just a dream, nothing practical, but if you believe, you
turn it magical!
"Your mind, your dream, your reality, and your fantasy."

BURNING WINGS

The voice stops, and someone throws a bucket of water onto the painting of my library. As it fades, I open my eyes, not really remembering where I am.

Serene is still next to me, but the pirate is gone, I can just see him ducking under the door of the stained glass house as I sit up.

"Wow," says Serene. "I'm glad I popped all those black balls. Let's get out of here before we fall asleep and can't get up." I shakily rise, and make my way out back into the cold.

☽☼☾

A train drives by us at the breakneck speed of about ten miles an hour, the conductor tugging on the string above the driver, choo-chooing by us. We board the moving train. I feel a bit dazed. Words still seem difficult, so I simply sit and appreciate the moment. Serene seems to understand my mood, and doesn't push. We hold hands and wait for our stop.

The train bounces in time to the music. A lobster sits down and shares a bottle of whiskey with us. He pulls bacon out of his pocket, as a chaser. He does not offer us any bacon or a name. Just when he seems to have fallen asleep on himself, he jolts up and leaves the train.

How long have we been on the train?

Once again time has stopped. So many people now have hopped on and gotten off.

Where are we?

Serene seems to read my mind, and we move towards

the door to investigate. We are exactly where we began. The train hasn't moved at all. Five minutes or five hours we will never know, as we walk away from it, again towards the crowd in the distance, which seems to have become farther away than before.

We walk so far away from the busy train, the footprints we leave in the dust stand alone. A large, green glowing art car is coming towards us. I can't tell what it is supposed to be, if anything, besides bizarrely beautiful. It is made of endless layers of delicate laser-cut wood. We jump on and make our way up through the hole to the second level of the bus. Finally, we are going somewhere!

The bus winds its way across the playa, towards the large crowd of lights, the same one we have been trying to get to for what could be hours by now. They surround a collection of people, on their hands and knees, arms raised to the sky in horror, hands blocking their faces to protect themselves: the same gods and goddesses I first saw after the dust storm in front of Cy-Top. They are twenty feet high and made of twisted metal pieces. Their hair is made of chains and hangs down, long and sad. Bursts of fire from surrounding art cars light up their faces for quick flashes, allowing me to see the complexity of their details, the realness of their anguish, for only split seconds at a time.

I see myself in them so clearly. I am their anguish, I am their rage. They look like how I felt in The Temple: desperate, raw, and pure: devoid of any mask.

Who am I really? Who am I, without any mask? Where does this pain come from?

"Why are they so sad? What are they afraid of?" I ask softly, holding Serene's hand. These are the first words I have spoken in what seems like hours.

"Afraid? They're not afraid! They are in awe! They are worshipping!"

"But, they look so frightened."

"No, they look like they have found something higher and more powerful than they are."

"What is worship? A surrendering? An offering? An exaltation?"

We all have something inside of us that wants to connect to a higher power; we must or we wouldn't be drawn to this place. It's human nature to want to belong, to be a part of something bigger than us. We have a deep desire to give as well as to receive. Sometimes one may be easier than the other. The divine is in all of us.

Again, I think back to my time in The Temple; of how I was in ecstasy and rapture all at once, recalling the liberation of acknowledging pain, which needed to escape to heal, even as I fought to keep it bottled up. I finally think I understand how I mistook pain for euphoria. After all, isn't love the fullest expression of euphoria? And isn't pain intrinsically linked to its inevitable demise? Is there such a thing as pain-free love? And if there isn't, is it really worth it?

That's the burning question: *Is my broken heart worth it? Can I heal?*

"They are going to explode the oil rigger!" Serene excitedly exclaims. "They're blowing up that thing! That's why everyone is here!"

FRIDAY: *The Edge*

The heat from the explosion takes my breath away, even with hundreds of feet of distance. I've never seen anything so big, bright and dangerous. It's baffling in its vigor. It's pure energy. It's senselessly excessive. The flames shoot up over a thousand feet into the air, before vanishing into smoke.

"It's a mockery of itself," a man next to me states. He is wearing a full-length, pink polka-dot faux fur coat, and has a week's worth of stubble on his face. He shoots me a sideways glance, to see if I am listening, before continuing. "The art installation raises awareness about modern dependence on oil. And so, to spread the message, they publicly waste 900 gallons of jet fuel and 2,000 gallons of liquid propane. I guess, at least, it looked pretty."

"And now, it's nothing but smoke." I answer, as I watch the last of the smoky mushroom cloud float up and away into the dark sky. The man sneers.

"Smoke and dreams," he says, before he walks away, rudely shoving himself through the crowd on top of the art car. His words echo in my mind for the rest of the night . . . *Smoke and dreams. Intangible illusions. Showing me over and over and over again the impermanence of everything except the individual moments where the sky is lit on fire and defies all logic, and for what? Smoke and dreams.*

I yawn and light a cigarette, just another symbol of impermanence, the tobacco turning to dust and smoke before my very eyes.

SATURDAY

Illusion is Just
Another Illusion

I came here looking for a party

I came here looking for a dance

I came here looking to escape

I came here for a second chance

IT IS SUNRISE IN BLACK ROCK CITY AND I am just arriving back at camp. At this precise moment, there are people in the city making love, drinking their last bottle of tequila, sleeping, wishing they were sleeping, meditating, and losing their minds. In any given second, there are incalculable possible experiences, although we physically exist only in one point in space. By now I have surrendered to the fact that there is no possible way I can experience everything in this place, and lamenting over that would only nullify my present reality. The best I can hope to do is sleep as little as possible, a goal becoming more and more difficult as the sun rises each morning.

Here, at Camp It's All Fucked, the first thing I see is a beautiful nymph, wearing a white dress, crumbled on the ground near my tent. It is Serene, and she is crying soft, luscious tears. Her dress is delicate and made of lace. It belongs on a porcelain doll on a shelf, not paired with brown combat boots, lime green ski goggles, and furry antennae; yet, it is lovely. Her brown nipples poke through the sheer top of her dress. I sit next to her, and cradle her in my arms. Her body easily yields to my embrace. "What's wrong? Why are you crying?" I expect a long dramatic story at best or, at worst, some drug-induced blathering; instead, she looks at me with a giant grin.

"I'm getting married!" she states brightly, through her tears. "I'm getting married!" She repeats it again, but this time to herself.

"To Torque?" I ask. For most people, this question wouldn't be necessary, but with Serene and Torque, you never know.

"Yes! To my soulmate!" Her eyes are wide and wild, and her pupils are shaped like tiny hearts. She looks like an anime heroine, ready to save the world, karate-chopping through the villains of the earth, all the while wearing a white lace wedding gown and combat boots. Right now, she is invincible.

Torque appears, in the distance. He is wearing an over-sized top hat, calf-high trousers, and a white and tan striped men's dress shirt with the sleeves cut off. His giant green snowboard goggles hang from his neck, as if they were another ornament. Serene ducks into her tent to find some special necklace, and I see Torque, pacing spastically in small circles and talking to himself.

"I am love. I am centered. I am worthy of love. I embody love. Up until now, I have been wary of Torque; not only do I not fully trust nor understand his personality's irregularities, but also, he has made it very clear that he does not like nor respect me. I am an alien to him: naive, young, and sanguine. To him, I have no comprehension of spirituality or darkness, nor any perceptible depth. That's fine, I'm used to being underestimated. *Not everyone needs to know about my evil clown.*

Again he turns to me, "Darkness is misperceived! It's a

trap! Death and birth are simply capstones of where every-one really is. Darkness is just death. It's needed for rebirth. Burning Man is a rebirth! It's your whole life in a single week! It's a grand totem to the process of birth and death! It's just Kali! We need the darkness as a catalyst for change!"

"Are you ready for change?" I ask quietly.

"All I am is constant change. This is a fact! But marriage? I despise the very definition. I despise conformity. I despise right wing traditions."

"No kidding, really?" I ask sarcastically; it is lost on him. Still, he paces. *I doubt he has slept.*

"And yet, isn't this the ultimate rebellion? To take on an institution such as marriage, which has become a parody of itself? One that supposedly exists for such pure reasons, and yet has served to oppress women and promote materialism? Take it back?" He stopped pacing, turned towards me, and looked deeply into my eyes (and, through them, into my soul). *He definitely hasn't slept.*

"I am reclaiming the institution of marriage. Marriage is life. Marriage is birth. I don't give a flying fuck about the pomp and circumstance of the procession, and the stupid fucking flowers, and the dress, and all that bullshit. I want to create something. I want the birth. There has been far too much death for me." He doesn't want an equal conversation, just an audience for his monologue, so I light a cigarette, in lieu of trying to respond. "Everyone I love is here! Even you! I fucking love you! I hated you, and now I love you! Love is everything! I love Rico! I love Archinta! I love Marson! I love Spruce Man! I love North! Where the fuck is North? He needs to be at my wedding." He turns to me again. "Where is North?"

"At camp, I'm sure. Do you need me to get him?"

"Yes! You get him! I need to get married! It is almost dawn! We will be in deep playa. Find the psytrance camp, and bike as far as you can towards the rising sun. That is where my destiny lies." He rushes off, leaving me alone.

The sun is almost up. The sky is a brilliant watercolor of every shade of pastel imaginable.

I discard my jacket, trading it for sunglasses, new cigarettes, and a bottle of champagne. I find a bike with a basket on it, toss the bottle of champagne in, and steal it, without a second thought, as off I go back across the playa, about two miles, to find North, to invite him to Torque and Serene's dreamy dystopian psytrance wedding.

For all the nights I've stayed up, and all the mornings I've watched the dawn, this is the first morning I am active, at this time; usually, I am snuggled up or just getting home.

)☼(

One hundred and eighty minutes ago, I said goodbye to Serene, and denied her invitation to return to camp.

One hundred and fifty-two minutes before this moment, I was dreaming of sleep.

One hundred and seventeen minutes ago, I found myself propped up on scaffolding looking down on a giant dance party, framed with pyrotechnics and found my old friend Peach. We jumped up and down in joy and hugged for what felt like forever. I remembered how to speak again. She gave me her favorite velvet hat to wear. I gave her a leather bracelet I sewed.

Ninety-seven minutes ago, I saved a girl's life with a lollipop I had stashed in my hair, and she rewarded me with a white pill, which I swallowed, before I remembered I wasn't supposed to take any more drugs.

Seventy-one minutes ago, I ran out of whiskey.

Sixty-three minutes ago, I smoked my last cigarette.

Fifty minutes ago, I began my walk back to camp.

Fifteen minutes ago, I arrived.

Now, I ride spastically back to the other side of the city, passing The Man on my right. He burns tonight.

)☼(

When I arrive at Cy-Top, it is quiet and dark. I find North's tent, unzip it, and gently snuggle him awake before whispering, "Torque is getting married. Come, now."

He recognizes the importance of this, and gets up immediately. Silently, he throws on a tank top, embroidered vest, and hat. He climbs on his bike, and off we ride again, across the playa (my third time in the past hour). The thought of questioning this rash decision does not even cross his mind, let alone leave his lips. He knows Torque better than most people, and therefore knows that logic has no place when discussing him.

The sun slowly emerges from its home behind the horizon, announcing itself proudly, illuminating the sky brightly, first slowly, and then, all at once. We ride urgently, aiming for the openness outside of 10:00.

We find the psytrance camp and, predictably, the same generic beat is still playing (a way higher BPM than I'm comfortable with at the peak of the night, and even less so at sunrise). Out from here, we ride into the open desert. Finally, we find them, amidst the empty space.

The sun is higher now: high enough to cast full shadows, but low enough that they are long, and extend across the cracked ground. If one were to judge us by just our shadows, we'd be very gaunt giants. Because nothing is as it appears here; our shadows join the collection of illusions I have encountered.

)☼(

We've missed the actual ceremony, and I'm disappointed, for I was looking forward to witnessing both the spectacle of their wedding itself, as well as the renewal in my faith in love I have been craving so desperately. But what remains of the wedding party is still picturesque in a twisted Mad Max meets Dali sort of way, and yet like most oddities here, it makes sense to me.

Serene and Torque sit on the dust, holding large, green plastic margarita glasses. Around them is their wedding party, about twenty slightly haggard friends, clad in torn lace, studded leather, and dirty furs. Everyone seems to have bottles of champagne in hand, and takes turns pouring the fizzy liquid into the happy couple's glasses. Serene mixes hers with kombucha. Marson is back, and now he presides over the festivities, wearing a top hat, spectacles, and a long cape.

)☼(

Four hours ago, I was dancing on a lotus flower.

Three hours ago, I rolled in the dust, making angels.

Two hours ago, I was spraying pee on my boots, behind an art installation.

One hour ago, I was almost in my bed.

Now, I am at a psytrance wedding, drinking champagne.

Reality is an illusion.

)☼(

I pop open my own bottle and run towards the bride and groom, the foam overflowing from the bottle. The wedding party dances around each other, laughing and singing, and pouring the wine into each other's glasses. As the sun rises higher, so does the temperature, and soon the ground is covered with piles of fur and leather. Everyone dances together. I stay off to the side, drinking my bottle, and smoking what may be my hundredth cigarette of the night. These are my campmates, but I am not sure whether this is my family. Not yet, anyway. I simply appreciate the beauty of the scene from afar, basking in the contact high I receive from their excitement.

Serene dances up to me with a huge grin on her face.

"Thank you for coming! Thank you! Thank you! Thank you! I love you!" I smile, putting out my cigarette and stuffing the butt into my portable ashtray. We spin in circles, laughing and smiling, before plopping down, together, onto the ground.

"I love you too. I'm so happy I'm here with you," I finally respond to her. Maybe I have found a new family, of sorts.

"The wedding was breathtaking. And then these Mormons came and wanted to know if they could marry me also! I told them maybe next year! But there was so much love in one place. And then the sun came up . . . It was like it rose just for us, just for our love."

"I watched it. It hovered above the mountains for an insanely long time, like time slowed down." I light my hundred and first cigarette.

"There is something so special about the sunrise, about fighting through the night to make it back to the light. Everyone is so raw and vulnerable at sunrise. It strips you down to who you truly are."

"No one can hide during the sunrise, huh? Whoever you could pretend you were during the darkness, when the sun comes up, it exposes the true self."

"And that's how I got married: raw and vulnerable, with nothing to hide behind, except, of course, my goggles!" Serene smiles the biggest smile I've ever seen, then she pulls out a tiny carved wooden box out of some fold in her costume, opens it grandiosely, and presents it to me: "Here, eat some acid."

SATURDAY: *Illusion is Just Another Illusion*

"Here's to new beginnings." I take the tiny blotter paper on my tongue, raise my bottle to her glass, and we toast each other, the new day, and each of our new lives. Each dawn brings new beginnings, and this one is no exception.

)☼(

I walk through the desert alone, wearing a cotton and lace white dress. A figure is in front of me, blocking the sun.

It's him. I fall to my knees and my dress splays out on all sides of me. It's really him. I stare up at him, at this beautiful damaged man that will be a part of me forever. In this moment I see the full spectrum of our love, the pain, the demise, the breathtaking beauty of it all. I see him in his imperfection so clearly, and yet I still love him.

"I love you. I love you here and now and I always will." *I shake as the words come out.*

He is silent.

"I thought I could live without you. I thought the pain would fade. I was wrong."

He is silent.

"Can't you see? There is nothing in this world that makes sense besides love! Even through the pain I still choose love!" The tears begin again, but they aren't water, they are blood.

He is silent.

"If you walk away from me, if you choose to turn your back on true love, you will regret it for the rest of your life." *My sadness turns to anger, and the tears sting as they roll down my cheeks and splash onto my white dress.*

BURNING WINGS

Incensed by the blood, I frantically claw at my chest, using my tiny bitten nails to scrape back the skin. Through the slippery blood I manage to get my fingers into the crack between the bones, and then with a primal scream of rage and unrequited love, I pry open up my chest so I can reach my heart. I gently pull it out, ignoring the snapping veins. It takes both hands to hold onto this slippery beating thing, full of the glass shards.

In my white cotton dress, now stained with blood, with a hole in my chest, I kneel on the dust and offer my heart.

"This is the most precious gift you will ever receive. If you walk away now you'll regret it forever. This is on you. For the rest of your life you'll have to know that you turned your back on love." There is no stutter in my voice anymore.

He is silent.

"So this is it? It was all just for nothing?" The bloody tears harden on my face in the dry heat.

He stares at me sadly, and finally he speaks.

"Once it was everything. Now it's just dust."

I spend the morning lounging at camp, unable to pry myself up from my beautiful nest of a beanbag chair. I'm in one of those dazes where I'm half awake and half asleep, unsure if the swirling patterns I see on the ceiling of our newly erected easy-up are my sleep-deprived imagination or LSD-inspired hallucinations. A spritz bottle and a six-pack of coconut water keep me alive. After hours of this, I realize that to eat would be an intelligent decision.

"I heard there's a camp called Erotic Eggs that will cook you eggs any way you want," Spruce Man suggests.

"While you watch porn!" Someone yells from their tent laughing. "Or you can make your own!"

"Porn and eggs? I could eat eggs and watch porn. That sounds about right," I respond, thoughtfully. We leaf through the Burning Man guidebook and camp directory until we find the camp address, just a few blocks away. "Ugh! I guess I'll get dressed."

In my ramshackle tent I find my lucky black bootie shorts and a comfy cotton striped bra I got from the little girl's section at Target. I pair these with my black platform boots and a collection of rainbow beaded necklaces. Of course my lopsided wings get strapped on my back. I've given up on my hair. It's a bird's nest of bells and knots.

We walk down the streets in a zigzag pattern; neither of us has slept, and we hope that eggs will revitalize us. I imagine perfectly poached eggs, atop an English muffin, smothered in Hollandaise sauce, hash browns and hot sauce on the side, and a mimosa, to boot. A gang of chisel-chested men, wearing tutus with long fake balls dangling down, struts past us, and I have to rub my eyes to make sure that their balls do, in fact, exist, and that they are fake. *They must be fake, right?*

When we finally find Erotic Eggs, it's underneath a few large easy-ups. There is a mahogany coffee table, covered with vintage *Playboy* magazines. The muscular man behind the bar is old enough that his skin has grown thin, so, when stretched tautly against his bulging muscles, it exposes every vein on his body.

"Do you have eggs? Can I get mine poached?" I inquire.

"Eggs? You want eggs?" He responds slowly, eyeing me with determination.

"This is Erotic Eggs, right'? We heard you had eggs?" Spruce Man asks, hesitantly. The bartender turns to him, finally taking his eyes off me, seemingly shocked to notice that someone else is in his domain.

He laughs. "We ran out of eggs on Tuesday. If you want to make some porn, we have a back room, and I'd be happy to set up the camera for you." He turns back to me. "I'm happy to join you." He smiles and licks his lips.

"We came for the eggs," I say, not swayed by his offer.

"No eggs; just sausage." I shake my head *no*. "Well, then . . . What to offer the beautiful fairy? Want some nitrous?"

Although he makes me uneasy, the allure of the drug wins out over common sense. I smile a fake smile. "Nitrous sounds like brunch to me."

He grabs a canister and a few cartridges from behind the bar, and plops down on the couch. I reluctantly move to join him. *I hate this game, but fuck it, it's Saturday.* I'm still feeling the acid and haven't slept. It's the perfect time for trouble. I sit down next to him on the couch.

"I'm gonna grab a drink at the next bar; meet me there?" Spruce Man asks, pointedly. "If not, I'll come back for you. Don't wander off, fairy!"

"I'll meet you there. Don't worry." Spruce Man leaves Erotic Eggs for the giant day party I can see, a camp or two down.

"What's your name?" I ask, as the bartender fills a balloon for me.

"Robin Jeremy," he replies, as he hands me the bulging balloon. I inhale, filling my lungs to their maximum capacity, and hold it there, with my cheeks full, for as long as I can, before I exhale. He watches me, as he takes his own hit, directly from the canister. "I like when your cheeks bulge. You look like a sexy chipmunk."

There is no response to that that doesn't sound bitchy or flirtatious, so I choose to ignore him, as I repeat my inhalation process, trying not to bulge my cheeks too much this time. Finally, on my third hit, I go into Magical Nitrous Land, where everything looks like a Stanley Mouse poster from the 1960s, and every sound has a tail. It's pretty and safe here. *I like this dream.*

It dissipates and, when I open my eyes, I'm still at Erotic Eggs, and Robin Jeremy is still staring at me. His hand is on my thigh.

I jump up, a bit dizzy, but back in control. "I have to go. Thank you for the nitrous!"

"Anytime, sugar. You know where to find me, if you change your mind." He winks at me.

I walk quickly out of the camp, blinking at the intensity of the noon sunlight.

Time for a change of scenery.

I head towards the music. There's a large outdoor dance party going on, on the open dust, surrounded by a collection of structures, modeled after an old western town. Two thousand people dance under the hot sun as a DJ spins a house track. I walk along the edge of the dance floor, still a bit hazy from the nitrous, which seems to have given the aftereffects of my acid a new lift. This is the kind of party that calls for ecstasy or cocaine, not LSD.

Cocaine sounds like a good idea right now, who here has coke?

I find the bar, and perch on a random stool nearby, observing the rowdy crowd. Two men are behind me, talking; one is wearing tight gold leggings, a plastic "$" necklace, and a white curly wig. His companion has on a loincloth and a pharaoh headpiece. Without meaning to, I eavesdrop on their conversation. . .

". . . she's hot as fuck, right? What was I supposed to do? I couldn't let her go!" The man in gold is talking loudly, as he makes large gestures with his hands. They might be spray-painted gold; my vision can't fully be trusted, at the moment.

"Wait, wait . . ." The man in the loincloth stops him with a look of disbelief and admiration. "So, you stole someone else's soulmate?"

"I didn't steal her, so much as accept an obvious gift from the Playa Gods. She went to some soulmate camp, picked a soulmate out of a hat, and it was a guy named Todd. So, she goes looking for Todd at 4:30 and E. I'm at 4:30 and F; she wanders into my camp, and I swear man, I knew I had to have her. She had on these tiny white bootie shorts, white push-up bra, and pigtails. Fucking pigtails! So, of course I go, 'I'm Todd.'"

"Dude. You stole Todd's soulmate! They might have

gotten married, had kids, the whole white-picket-fence bull-shit. . .”

"Dude. Fuck Todd. Todd could have been a murder-er. Or a stage-one clinger. Or had a tiny dick. We fucked all fucking day in my trailer, and then all night. I made her fucking burn.”

"Your karma, dude. It’s going to bite you in the ass, one day.”

"The best part? She kept screaming ‘Todd,’ when she came. . . .”

I get up. *I can’t listen to this bullshit anymore*, and I don’t have the composure to call him out, let alone wth eloquence. I wiggle up to the bar; it’s long and crowded. The bartend-ers all look like models: the girls have tiny skirts, platform boots, and yarn braided into their hair; the men have short shorts and perfect abs. They dance around, taking orders and dumping obscenely large amounts of vodka into blend-ers, along with frozen fruit. Within minutes, one of the guys makes eye contact with me, smiles, and saunters over. He grabs my princess cup, and fills it to the brim with pink vod-ka slushy. I thank him, grin in delight, and take a sip of the sugar alcohol concoction bestowed upon me for no other reason than I’m a girl. *I like this carnival bar.*

I saunter away, and find Spruce Man down the bar. "Hey!" I call out in greeting, as I poke him.

"Yo! How the hell did you get a drink? I’ve been waiting for like thirty minutes.”

I shrug. "Boobs?”

A woman next to me, wearing a see-through tight mesh

tank dress, turns to me and winks. "You can get anything in this place with tits or a bottle of whiskey. Watch this." She pinches her nipples until they are fully erect, and then gracefully shoves her way to the front of the bar. Within thirty seconds, she is given a drink, much to the annoyance of the four men surrounding her. She leans up and over the bar, kisses the bartender long and hard on the mouth, then comes back down to the floor, straightens her skirt, turns to us, and winks.

"That's such bullshit," says Spruce Man.

"I'm sorry? Kind of. Here, have my drink; I'll get us refills from now on." We move away from the bar, and into a shaded area. The crowd grooves, as though it is one. Everyone is dressed to the nines. A bunch of men—*how does every man here have a six-pack?*—wearing tutus spray the crowd with giant water soakers. Someone keeps on blowing a horn and, each time, everyone cheers, like it's the first time in the history of the world anyone blew a horn.

"Ugh! I'm so confused. This is Spring Break." I say to Spruce Man, as I down my cocktail.

"You just hit your wall, is all. This is so your scene. And this track is sick! I didn't think anyone else had this remix."

"Whatever. Everyone here sucks. I'm getting another drink."

"If everyone here sucked, then that douche at Erotic Eggs wouldn't have been up on your flat chest so hard." That at least gets a laugh and a smile out of me. Maybe I am being a bitch. I need some sleep. Or some cocaine.

Where can I get some coke?

SATURDAY: *Illusion is Just Another Illusion*

I get us another round of drinks at the bar. This time it takes me a few minutes, but I'm still way ahead of Spruce Man's wait time. My flat chest still works for something.

When I get back to our sitting area, our bags are still there, and Spruce Man is out dancing, a few layers deep into the crowd. He beckons me to join, but standing up is awful. I settle back down, light up a cigarette, and resume people watching. I'm impressed by everyone's sunglasses; I didn't know that they could be so big, so gold, or that so much glitter could be contained on such a small surface.

A couple bounces in front of me. Literally, they are bouncing off the wall. The guy is wearing black, studded shorts, a leather Peter Pan style hat with butterflies on it, and leather boots. He must be six and a half feet tall and really good at bouncing, so when he reaches maximum bounce height, I swear he makes it to eight feet tall. His girl is Latina and petite, in a purple tutu, a purple sparkly bandana, purple heart sunglasses, and purple heart pasties. She bounces as well, but her maximum bounce height is only just his standing still height. I wonder what drug cocktail they've ingested; their bounciness is very impressive. They are trying to tell a story to their non-bouncing friend, who, ironically, is dressed like Tigger.

"It was the longest ladder in the world!" she says

"But we climbed up, up, up, up to the top!" he says.

"And on the very top-."

"There's a tiny platform-"

"But since the semi-trucks-"

"Are all metal!"

"It was so hot!"

"Oh, my god, so hot!"

"And we ran out of water-"

"But, we had acid-"

"So, we took the acid-"

"And then we couldn't get down-"

"Because the ladder was so long-"

"And moving-"

"And, everyone that came up the ladder-"

"We asked them for water-"

"But they only had drugs and alcohol-"

"So, that's what we did!"

"All the drugs!"

"And all the alcohol!"

"But we finally-"

"Got down the ladder-"

"And didn't die!"

"And now we're high!"

I'm getting dizzy, watching them. Thankfully, they bounce away onto the dance floor, where she climbs up on his shoulders. He continues to bounce. I cringe each time, expecting her to go flying off, like a tiny doll. Miraculously, she stays on. Her platform boots hit a few bystanders along the way, but they've already bounced away before anyone can protest.

I'm almost done with my drink, so I head back to the bar for another. As I wait, someone backs up into me, while waving his arms, and spills the rest of my drink down my legs and belly.

"Dude!" I exclaim.

"Fuck sorry . . . Oh hey! What's up girl?" It's Coco, my DJ friend from San Francisco.

"Hi sweetie! Great set on Wednesday; that Doors remix blew my head open. *Literally*."

He smiles, rubs my back, and says: "Want to get out of here? My RV is super close, and I really want some blow."

"You are my personal savior. Let's go."

)☼(

I'm supposed to do something special before I take more drugs, but I can't remember what. It's important. *I'm supposed to meditate?* I snort a line of cocaine off the peeling linoleum table. Can you meditate on cocaine? *Probably not*, I decide and then do another line, dropping my tiny straw on the table to signal completion. The straw promptly rolls off the table and disappears forever.

"It's fucking bullshit. Back in the day there wasn't this house music shit. The ravers stayed in their zone. They were the laughingstock of this place. Now they're everywhere!" I'm in an RV from the 1970s, with my DJ friend Coco and some crusty testosterone-filled ex-fitness athlete turned blasé hulk-like burner, who has more white powder stuck to his low-hanging nose hair than in his actual nostrils.

"Music is the heart of the city. The bass is literally the heartbeat. You can hear it everywhere—" Our resident music nerd romanticizes the music, before being cut off by the large troll.

"—damn fucking right I can hear it everywhere. There was pure silence in this place, before all you little monkeys showed up with your fancy sound systems and decided to make this place your playground." The shaggy ogre smacks the table to make his point, and the remaining powder dances with the vibration.

I silently take the rolled-up Walmart receipt from his hand, and help myself to the rest of the cocaine. For some reason, he likes me, and I don't want to push my luck by speaking. Coco is getting frustrated now, trying to keep his cool. His curly pigtails and antennae probably help.

"Cities change. This is a city. The music brings new life."

"I don't come here every fucking year to build and clean up, so you assholes can play kiddie rave. And what the fuck is up with those throw-away glow sticks? You all are the worst hippies, ever. Can't you bottle up fireflies or some shit?"

"Listen, the music isn't going anywhere. It's just getting bigger and better. I even heard that Daft Punk is going to play a show at the trash fence, after the burn. It's probably bullshit, but you never know. . ."

Right then, I remember what I'm supposed to do: *Next time someone offers you a substance, instead of taking it blindly, stop. Meditate. Ask yourself what you are trying to accomplish with the experience. Identify the spirits. Honor them and ask for guidance.*

"Who the hell is Daffy Punky? Another douche from Vegas? Does he have his own reality show? Does he bring a harem of Swedish models? I was almost on TV too! Fucking body building olympics and it fucking fell through. Fuck them."

The greasy ape-man is getting riled up, now he stands up to gesture as he continues: "I bet they wish they could see me right now! Look at this fucking ridiculous life! If this isn't good reality TV what the hell is? Shit . . . I'd suck my own dick!" The large scary man that weighs twice as much as me stands up to pace as he rages. He is not able to pace far in the small RV and it shutters as he stomps. I cower a tiny bit lower on my seat.

"I wish I had blown the fucking man up early! About fucking time someone brought back some fucking havoc. I can't even deal with this pretty little sparkly festival anymore!"

Fuck, man! What do I ask these spirits for? I try. I close my eyes and take a few deep breaths. My heart is racing at an insane pace. *What do I want from cocaine?* I think about what I know about the drug: its quick lift to heightened alertness, and its ability to engulf the user in its excess of thoughts and action. I go over the week, and what I have been given, for better or for worse, and all I can come up with for this experience is *don't let me sleep*. There is too much here. I have only a day and a half left. I need all the experiences I can possibly have. I need it all. Sleep is for quitters. I am invincible.

"Don't get me wrong. I'm grateful for the work you do. I couldn't handle, whatever gnarly work you do showing up early, physical labor and all that, but I'm here working my ass off, too. You think it's easy to play a set on a moving art car in a dust storm?" I can still hear Coco through my hazy thoughts.

I open my eyes wide and look around, really look around. I'm suddenly hyperaware of my surroundings. I'm in a crusty old trailer, shoving white powder up my nose, listening to two jaded burners exchange spars over whether or not music is a good thing? I'm an extra in a bad low budget B-movie, without a plot.

I have to go. I need some crystals and sage, right now.

"Oh, excuse me. I didn't realize pounding rebar for a solid month was as hard as playing your iPod, while driving at 5mph. You call that work? My ass!" Our resident barbarian is now breathing hard in anger. His whole face is the same delightful shade of red as my sparkly lip-gloss.

"Back in my fucking day it was pick-up trucks, rifles, and a good old fashioned 'fuck you!' to everyone. Myself included! Don't think that I don't have a sense of humor!" He turns to look both of us in the eye, with a cynical mischievous grin, daring us to disagree. The muscles in my face seem to be rendered practically useless by the drugs and lack of sleep so I can only imagine that the corners of my mouth curve up slightly in appreciation.

Carelessly, he dumps another pile of white powder onto the counter and roughly chops it. His movements are erratic as he plops back down onto his seat, sticks his nose into the pile, *Scarface* style, and inhales deeply. He lifts his head up a few inches to glare at Coco, his lips curl up into a sneer, and then his head drops back down onto the table. He doesn't move a muscle, as the cocaine settles around him. My gaze rises to find Coco's eyes, and we hold our breath anticipating another explosion.

His nostrils begin to move slightly. My body tenses, expecting the eruption. Instead, he begins to snore. Coco and I both begin to snicker. His whole face, even his eyelashes, are sprinkled with cocaine.

Soon, we are laughing uncontrollably and I begin to sob. When I have control again, I stand up, brush off the loose powder on my bra, and snort another line. I bid goodbye to my friend, and the finally peaceful, now sleeping, jolly giant.

"Thank you for the hospitality, but I have to go meditate or get drunk."

"Don't miss the burn!" he reminds me, as we hug goodbye.

Shit. The burn.

How have I forgotten?

What did I do all day?

What now?

Back to camp?

Do I have any drugs on me?

Have I eaten today?

I stop at a bar, to ponder this last question. I drank champagne this morning, along with a micro- dose of acid. I drank strawberries and rum this afternoon. I just did about a half of a gram of cocaine. But human maintenance? Non-existent.

Just then my stomach rumbles. I run my tongue along my teeth, and they are thick with dust-coated plaque. My throat is sore. My feet hurt. I am thirsty.

I now remember cocaine's descent.

There are people everywhere, and no one seems to notice I am fast becoming destitute. Even the bartender hasn't said hello to me, yet—and I'm not wearing a shirt. Something is wrong, here.

I look down at my black boots. They are no longer black; they are dust-colored. Above them, my dirty legs show through my wide mesh fishnet tights. Six days ago, my legs were carefully shaved, and now their prickly stubble serves only to attract more dust. There are patches where I spilled spirits, and the dust dried there, in almost psychedelic patterns. I'm wearing my favorite black bootie shorts; no, I can't think about my vulva now. It, too, has grown out its careful Brazilian shave—not to mention I haven't found a porta potty with toilet paper all day. The thought of sex repulses me—I'm glad I got my kicks, earlier in the week. My torso is bare, except for an old, pink-striped training bra. I don't remember putting it on. It's hideous.

Why the fuck would I wear something so ugly in public?

My hair is wild and half dread-locked. Thank god, I still have my wings!

I feel nauseous, and am suddenly aware of how disgusting I am. Gracelessly, I hop off the bar stool and head back out to the street. I wander aimlessly. The late afternoon sun is high, and I am tired.

Don't go to sleep.

I smell pizza. I climb over a pile of overturned camping chairs and find a group of women around a pot of spaghetti.

"Do you have any food for a hungry fairy?" I ask meekly. They look over at me.

"Sorry honey, this is the last of it." I pout and flounce away, embarrassed for asking, and even more embarrassed that I was denied.

"Hey." She calls me back over and hands me a giant bottle of water. "Chug this. Also—best advice I can give you for staying together is to use the sunrises and sunsets as a reminder for human maintenance. Drink water. Brush your teeth. Change your panties. You don't want to meet the love of your life with dirty panties, do you?"

I nod, still embarrassed, chug the water, choking a little, and scuttle away.

I walk and walk and walk, until I hit Esplanade again. I see people everywhere, and I am lonely. I smell food everywhere, and I am hungry. I am tired, and I am not allowed to sleep.

I am becoming more destitute.

Don't go to sleep.

Standing upright is becoming a chore.

My footsteps grow closer together and slower. My eyes begin to close. I force them back open. They close again, and I remember how it would feel to rest, to simply sleep.

Don't go to sleep. Stay on your feet. Don't go to sleep.

I can't resist the temptation. I stumble, and the ground calls me closer to it. Sleep. Just then someone grabs my hand and pulls me into a giant bear hug. I melt into the embrace, partly from physical exhaustion, and partly from relief at being touched and held.

Human beings are made for contact and companionship. Although we tend to marginalize this urge into the purely sexual, a hug at the right time can change a life. I think most the time strangers have sex it's just so they can have someone to hold after. It makes sense that the worst punishment you can give to someone is physical isolation. Emotional isolation we do to ourselves.

When my rescuer finally releases me, I look up to see who it is. My clown stares back at me. His eyes match his mischievous grin, daring me to pull away from him. I don't.

Sweetly he takes my hand, gently opening my fingers with his, so they can slide in between mine, in a full clasp. He pulls me along the street, steering me to avoid the constant stream of swerving pedestrians that I threaten to bump into, in my delirium. Over the course of the week, I have become accustomed to the unfamiliar becoming the familiar. It seems perfectly normal that this clown used to cause me annoyance, even utter fear; yet, now he is my knight, leading me to safety.

"Where are we going?" I ask.

Smiling knowingly, he doesn't respond with words; rather his twinkling eyes tell me to trust him. I do. His eyes are no longer bloodshot; now, they are clear and white. We have traded eyeballs, it seems. We turn up another street, and into an open circular courtyard. He releases my hand, points me towards the east, and gently pushes me away from him, like a mother bird, pushing her baby out of the nest to fly. Hesitantly, I walk east, unsure of my destination. And then, I see . . .

A noodle cart. A fucking noodle cart. A FUCKING

NOODLE CART!

Noodles. Noodles. Noodles. Noodles.

I am saved.

A very nice, small man, named Shin, and my evil clown, are my new heroes. Shin has a white noodle cart, decorated with a gold and red dragon. I watch, as he expertly dishes out a serving of loose flash- boiled noodles into a wooden bowl, pours broth over them, and then garnishes them with an assortment of liquid and solid condiments. He hands me the hot bowl, and my eyes tear up in pure gratitude. Not once, in the history of the universe, has there been such a grand gesture, as the gift of this steaming bowl of noodles; never mind that the temperature on the playa is over ninety degrees Fahrenheit.

I crouch down on the dust, and frantically slurp the steaming noodles into my mouth. Bits of fried garlic and dried shrimp get caught in my teeth. The broth burns my tongue; it is so salty and vibrant, I can't stop my consumption. A warm sensation grows in my belly, and I begin to feel whole again. The broth is so rich and flavorful, I could drink it forever.

When the bowl is empty, and my belly is full, I melt into the dust in satisfaction, physically exhausted from my excess culinary bliss. In this land of dreams and wonder, the simplest things have yielded me the most pleasure: a warm fire, soup, clean toilets, the sunrise. . . It's almost as if all the excess has a greater purpose: detaching us from our default routines, where we take our lives for granted, and breaking us down to our basic needs, so we can truly appreciate the primality of living. Away from the monotony of city life, when confronted with excess, the beauty of the mundane reveals itself.

Back at camp, after reluctantly napping on a partially-deflated raft, with a giant stuffed turtle, I give full attention to my personal hygiene. I strip off my disgusting clothing, and bathe myself with baby wipes. It takes twelve to wipe off my entire body, including my lady parts, and the cracks between my toes. Next, I smear lotion all over my parched skin, rubbing it in furiously, until every streak has been absorbed. I brush my teeth for at least five minutes, and then floss and rinse with mouthwash. I dress in warm cleaner clothes—although nothing is completely clean, in my dust den of a tent. I refill my flask, find an unopened pack of cigarettes, and again put on my broken wings.

I will try to remember this every sunrise and sunset. Maybe.

Camp It's All Fucked is slightly less fucked. Serene and Torque are missing—presumably on their honeymoon—however Rico, Archinta, and Spruce Man are gearing up for the night, busily cracking open a full box of glow sticks to decorate hands, hair, bikes and bodies.

Archinta is on a tirade. She tried to commandeer a neighbor's art car to throw a party on for the burn but was rebuked. She is not used to rejection. "I was so polite! I mean, we have the DJs, we have the ladies, what else do you need for a party?"

Rico rolls his eyes. "Even here, my dear, there are rules. You heard the man. . . You need a *legal* driver, spotters, registration with the Department of Mutant Vehicles. It sounds like a hassle to me."

Her eyes flash. "What's the point of building an art car if not to attract humans that are better looking and more fun than you to dance on it? It seems like a complete waste to me."

"You want an art car? Build a fucking art car!" They wander away, still bickering. I light a cigarette and sit on my favorite beanbag, waiting for the rest of the crew. *I'll just close my eyes for a moment. . .*

)☼(

"Wake up fairy!" Spruce Man kicks the beanbag and I jolt up, spilling a drink in front of me with my clunky boots. There's a hole where my hand dropped the lit cigarette, and I dust off the ashes, blinking my eyes. *No more sleep!*

"No more sleep! The Man's about to burn!" He reads my mind and hands me a can of beer.

"I'm coming! I'm ready! Let's go!" I chug the cold beer, holding back vomit, and we're off again, ready for the next spectacle. The sun has set and the stars begin to dot the sky. The city is again transformed into lights and lasers. They share a bottle of whiskey, for once I shake my head no as it is passed to me. *I can't.* The ground thuds with bass music as we make our way towards the center of the playa. Stimuli are everywhere. Lights and sounds. I can no longer smell anything.

Tonight, finally, The Man will burn, as scheduled. He is completely rebuilt. He rises tall and brilliantly lit, amid the glowing humans and vehicles that circle him. The people on the ground, in the front row, form a barrier between the crowd and the openness which surrounds him. An aggressive excitement that intrigues me is in the air. So far, I've seen no real violence, yet I can feel the energetic shift from the beginning of the week. Sleep has been traded for sunrises, water forgone for bourbon. Clear minds have been exchanged for hallucinogens. Saturday feels like the wild card it is.

The art cars compete acoustically, each one trying to drown out the next. I turn to ask Spruce Man how many types of music he can distinguish; he is gone. I turn the other way, and the rest of my camp is gone as well.

Should I try to find them or stay put?

Before I can answer my own question, small fires ignite in the middle of the circle around The Man, and the crowd begins to cheer. I'm too short to really see, so I climb a giant art car behind me that looks like a river boat. From the first level, I climb a spiral staircase to the top deck, where I weasel my way under the crowd, until I find a tiny ledge from which to dangle, to watch the spectacle below. Fireworks light up the sky, brighter than any Fourth of July celebration. I still have 2CB with me, and now seems like the perfect time to take it.

Even with all the chaos around me, I turn my gaze inwards and do my best to focus.

SATURDAY: *Illusion is Just Another Illusion*

Spirits . . . What do I want from you? What do you want to show me?

I open my eyes to lights and sounds and cheers. Chaos. Competition. Confusion. That isn't what I want. Peace and calm? Neither. I want something in between these two extremes. Again, I close my eyes and ask for guidance.

Break me open. Shatter illusion. Show me truth. Shatter illusion. Show me myself. Shatter illusion. I can take it.

I open my eyes to swallow the tiny capsule of truth, gulping it down with my last remaining water. The fireworks continue, all green. They illuminate The Man completely, mimicking the green lights that have adorned him at night. Over and over, the lights flash, until an explosion of fire erupts, covering The Man in flames, all the way up to his head. When they dissipate, his whole base is left burning. The crowd goes wild.

The fire that began suddenly, spreads slowly, like taking a sip of whiskey and feeling it overtake your whole body, inch by inch. It's a delicious tease to watch the flames lick the dry wood, steadily consuming it, one lap at a time. With every foot the flames climb, the crowd roars louder and louder. I scan the crowd to see screaming faces, partially illuminated by the fire's light. Everyone is united in emotional attachment to The Man.

I feel isolated in my non-attachment. Perhaps for me, he died on Monday. I remember passing him by, that first day, and being unsure . . . and how I felt almost relief, as he burned. No matter the reason, this feels like it's just for show. The Man seems shallow and insignificant, compared to the light of the morning sun or the poetry of The Temple. Or perhaps, I am disillusioned by masculinity. Nonetheless, watching his demise in its entirety seems essential to my experience, here. The week has been full of dismantling illusion, and perhaps The Man is just another illusion.

Maybe love as I think I know it is just another illusion, how much of what I feel is real?

Then I realize, The Man is *him,* the dark masculine, the heartbreaker. And he could be anyone, could have been anyone. That first dark love that will haunt me forever, that will imprint its scars on anyone else I ever love, that I will always compare both the passion and the pain to. He is inside of him, and I have to burn or accept him, turn the pain into growth.

Higher the flames climb. The crowd continues to cheer, but loses some of its vigor, as the minutes roll by. This is taking an excruciatingly long time. I can feel the drugs begin to kick in. My head is getting warm, especially behind my ears, and behind my forehead, between my eyebrows. After what seems like hours, the flames finally engulf his head. Still he stands tall, though covered in flames. I begin to respect him more: this is quite an impressive display of macho stamina.

At last he falls. Now, I scream with the crowd, using what feels like the remainder of my vocal strength, to express my pure unbridled emotion. I flash back to the fight in the dome on Wednesday, how I became one with the other voyeurs, living vicariously through the fighters, becoming almost sentimentally involved with their triumphs and failures. I am there again, although now I am one with the crowd, and one with the raging fire. The screams of the crowd, which seemed completely random, now echo around the circle of The Burning Man, like a sound wave.

The effigy is now burning timber, and then smoldering embers, dotted with smaller flames. The barrier that held the crowd at bay is released, and I watch the masses flood into the inferno, getting as close as they dare to his remains, now small bonfires of wood still burning. I have no desire to join them. He is gone, but the pain is still inside of me. I know where I am at home, and it is not here.

I push through the crowd, suddenly feeling claustrophobic among the tightly packed groups of people. After I finally get beyond them, I realize how cold it is alone. I wrap my arms around myself, and begin to walk aimlessly through the dust; it hangs low suspended in the air, hovering above the playa like fog, backlit by the fires and roving lights that characterize the playa's nightscape. The dust seems gentler tonight, as if The Man burning was a sacrifice to appease its pain, an offering in gratitude for its allowing us to dwell upon it.

I wander aimlessly, finally choosing a flame in the distance and walking through the fog-dust towards it. When I arrive, I warm myself at a mobile fire pit, attached to a bike, accepting a giant hug from the man who built it. Like bugs to a light, soon there is a tight group of people cloistered around the fire, and I fully appreciate the beauty of the gift of warmth. A young boy, perhaps seventeen or eighteen, huddles next to me. He is wearing a warm canvas jacket, and has curly untamed hair (now covered with playa), and bright, yellow eyes, that twinkle like Christmas lights.

"I walked here," he says to me without looking at me.

"So did I."

"No, I mean I walked from Gerlach. I hitchhiked from Tennessee, and walked through the mountains from Gerlach."

I nod at this, without fully processing the data. His story sounds familiar, but I don't think on it very hard. My brain is mush, and the fire is made of mandalas. I watch triangles spin, surrounded by circles, and lose myself in the patterns they create. They swirl together, and then rise up to the sky, in a DNA helix formation. The stars join them, and soon the sky is another art installation of twirling energy.

I blink, and I'm alone on the playa, sitting cross-legged. The fire is gone, and so is the boy. Then, all of a sudden, I remember standing around another fire, three nights and a million lifetimes ago, and hearing about him.

Some legends are true.

Finally, warm, I look around the open desert, and know where I need to go: The Temple.

As before, her energy draws me in, before I am inside of her. At night, she is still beautiful, although I prefer her during the day. The mood here is in stark contrast to that of the burn. Chaos has no place in her. She is sanctuary.

Even the people inside of her, seem unaffected by the ruckus, a half mile away. Her aura has grown throughout the week, fed by the many offerings given to her. Initially, she was pure and white, brand-new, and untouched by pain and suffering. Now, if you look closely, she shimmers a thousand colors of the rainbow, a thousand shades of black, white and gray. Again I pause to read the words.

if there is no tomorrow only today this moment then i die happy
i have found joy i have found freedom i am whole

In under a week, she acquires tens of thousands of scribbles, poems, and prayers.

Grammy I took you for granted. Your strength scared me when I was young, and then when I was old enough to appreciate what you had been through to attain it I was already far away. First I took you for granted, and then I took your strength. I thought it would keep you alive forever. How wrong I was. I wonder what you would think of me here dressed like a rainbow with a pharmacy in my bloodstream. You would be horrified, but perhaps, also proud of the strength it took me to get here.
—Katira

The Temple is full of stories of completion, and yet, still, she is missing some.

Finally, I write my own story.

Most of the space on the walls has been taken already,

so my own writing becomes a part of everyone else's. Our stories are all so different, and yet they are all the same. They all speak of yearning for something more, for wanting to right wrongs done in the past, of hope for a better future, of creating true connection with others.

There is no greater gift then the gift of love.
And no greater gift to give in return but
that of an open heart.
May my heart stay open.

My story is identical. I write about my own tender, broken heart. Of all the people I have loved in my short time on this planet. Of how they hurt me. Of how I hurt them. Of the joy we shared together, and the pain of releasing the promise of the future, that joy inspired.

Love is pain.
Life is beauty and pain.
Love is beauty.

How can all these statements be true at the same time? And yet they are.

My words weave around the offerings of others. From a distance, it looks like a distorted tapestry of scribbles, but like a true tapestry, until you look closer, you can't truly appreciate the details of the design: all those tiny threads, perfectly woven together to create something larger.

I came here looking for a party
I came here looking for a dance
I came here looking to escape
I came here for a second chance

This whole city represents that as well, no one could build this without help. This city was built with sweat and love, and a lot of whiskey. From a distance, it looks like a dusty carnival, but once you allow yourself a closer look, you realize that beauty is in the details.

I lose myself in the lights, but when
the sun rises I am alone.

Instead of fearing this solitude,
I walk alone to the edge. I am alone and I
am OK.

Still I write. My story weaves in and out of itself, shooting forward and then returning to earlier ground, to catch up.

Is there even a future and a past!
How would the world change if we
only lived for NOW?

As I write, it feels like my whole past happened at the same time, as though every single event that impacted me so greatly, occurred all at once. I remember being told that all life exists at the same moment.

Time is an illusion.
Separation is an illusion.
Everything you think is real
is an illusion.

Right now, I am buying my ticket, arriving at the gate, vomiting behind the tent, and riding to Torque and Serene's wedding.

My pen dies. The dust has clogged it. So, I write with invisible ink. It will all be burned tomorrow, anyway.

Just because you cannot see something, does that
make it any less real?

I cry softly as I write. I am happy, I got my giant choking sobs out earlier this week; for now I can cry gently as

SATURDAY: *Illusion is Just Another Illusion*

I relive all the great moments of my past, all the decisions that resulted in my presence, at this moment in time.

> And now the dust has settled
> And now that the music is gone
> I sit alone in solitude
> And realize it was ME
> I was searching for all along

I come across a heart, drawn with what looks to be human blood. I stop to admire it. It is raw. I can feel its intensity. I find another pen, and spend the next few minutes, writing four words to him, in large lettering across the blood heart.

> Tragedy I Release YOU

I etch it in as dark as I can, so that each letter of each word is indented into the wood. Below it, I choose to write my longest and darkest letter, to the first man who showed me what true love and true passion were. He also showed me what it meant to fall so deeply in love that all warning signs are ignored. He called himself Tragedy; I should have listened. He showed me how intensely I could feel pain: what it meant to be left broken, a cowering pile on the floor, a shadow of who I was before. His betrayal was a thousand shards of broken glass, discarded inside my heart.

Also, he showed me how strong I could be: that if I could fight through that pain and still love, that life might be worth living, after all. I'm not over him yet. I have stopped allowing the strange mix of truths and lies he left inside me to rule my head.

Parts of me still belong to him, but not as many as did a year ago. I have begun to pick the largest slivers out of my heart and, although the tiny ones still remain, I know they will merely require more time to extract. There is hope. There are rainbows. The darkness is real, but so is the light. I finish my long letter to him, and sign it with my name. I wipe a tear away, and I leave the blood heart.

I find a clear piece of wood next to a hanging mobile and I write a poem in real ink with my new pen.

Life is a phoenix
Young and vibrant one second
Burnt and decayed the next
A constant renewal
Societies rise and fall
People live and die
Without end, there would be no beginning
Nothing is permanent
Except for a moment

SATURDAY: *Illusion is Just Another Illusion*

Like the ecstasy of now
After you break my heart
(You will, and it's okay)
I know
That when I stop my tears
I'll look back and smile
Because
I would rather have loved you
Innocent and pure and true
Than held back
And wondered
"What if?"
So, bring it on
I'm not scared by what you
Or anyone else can do to me
I'm only scared of what I can't do to myself

I vaguely remember writing that poem, in pain. I see now, I wrote it to leave it in The Temple. Whoever I was in that moment, was simply preparing me for who I am in this one. I wonder who I am preparing to be, now.

I sit for a long time, rereading my words, and then I'm finished. I've completed a cycle. I can almost leave, now.

Almost.

I need to leave more than just words, in here. I must offer something more sacred to this holy place.

I take off my most prized possession: my wings. I look down at them, and another tear drips down my cheek. They aren't bright and shiny, like they were a week ago. They are dirty, misshapen, and full of quick repair jobs. The beads and bells still decorate them, and now they have memories on them, as well: tiny emblems, glow sticks, feathers, little treasures I've been gifted or found on the ground throughout the week. They show my journey. In these wings, I have lived a full lifetime.

A piece of paper blows toward my feet; I stoop to pick it up. What messages does the universe have for me?

ILLUSION IS JUST ANOTHER ILLUSION

I think of my clown and smile. It's true. Illusion is just another illusion.

Time is an illusion. Suffering is an illusion. Separation is an illusion. No one ever really owns anything or anyone. Instead of trying to pin down experience, or physical ownership, be grateful for the experience of living. Living in the moment, there is no room for illusion. When we give, when we release, we honor the moment.

SATURDAY: *Illusion is Just Another Illusion*

I set my wings down on a raised area, in front of The Temple's entrance. My hands feel lighter, as I release them. I walk out of The Temple, proud, wingless, hopeful, with my head high.

SUNDAY

The Last Sunrise

And now the dust has settled

And now that the music is gone

I sit alone in solitude

And realize it was ME

I was searching for all along

SUNDAY: *The Last Sunrise*

JOURNEYS NEVER BEGIN OR END IN THE desert, at least, not on purpose. The desert is an interlude, an obligatory pass-through, on the way to somewhere else. And yet, the desert is everything. Amidst the constant evolution associated with the intermediary phase of self-discovery, the highs and lows themselves become tiny beginnings and endings. In the open space that seems lifeless, there is viability. In this short week, I've already been reborn a hundred times. I've embodied a thousand archetypes. I have lived a million, tiny lives.

Still, I have yet to find any true, tangible version of who I am. If anything, I am more confused than ever by my existence in this party-ravaged human form. The week has not been kind: my usually smooth blond hair is in knots, tiny sores cover my tongue from forgetting to brush my teeth, my feet are cracked, and the tattered dirty scraps of clothing I wear, hang from my body, newly gaunt from hardly eating. My wings, which gave me some identity, are broken and sacrificed; who am I without them?

It's almost sunrise again. My final one. I wear my black boots, shredded pink fishnets, torn black pleated mini skirt, and a black lace bra. As my mind wanders, lost in an ongoing existential loop, I dip the ends of my staff into a plastic bucket, full of white gasoline.

A girl with a dreadlocked asymmetrical haircut lights my

wicks. I forget her name. Perhaps, *Dragonfly*? It doesn't matter. I walk into the openness, towards the place where the sun will rise. There is no stage here, just the dusty ground. There is no audience, except a few small groups of cuddling humans. There is just me and my fire, in between The Temple and the sun.

I dance as if I've never danced before. There is no music paying and yet I can hear it clearly. There is no urgency in my dance; there is just pure being.

Dust below, stars above, and the sun emerges right in front of my eyes. A gong is struck in The Temple, and it vibrates through my body. A few people begin to cheer. The sound is reverent and holy, not a violent cheer, like it was the night before, as The Man burned. Now it's slow and deep-throated.

The bottom of the sun's glowing red sphere clears the horizon and begins to hover in the sky.

This will be the last of the sunrises I will see, this week. I am alert and present. The Temple sparkles in the new light. I can't imagine The Temple, no more. I can't imagine this place, no more. How can I leave? *I am home.*

I dance. The flames whip next to my face and around my body. Still, I dance. The sun rises higher. An art car circles near, and I can feel the music from its subwoofers. I dance faster to its beat, still in control. The flames make a delicious *swoosh* sound, every time they buzz by my ears. My fire dims, as the sun rises higher. I dance. Now, my flames have extinguished themselves; still, I dance. I don't need the fire to worship. I am my own fire.

SUNDAY: *The Last Sunrise*

Gradually, my movements become slow and calculated, then sedated, and finally, I release onto the playa, arms and legs spread wide, my staff next to me. I can feel the heat of the sun, as it washes over me. It's such a relief, after the cold, long night. The rays warm my tired body, melting through the layers of fishnets and cloth.

I smile in gratitude for the amazing week I have experienced, for every high and low, for every tear and smile. I think of the many weeks leading up to this one, and about how little I live, on a day-to-day basis . . of all the monotonous days, simply going to work, to the same bar, back home. . . In these past six short days, how much growth and beauty I have experienced.

It would be too easy to fully credit the drugs. Yes, the drugs have taken me to new heights within myself, and helped me come to terms with what I have kept bottled up, but there is more than that. The drugs have broken down barriers, yes, but after the walls come down, I am left with just myself, whoever I am. I am beginning to be okay with that.

More than the drugs and sleep deprivation, there is an incredible power here: a power to be free, and be true to the soul's purpose. I've found this through play, prayer, comedic banter, and the simplicity of being alone. There is a collective consciousness here, that allows my psyche to operate on a new frequency. The right people appear at just the right moments, and I get exactly what I need, at any given time. There is order amidst the chaos, an order founded on the principles of play and love and excess.

BURNING WINGS

They call real life the "default world," and the name suits it. How many actions do we merely repeat daily, out of habit? How many of our actions, on a day-to-day basis, are intentional, and how many are simply repetition? Is our "default" a reflection of ourselves or our environment? Who do we become, when we remove our defaults and simply live? There is no default for me, here; every moment brings a new experience. I have no idea what will happen next.

Just now, I remember the DMT in my waist pouch. I've been saving it for the perfect moment, and this feels like it. DMT is one of the strongest hallucinogens known. I've been told that, for five to ten minutes, it dissolves all semblance of real life, and can take the user into alternate realities. Rico says that he meets alien creatures from other dimensions, and is slowly trying to learn how to speak their language. He says he has the linguistic concept down, but the grammar itself is highly irregular.

The physical drug manifests itself as tiny balls of orange paste. I bought my first "special" pipe in preparation for smoking it, a small cheap glass tube with a large orb at the end (I'm not sure if it's a meth pipe or a crack pipe, Spruce Man called it a tweaker pipe, but my intentions are more pure.)

I set myself up, sitting alone on the dust, legs crossed, close my eyes and take ten deep breaths. They take a long time.

What do I want from this experience?

I ponder.

I want to connect with something larger than just myself.

SUNDAY: *The Last Sunrise*

I want to know that all of this has a purpose.

I exhale, bring the pipe to my parched mouth, and inhale deeply as I light the exterior of the round glass. Instantly I am greeted with a rush of thick smoke into my lungs, and an intense natural but slightly chemical smell like an ancient otherworldly tree of wisdom burning in offering.

My vision begins to pulse as I struggle to hold the smoke inside of me for as long as possible; rushing towards me as the open playa and bright sun morph into something that wasn't there before. I can still see them, but they are no longer of this planet. I exhale soft smoke into the dry clear morning air, where it quickly dissipates like an offering.

The playa cakes in front of me are outlined in rainbows.

I am losing control of my limbs, but not in a violent way like the ketamine. I use my last awareness to repeat the process, taking a larger and slower hit this time.

Again the smoke enters my lungs, and this time the change is more pronounced. My body loses its form and I lay back in wonderment, forgetting to hold in the smoke any longer, allowing the exhale to occur naturally.

There is a dull humming, almost like the art installation from that first night, and I can also hear the music from a camp nearby. This music seems to guide the visions, gentle cornered geometric shapes pulsing and dancing together, melting what once was. When I close my eyes, they intensify even more.

Radiantly proud, forever spinning and morphing, the colors and textures create a three dimensional playground of extendable tubes that dance with each other. I watch in amazement as they take me with them into themselves, then back out again, moving slowing in time with the music. I move my eyes behind my lids, and they exist in every direction. My eyes are faced backwards, and the visions are not just in front of me, they are actually inside my own head.

I begin to sense the presence of other beings, other light forms watching me, but as I search for them in the forever expanding playground, they shift and disappear from view, like they are playing hide and go seek. I giggle, and the human sensation feels strange, like I'm speaking another language than the one in this land.

Human giggles seem to amuse and even please the beings, and without allowing me to catch a glimpse of them, they somehow implant a rainbow funnel in my third eye, the tunnel stretches from it into my head, through my body, and into the depths of my soul. They dump colors, shapes, and energy into it, still shapeshifting and vibrant, and I am paralyzed in amazement and gratitude for the gifts they are offering me. For these are true gifts, true offerings, I have somehow deemed worthy and they want me to know that they care about me, and they want me to take their magic with them, back into the dust, and into the default world.

Again I giggle, and open my eyes. The playa is still dancing, but at least I recognize it, and the creatures are done with their task. I lay there for a long time, still marveling at this other world.

When I get up, there is a shaky clarity around me. Each color and texture seems to be accentuated, and conducts new life. It strikes me that nothing has actually changed but my perspective, and with this new perspective, I am able to see the beauty and life in each particle of dust, each molecule of air, and even in the tiny humans that are biking across the playa, some bright and fresh in sunglasses, and some haggard and trailing large fur coats off of their bikes, eyes uncovered and squinting in the sun.

Laughing at the absurd beauty of life, I get up and walk towards The Temple, now even more radiant and majestic than before in the morning light and in my new eyes, if that is possible. She is not empty. The wanderers are here to worship. Some sit in prayer, some walk slowly, simply gazing at the writing on the walls. Others add their own messages, on the last day before she burns, tonight. I sit down in one of The Temple's wings to observe the pilgrims. A man sits next to me. He wears a purple beret and a worn lavender suit. He turns to me and quite seriously asks, "Want to know a secret of life?"

"But, of course." I respond.

"If you think you can, then you're right. And if you think you can't, then you're right. You're always right. Just make sure you're right about the right thing."

I have no witty or analytical response. What do you say to this simple wisdom?

He's right.

Our minds are our most powerful tools; it is inside them that all decisions and manifestations begin. The most difficult part of making any substantial change to our lives, can be the admission that the old way no longer works, and it is time to move on. After we've accepted this within ourselves, real change can occur. For months now, I've felt disenchanted with my life, and have struggled with change. Being here helps put it all into perspective: *I'm ready for more.* I sit down in the center of The Temple, next to a few piles of stones, stacked precariously on top of one another, and continue my existential wondering.

More what?

I wish I knew. More realness. More spirituality. Less bullshit. More play and dance—but I want to play and dance with a purpose. I want to celebrate, not escape. I want to bring intention into all that I do; I want to know that I have an objective, that my actions, words and thoughts serve something.

I see so clearly, in this moment, that it all must be for something greater.

It must be. It has to be.

Don't I always have the power to tap into something deeper? To take a few extra breaths, before reacting blindly? To consciously choose when to work, when to play, when to shut down the mind, and when to lose myself in it? And now, I give myself permission to lose myself in my thoughts.

Isn't it all just an illusion?

By this same logic, I can validate any frivolous action as being "mindful," when in fact it's just another default.

Fuck. It is all just an illusion.

I curl up in fetal position, using my arm as a pillow, and I watch a couple in their thirties walk through The Temple, holding hands. They are both in white priestly garb, from head to toe, and when I squint I can see behind each of them, beautiful white wings, attached to their backs, feathers trailing behind. Both of their faces are decorated with gold and white paint, and while they match materially, their connection is deeper than just their clothes and embellishments could ever represent. They seem to move as one, seamlessly transitioning from leader to follower, as they tour The Temple, taking in the various blessings and curses, etched into the walls.

When they get to the portal that looks out to the deep playa, he holds her close, for a moment, and whispers something in her ear. She smiles and closes her eyes, as he releases her. The sun shines on her face, illuminating her flawless skin and flowing dress, and reflecting in her gold jewelry. The man takes something out of his pocket, as he walks in front of her, and then kneels down on one knee. Hesitantly, he reaches his hand up to hers, and then (she must have opened her eyes) she shrieks, as he slips a ring on her finger. A second later, she is in his arms, legs wrapped around his waist. He twirls her in circles, as they hold each other, gently crying together.

Yes, ecstasy can look exactly like pain, I think as I shut my eyes, hardly realizing that I too, am crying with them. They are my last vision, before I fall asleep on my tears.

)☼(

It's a strange thing to watch your body being sliced open. There isn't a way to observe a limb severed or internal organs exposed, without completely leaving the physical body. We are born, knowing that certain things are best kept contained . . . blood, guts, and emotions, better felt than shown. I ponder these thoughts as I observe my heart, exposed from the wound on the left side of my open chest.

It's a beautiful thing, the human heart. It contracts and expands, like life itself. The veins on it look like tree roots, anchoring in the blood vessels to the beating organ. I didn't know that the color, red, could exist in so many variations at the same time.

The gnomes have nimble fingers. They operate smoothly and quickly with their tiny hands. Previously, I thought them cynical, unemotional, and, overall, unattached to humanity, yet their work ethic is unmatched. They move confidently, methodically, and with precision. The blades they use to slice open my chest appear to be hand-carved, and yet as evidenced by the clean cuts, as sharp as any steel scalpel. The skin was the easy part. It opened quickly and cleanly, even as my red blood poured out. It was the cutting of the breastbone that truly impressed me. They put aside their scalpels and took out tiny blade-saws; each taking two of them, to coordinate cutting through my sternum. They spread it open, to expose my pulsating, live heart. With each beat, it seems to double in size, and then retracts back to a fraction of what it previously was. It's an incredible thing, to witness the heart's fullest capacity, and also how sad it can appear, when empty.

In this vulnerability, I feel my emotional, rather than physical, pain, as I observe this open surgery. Perhaps, what shocks me the most, even though I already had some idea of the damage, are the razor-sharp shards of glass, stuck in the heart. Some are fully exposed, some half, and some are just tiny slivers of glass: so tiny, in fact, that they look like stray glitter. I am grateful for the professionalism of the gnomes, as they take on the thankless task of removing these shards, one at a time. If they had the compassion to look at me, to make eye contact, to acknowledge the depth of suffering it took to lodge them there in the first place, I am sure I would lose my own composure, and, reliving my own agony, my own heartbreak, my unbridled emotion would dominate whatever magic anesthesia I had been given, and my body would rise in protest.

The shards hurt. I can feel them, as truly as I see them. When each shard is removed, real, true blood drips out of the wound. My heart is covered with dried blood, from each of these incisions. With each pulse of the heart, the dried, cracked blood spreads, and the scabs break open in geometric patterns, much like those on the edge of the deep playa. With each contraction, the created shapes again condense into a wrinkly, seamless wall, protecting the last few unspoiled patches.

With each shard of glass they remove, I cringe, reliving the intense emotions that allowed them to lodge there, in the first place. Every kiss, every promise, every lie, every tear, is a shard. For every tiny sheer glass piece one gnome dislodges, another gnome, with a needle and fine gold thread, stitches the open wound back up. It's ironic that the smallest pieces require the least thread, for those are the ones that hurt the most. When they are done with each shard, they tie the gold thread in a bow, like it's a present, just waiting to be opened again.

)☼(

I open my eyes; the couple is gone, and the sun is high above me. I fell asleep again. I turn over and in front of me in giant red lettering on an American flag I see:

GOD BLESS BURNING MAN

I yawn and stretch my full body, arms over head. I yawn and stretch my full body, arms over head. *Where is my water? Where is my staff?*

I find my bottle and the last few sips of water, before standing up and mentally readying myself for the journey back to camp. My staff is next to me, right where I left it. I pull myself upright, my strength for this basic task is a miracle. The Temple is calmer. The walls are covered, like the pages of a high school yearbook, the writing twists and contorts around each other making new passages hard to follow. There are more notes now too, in addition to the photos, drawings, and memorials.

Love is the only thing we can perceive which
transcends both time and space.
-Rave Daddy

Don't start to read! You'll never leave! I tell myself, but of course my eyes land on a blue piece of paper, tacked to the wall with a pushpin, and my vision dances along the words, written with evenly spaced sprawling natural hand writing..

231

SUNDAY: *The Last Sunrise*

It's like we're trying to complete a giant puzzle of a beautiful magical vignette but we keep dropping the final few pieces (and the pieces are really tiny) that will complete the image, and as we bend down to pick them up we knock over a few more that we had figured out, and I know we should walk away from the puzzle but what I can see is so gorgeous and I've worked so hard to get this far, I want to see what it looks like when it's really complete. And you're just laughing at me because I'm so serious about this silly puzzle and alternating between pouting and giggling, and without me you might have just left the whole dang thing in the box, (which in retrospect could have been a really smart idea) but now we've seen the puzzle and touched it and it's such a nice puzzle and even though you're laughing at me, you're now just as intrigued by the puzzle as me, and you want to see what it looks like just as bad as I do but you keep on talking about all these other puzzles we could be working on and you're right, there are other puzzles, but I haven't found another good puzzle yet and I really like this one, and by now we've lost the box anyway, so now we have are these pieces all over and it's not like we can just put the pieces all tidy away in their box, we would have to throw them away or put them in a zip lock bag and that just doesn't seem right. It's a really, really nice puzzle and even if we haven't finished it, it's still really pretty.

This one makes me smile. It's a love story. What if we were all just puzzle pieces, each with a perfect place to fit within a meticulous lattice? Where do I fit? Do I have any of my other connecting pieces?

It's like that wizard boy was saying on the first day in the floating treehouse . . . We're all just pieces of a giant puzzle.

I walk slowly out of The Temple, staying in the last bit of shade, for as long as possible, before stepping out into the radiant sunlight, and beginning the mile-long trek back home, removing a piece of myself and readying for the next connection.

)☼(

The sun burns; my black clothing is a magnet for its heat. I thankfully have an old pair of scratched sunglasses with me, but I wish I had more water. I walk as fast as I can, but there is a pep missing from my step.

This is work. My vacation is your worst nightmare, is fucking true.

What if *we* controlled our nightmares? What if our nightmares served to push us farther into our true selves? If our dreams are hopes for the future, then are our nightmares just scars from our past? And what are scars for, if not to heal old wounds, and remind us not to make the same mistakes again? When I think back upon my short life, I see that I have grown the most through struggle and heartbreak, that the nightmares have helped me to get closer to owning myself, even if I am still far away from truly mastering that concept.

Who am I? Will I ever know? I BELIEVE I can try to find out!

This perks me up, remembering that if I believe I can, then I CAN! If I believe I am, then I AM!

"Need a ride?" A man in a loincloth and tennis shoes, driving a pedicab, slows down to my right. His dark skin, covered with playa, is a rare shade of dusky lavender, and his afro could rival Jimmy Hendrix's. His cab is covered with a white sheet, on a sloppily welded frame. The seat is made of Walt Disney logo embossed linoleum. I can't control my excitement, being able to sit in the shade.

"Yes! Yes! Yes!" I exclaim, as I hug him, before hopping in and relaxing onto the seat; my sweaty thighs promptly stick to it. He has a small stereo attached to his handlebars and it plays The Beatles' "Lucy in the Sky with Diamonds," proud and staticky, as if it were an original record. I close my eyes and let the music carry me.

"I bet you've been one of those girls," he says with a smile.

"Huh? Me? What do you mean?" I ask, with a dry laugh.

"I can't see your eyes, but I bet they're kaleidoscopes. And I'll double down and place a second bet: I bet you've been 'the girl who's gotten away.'"

"You tell me." I say, and I take off my glasses, blinking at the sunlight, constricting my pupils. He stops the cart and stares into my eyes deeply, as I wistfully answer: "Maybe I've gotten away from my fair share, too. Not on purpose. I don't like making other people sad. Sometimes, I must. It's a side effect of love. Isn't that funny? The way that love hurts so good?"

We ride through the dust. He doesn't ask where I am going, he just pedals slowly, in the direction I was walking.

"I like the way you smile. You've still got a lot of love to give."

"I like smiling, even when it hurts. Sometimes I smile so much, my face gets sore. I don't know if I believe in love anymore. Not like I used to."

"Love is an illusion. As is all life. And yet it is the only thing truly worth living for. Where are we headed?"

"Everything is an illusion, why should love be any different? 9:15 and D. What's your name?"

"Rugged Richard, at your service." He pedals a little faster.

"They call me The Fun Fairy, but I don't have my wings anymore, and I haven't seen my fairy guide in a day or so. She's probably an illusion as well, but that's to be expected, right?"

"Are you one of those princess girls?"

"Am I that transparent?" I laugh. "From as early as I can remember, I gobbled up every princess story, every teenage romance paperback, and every movie with a happy ending. I believed, without a shadow of a doubt, that love was forever. There was no spectrum of love. It just was. Or else, it was not. There was no spectrum. No illusion. Just black and white. Simple."

"Ah, honey. Trust a black man speaking truth to a white girl: it's all spectrum."

SUNDAY: *The Last Sunrise*

"Love has to be more than a single spectrum. I want it to be simple because I believe in it so truly, or I did . . . No . . . I still do . . . I think . . ." I trail off.

"You are so right and so wrong, at the same time. Explaining love is like explaining quantum physics, of which (lucky for you), in my other life, I am a professor. I'll explain it like geometry: it's so much more than a spectrum; it contains many axes, as well. Every relationship, romantic or otherwise, has an infinite number of moving parts. Sometimes, I think it's all perfect, that it's all fate, and sometimes I think love is just a series of happy accidents, that there is no order. And then, every time I fall back in love, my faith in fate and in quantum physics is re-established, beyond any doubt."

"I used to define love in terms of relationships, but they are two very different things. The kind of love that I used to fantasize about, as a girl, is very real, and can be the spark to ignite a relationship, but that's not what keeps love alive."

"Ah, listen to your wisdom! Yes! Relationships, like all living things, need to be fed and nurtured. When the spark, when the sex appeal fades away, what is left? Friendship, community, understanding, trust. These are all essential for longevity. These are your foundation. Without them, it just fades away, like a sunset. And so, the dismantling of a partnership is more than just saying goodbye to a lover. It's a re-evaluation of self, and an acceptance that something which you knew to be an absolute truth, is no longer true. When we believe fully that we are meant to be with someone, and then, years later, we realize that is no longer the case, it makes us second guess everything else we believe to be true in life."

"So, if I was so wrong about love, what else am I wrong about? What other lies am I telling myself? If the heart can lie, then what can I trust?"

"Your gut."

"What does that even mean? I don't know if I understand my gut. I thought my heart was my gut." We arrive at my corner and I sit in the cab, still lost in thought.

"You still have a lot of learning to do, but you're on the right track. Keep your heart, keep your innocence; there's more for you to find. You're young. You'll be fine."

)☼(

Back at camp, I force myself through the ritual of personal hygiene: toothbrush, baby-wipes, new clothes, and water. My final day clothes are bootie shorts and a sarong. That is all I can manage. I don't even put on my shoes. I consult my drug bag. MDMA and mushrooms seem the most aligned with my mood of the moment. I add them to my side bag, and head into the kitchen to see what is going on in camp.

Serene and Torque are back. They are radiant, and seem remarkably well rested for newlyweds who married on acid and had their honeymoon at Burning Man. Serene describes to me the perfect luxury playa hotel they stumbled upon, and where they spent the night. Of all the things I have found on the playa, nothing comes remotely close to the luxury she describes: a Bedouin-style tent, with Moroccan lamps, and oriental tapestries, hanging from the ceiling and walls. It sounds like heaven.

Torque is grinning a giant stupid grin, and with it he has been reborn.

Spruce Man is gone. Rico is off somewhere, probably the Temple, heartbroken. Archinta has decided to leave him, for a new lover she met this week. This news is a shock to me, but then she is born to shock. When her forthrightness and solid crass isn't enough, she softens as she did to me, and shocks through vulnerability. I could learn something from her. There is no logic in her flame; also, by default, no falsification. I wonder what it would feel like to be like Archinta or Serene, right now—enveloped in the sweet rapture of love, and precariousness, so trusting in human emotion, that there is no room for doubt.

I shake all this off. This is neither here nor now. I eat some granola and goji berries, soaked into submission with organic hemp milk. I have one day left of adventure, and I don't want it to go to waste. Personal hygiene is a necessary evil.

I meditate on the drugs. The MDMA is for opening my heart. The mushrooms are for opening my third eye. I choose my heart.

Spirits, help open my heart. Help me give purely and truly. Help my heart heal, through the healing of others. Show me truth through love. I am open.

I eat two finger dips of MDMA. To embark on this heart journey, I need my tools. I refill my water bottle—already empty, grab my bag of crystals, my princess cup, and my flask before I head out, alone. My body is sore and, even in its weakness, it feels stronger than when I arrived. I have allowed the unessential to melt off, and I am left with what I truly need.

)☼(

I wander the streets, unsure of my destination. A large sunburnt man, sitting in a folding chair next to the road, calls out to me: "Hey, you! What are you looking for?" I walk over to him, and stand with my hands on my hips.

"I'm not actually sure."

"Have you looked inside? Usually, when we think we are lost, we already have the answer inside of us. We just haven't asked the right question yet." He adjusts his position, rotating his body forward so his slouch transitions into a forward lean.

I cock my head to one side. "We can't get the right answer if we don't ask the right questions?"

"Exactly," he laughs.

"So, ask me a better question," I challenge.

"Well, then." He cocks his head to mirror mine. "What does your heart desire?"

"To give freely, without expecting anything in return." I respond without having to think.

"Well then," he says again. "Come here, I have a gift for you."

I walk towards him, and he produces a welded, heart-shaped necklace with the familiar)'(inside of it. He hands in to me, and I hang it around my neck.

"Good luck, sister. May you accept this gift without my needing anything in return. And may you discover how to give, in the same manner."

My new pendant hangs perfectly on my chest, right below my mood necklace. It is a pale blue, at the moment. I smile and bow my head slightly, in gratitude.

Camps along my path have begun to pack up. Perhaps a fifth of what was, has now been taken down, as the city's residents prepare to depart. Many bars are closed or in half disarray, as supplies are packed up. Yet, the streets seem familiar. I've been on this block before. On Thursday.

Was that only three days ago? It seems like a lifetime ago, now.

And then, I remember: It is Taylor's birthday! Taylor, my fairy friend, the embodiment of love and innocence. My head grows warm, as the drugs begin to take effect, and the little light inside my heart expands, with an undeniable need to give, and to honor her divinity.

I realize I am directly in front of Gnome Adoption Camp, or its remnants, where just a few short days ago Taylor was denied her gnome. I'm amazed I can still recognize it; the main Gnome Dome no longer has a cover on it, it is now an empty skeleton, a three-dimensional spider web. I stand in the center, finally beginning to recognize the impending finality of this week. I look up to make sure there are no rainbow spiders here, and it looks safe, so I sit in the center to ponder. A tattooed man, wearing combat boots and cargo shorts, greets me from the outside.

BURNING WINGS

"Hi! Can I help you?"

"Hi! I hope you can! It is my fairy friend's birthday, and all she wanted this week was a gnome to call her own! We came here Thursday to adopt, but you were out of gnomes. . . Do you have perhaps a gnome keychain? Or a cardboard cutout? Or a gnome card? *Anything!*"

"We've been packing up all day. This is the rest of it here." He beckons me over to him, amid piles of miscellaneous debris and boxes. "I'll see what I can find, but no promises." He opens tubs, peeking through piles of fabric and decor in some, tools and hardware in others. "I'm not sure. . ." From the third box he opens, he pulls out an object wrapped in newspaper. When he unwraps it, it is a gnome. He stands upright and is dressed in a red suit. His hat is pointy, and his whole body is miraculously untouched by dust. He is perfect. He looks at me mischievously, as if daring me to journey with him.

"Looks like the playa has blessed you. You know the rules, right?" the man asks me with a grin. When he smiles, his whole face is highlighted with beautiful lines. He has spent most of his life smiling, and it shows. I shake my head.

"Gnomes are earth creatures. They like to be low to the ground. They prefer forests and wooded areas, and aren't too happy with the desert. They can be good luck charms, if you are kind to them, but if you do them wrong, be prepared for bad luck. They seem docile, but they are very observant, and hold grudges for long periods of time. They are also very wise. Listen to them, and they may tell you the secrets you have been waiting to hear. Gnome adoption is a responsibility. Generally, we have forms and ceremony. . . But this one obviously wanted to leave with you, or else he would have stayed hidden. Treat him well."

"I will. I promise. Thank you so much." I take the gnome from him, and cradle him in my arms.

Now I have a love mission, I must deliver this gnome to Taylor, across the playa at 2:00.

Remembering the time I crossed the playa during the dust storm and the dust tried to kill me; even though the wind is calm now, I decide to follow the Esplanade there, and see who I encounter as I travel. I have a spirit mission to fulfill, and shortcuts have no place in spirituality. I hug my tiny gnome to my chest, as I set out towards the main drag. To be a true gift, first he needs to be wrapped.

I find my favorite lemonade bar, and my patron bartender, Loveless, is on shift. I smile, and get out my princess cup. "Loveless!" I happily exclaim, when she sees me, "I'm not sure if you remember me, but I met you on the first day. You gifted me this cup and I've had it all week."

"Of course, I do, sugar! You're the Fun Fairy, right? Where are your wings?"

"I left them in The Temple. It didn't seem right to hold onto them. I wanted to offer a piece of myself to this place."

She nods. "I am sure you have received as much as you have given. Lemonade?"

As she pours me a drink, I place my gnome on the bar. He stares at me mischievously, as if to say, "*I see you. I see you truly. I see past your bullshit. I see past your disguises. I know who you are; do you know?*" I stare back at him, unsure if his words are from him or me, then shake it off and tell Loveless about the gnome and about Taylor.

"So, if this gnome is a gift, then he must be wrapped." She looks at him deeply and asks him, "May we adorn you?"

I hear his response, *"very well, if you must."* Loveless must have heard him, too, because she nods and walks away from the bar to her camp. She returns with special fabric and ribbon. Together, at the bar, we wrap the gnome in red jacquard cloth and purple ribbon. We leave his head exposed, out of respect. The wrapping job is a bit lumpy, but the luxurious fabric makes him look awkwardly regal, like a tiny king who has not grown into the opulent adornment befitting his station.

"May I ask you something?" I say to her.

"I think you just did." She smiles and laughs. *I love her laugh.*

"The last time I saw you, you spoke to me about removing social defaults, and trapping into who we truly are. In this week, that I've been here, I've shed so many layers of myself and re-found myself so many times . . . I'm like one of those dolls that keeps on opening, there are so many layers of me. There isn't just one answer, is there?"

She refills my glass, and ponders my question. "Wouldn't that be boring? To stay the same person? To never grow or evolve?"

"Yes, but shouldn't there be just one me inside? One true me?"

"The true you has many faces. If you choose to live your life fully, then you choose challenge, you choose dismantling, you choose growth. You also choose wisdom, joy, and love. They are all connected, and the good and the bad times will both test your resolve, in different ways."

"So, there is no end? What about monks and meditation and being zen? Nirvana? Shibari? Is that an end?"

"You are asking the wrong person about that. I was raised hardcore Catholic. I was taught to embrace suffering, and not to trust joy. I shunned that. I trust joy now, but that doesn't mean I've shut out suffering. I'm a doer. I keep on finding more things that bring me joy, and each brings more challenges. Look at it this way . . . say you climb a mountain. A big mountain. You spend all this time dreaming and planning, and then you actually do it. It's the hardest thing you've ever done, and you fall hundreds of times. But, you get back up, and you climb it. Can you see it?" I nod. "So, what the hell do you do when you get to the top?"

I mull this over for a minute. "I guess I'd have to get back down? Where else to go?"

"And then what do you do? Are you fulfilled because you climbed one mountain?"

"I guess I would want to help others climb. Or else I'd find another mountain."

"Exactly. There's always more."

The gnome looks at me.

"Listen to your elders. There is no shortage of mountains. Plan carefully."

Next, I find a lime green and hot pink bar, where I make friends with one of the founders of the camp, The

Empress. The Empress is on her tenth burn and is in love with my mission.

"How fucking lovely! We need more fairies here! Less sparkle ponies and more honest-to-god fairies! Hell yeah, sweetheart! I have some pipe cleaners and ribbon! Let's get this gnome into shape!" And so, as we drink vodka and spiked with enough V8 Splash to change the color, but not mask the cheap liquor, we decorate the gnome with spiraled pipe cleaners and ribbon. He is not pleased.

"Sorry," I whisper to him, "just another few blocks and I promise to take all this off."

I leave, holding the gnome tightly in my arms. He has grown warm and a bit heavier. I stop at a gazebo-shaped bar, and drink ice cold sake with a half-awake young hippie boy. He slurs his words, as he tells me about his recent two-day acid binge. He stares into the gnome's eyes for a long time, his chin on his hands on the bar. I watch as his eyes grow wide and then he begins to nod in agreement. "Yo! This gnome knows what's up."

"Oh, yeah? Is he talking to you, too?"

"Dude! He told me I need to stop vagabonding and stay in one place, to plant something. I've always wanted a farm. Wouldn't that be the coolest, to just watch things grow all day long?"

I smile. He has just gotten a little bit closer to climbing his next mountain. I explain my gnome mission, and ask him for paper and art supplies to make a card. He stares at me, not understanding the magnitude of my quest. I offer him some MDMA, and he accepts a lick off my finger. With this bribe, he slowly walks off to search.

I glance at the gnome, turning him to face me. He stares back at me, as he does, with a deviant sort of wisdom. *"And . . . what do you want to grow? What happens if you actually focus on creating something larger than yourself, instead of looking for others to provide it for you?"* I blink in astonishment.

What do I want to create? What can I grow?

The boy returns with a Burning Man postcard and a few ballpoint pens. I don't share my own gnome revelation. The card shows The Man—or another reincarnation of him—fully ablaze. It's not as sweet and romantic as I would choose for Taylor; it is what the universe willed for me, so it will be my medium. I compose a rambling, but loving, letter on the back of the postcard. He signs it as Sake Tim; his writing is loose and sloppy compared to my intentonal, if scribbly, hand.

I am about to leave, when I feel a presence behind me. I turn around I am greeted with the biggest smile I have seen so far today, if that could possibly be quantified. I jump into Flook's arms, feeling that giant beating heart, and know without a doubt *I am home.*

"You're here! It's you! How has your week been? This is my gnome, kind of. He's been talking to me, but I think sometimes all the voices I hear here are just things I already know, or answers to questions I haven't answered yet. Like the way you gave me the ticket as the answer before the question." I ramble, excitedly.

His smile doesn't fade as he responds. "I'm glad to see you again, and I'm glad you're still standing and smiling! My week has been typical. I don't really party anymore. I come here to work and be a community servant. I fix shit, I solve problems, I help run camp, I fix art cars, I rescue refugees. I look for opportunities to serve my community. My favorite thing in the whole world is seeing the people that I love smile."

"I'm smiling so big right now!" I say.

"Yes, I can see that." And then the impossible happens: his smile grows even larger.

"I feel like everything is here, that every hour is a different card in a tarot deck, that all of life's lessons are encapsulated in this short experience, and yet it all connects to something bigger and deeper than I can even imagine." I pause, and then laugh again. "Do I sound like a hippie? Shit! I've gone full circle since rebelling against my parents. I'm in the dust with a talking gnome. This is everything, and it's nothing at the same time."

"Our lives are merely a flash of lightning in the flow if time. Our egos and self-importance create an illusion of significance, straying us from the path of harmonious symbiotic existence with the environment. We are here for such a short time." His smile grows older and wiser, and the lines on his face deepen.

"But each moment can be a lifetime. Or is it just an illusion? I'm not sure it it's the dust, or the drugs, but I've been having a hard time separating what's real from what isn't, but then isn't anything real that we think is real?"

"Illusion? I've noticed many people seem to think drugs and the visions and realizations they give us aren't reality.

They are absolutely reality. The universe is simply varying expressions of energy." He bursts out laughing and manages to choke out his next thoughts, "What the fuck is energy?" This is the funniest thing in the world to him, and he laughs so hard he begins to tear up and cough. It's contagious, his energy. "So how can we say anything isn't real? Or an illusion? Matter is the crystallization of energy. Our lives are the crystallization of our desires, our manifestations, our ideas. . ."

"It's like you're speaking from The Temple walls." I close my eyes and I'm back there, reading handwriting on the rough wood. "It will all burn tonight, but I hope I will remember it, I hope it's not just a fleeting dream."

"I feel life's fleeting nature is an expression of impermanence, offering us lessons of detachment. Because of our perspective and seemingly long lives we can achieve freedom and adaptability in realizing change is the only constant." Flook loses himself to laughter again, his head falling onto the bar, somehow this wisdom is hilarious.

Nothing is permanent except for a moment.

The gnome rolls his eyes at me. *Silly hippie. Everything is fleeting and yet a moment can be more permanent, more impactful with intention than a lifetime of fraudulent living.*

"Holy shit. I love your gnome. Enjoy each moment you have with him. I love you kid. Thank you for reminding me what it's like to experience this place from a fresh perspective."

"Thank you." We hug, for what might be the last time, and I begin to tear up with emotion and gratitude.

BURNING WINGS

He sees my tears, wipes one away, and says: "After so many years, I get lost in memories and service, and have to live vicariously through virgin eyes, *through your eyes*, is the biggest gift you could ever give me. I'll take your energy, your smile, and your light, over any fancy thing you could have possibly purchased. Thank you."

We leave together, and then walk away from one another in opposite directions. The playa is soft under my bare feet. I try to walk straight, planning to go straight to Cy-Top, when a ramshackle, black Bedouin tent pulls me in; incense burns and dark music plays. I sit at the low bar, on a dusty velour pillow that was black once. The bartender is skinny, with a mohawk and giant, stretched ears. "Are you here for the bondage workshop? The teacher flaked. Fucking *Gucci* asshole." He half greets me with a question, without really making eye contact.

"No, I just wandered in. I'm on my way to deliver this gnome to my friend for her birthday." I set the gnome on the bar, and turn back to the bartender with more attention than he offered to me.

He cocks his head as he peers at the gnome. "He hates this shit you know. Gnomes like cool dark earth, not sparkles and dust."

"Yeah, I know, but it's for a good cause."

"Ha! That's funny! Usually, I have to justify the darkness to people, and here you are, justifying sparkles. I guess it's all balance; the darkness is important, too. Whiskey?"

"Sure. I have darkness too, you know," I tell him, as he pours us each a shot.

"No shit, we all do. Have you embraced it? Have you accepted and embodied it as a part of you?"

"I'm working on it."

"It's work that never ends. The more you repress, the more the shadow comes out in unexpected ways." He raises his glass to mine. "To our shadows, our true selves. May you embrace them before they fuck you." I clink mine to his.

"Mine was an evil clown. He stalked me and I hid from him, and then I accepted him, and he helped me find noodles." *I try to bond with him.*

"I have no fucking idea what you are talking about, but it sounds awesome."

"Is the shadow just our inner darkness? How much of it can we control?" Now I'm getting somewhere with my new punk guru.

"Oh shit. Where to begin? So, if our shadows are ignorance, shame, wounds, and delusions—all the stuff we have inside of us that we repress, and if we acknowledge they are all created by fear and ego, then we have to look at how they began. Most of us have wounds from our childhood, some are from past lives, and some are fresh. It depends on our state of being, when we created these wounds, how deep they cut, and how we dealt with them. Hypothetically, we can control all of them, which requires some serious work and dismantling. I'll talk to hippies who talk about 'blah blah blah love, blah blah blah light, blah blah blah,' and it's bullshit. Our wounds ARE us. Our shadows ARE us. To overcome them, we must embrace them, fully. Shutting them out is how we got them in the first place."

"I keep discovering new wounds inside—" I stop in amazement. "This whole time, I've been so caught up in growth and shedding layers and finding more pieces of me—and each new piece I find is linked to shadows I have hidden."

It's so simple. How did I miss this?

"Ding, ding, ding, sweetheart! True growth comes with shadow work, and the first stage is recognition." The gnome looks at me, approvingly.

"Let's drink to that." He pours another two shots, larger this time. "To embracing the true self and all the bullshit that goes along with it." I clank my glass against his, take the full double in my mouth, and hold it there, so I can embrace its burn, before I swallow.

"Can I gift your gnome? He's craving darkness." He pulls out a black screen-printed bandana and ties it around the gnome's neck, blocking the sparkly curly bows. "That's better."

)☼(

When I finally arrive, Cy-Top is in full swing, getting ready for their last night of music and play, while simultaneously breaking down their community dwellings. North is predictably, fiddling with the speakers. I still don't pretend to understand the magnitude of all the switches and wires and buttons he commandeers. I slink up behind him, engulfing his slender body in a hug.

"Hi, pretty lady! What have you been up to?" he says, as

he turns around.

"Shadow work, more existentialism, and gnome adoption. You?" I offer him a finger dip of MDMA.

"About the same: subtract the gnome, and add in too many hours of sound system tinkering." He licks my finger, keeping it in his mouth for a few seconds longer than necessary.

"It's Taylor's birthday, and I brought her a gnome! Can we find her?" He nods and smiles.

She is easy to find, lying on her back on an old couch, in the camp area. I bounce on top of her, squealing. "Happy birthday, sweet fairy goddess!"

"It is my birthday! What a perfect sublime surprise to see you! Your presence is such a gift to me." She hugs me back with vigor, and we are intertwined in the center of the storm together, again, two twins in the womb.

"Someone wants to say hi to you!"

"Who is it?" she asks back, excitedly.

"Just come and see." I offer her my carefully wrapped package with both hands—I have covered his face for this moment. She takes the time to read the silly card, before opening her gift.

"A gnome! A gnome! What a thoughtful and heartfelt offering. Thank you again for your kindness dedication and love. I appreciate you as a friend and I admire you as a woman. Thank you for being exactly who you are." She beams that radiant smile that I know and love, as she cradles it in her arms, every bit the proud gnome-mama she's always wanted to be. The gnome looks frightened in her loving arms. *Sorry . . .* I mouth to him. *Have fun making her accept her darkness.* He rolls his eyes and, I swear, I hear him sigh.

North squeezes my hand sweetly and smiles at me. "Want to shower?" he asks.

"Shower? Like with water?" The concept seems foreign to me; I haven't washed properly all week. I've worn my dust and grime like a badge of honor. And now, nothing in the world sounds more divine than being clean.

"Well, I have a kiddie pool and a few gallons of water left. Nothing fancy."

"That sounds like heaven."

We take turns, standing in the kiddie pool, pouring water over ourselves and washing with mint-scented natural soap. My skin tingles and erupts into tiny goosebumps under the cascading liquid. This simple ritual makes me feel like a new person. Again, I am blown away by how the simplest things I take for granted in the default world become profound here.

Fire. Water. Toilet paper. These are things that bypass illusion, all by themselves.

Sparkly clean, I hug North goodbye. As I walk away from him, I feel something shift inside of me. *I'm not in love with him and I don't want to be.*

My heart is not sad to be saying goodbye, but my mind is. From a rational place, it would be good for me to fall in love with someone solid and trustworthy like him. He is such a good solid man, and he makes sense in my life, but something is missing. You can choose your lovers, but you can't choose who you truly love. It's at the dubious mischievous command of the heart and of the soul.

I am still the lovestruck fairy princess of my childhood games, and I crave love so vigorously, but I think I would rather not be in love than be in love with the wrong person. Or in a false sort of love. You can't heal a broken heart by simply filling the hole with another. *I must find a way to fill it myself.*

It's very simple yet profound, like most lessons here, that I can care deeply about someone, their energy, the conversations, the spiritual connection, and the physical, but that can also be where it ends. Love has many expressions, and it's ok to simply enjoy beautiful moments with another without needing to quantify or push it to where it doesn't naturally want to travel. And perhaps the friendship that will result will be more fulfilling than a failed love affair.

Feeling sexually and emotionally empowered, but also a little sad, I sigh and begin to head back to my camp.

)☼(

It is late afternoon. I eat more MDMA. This time, I cut through the open playa, taking a slight detour to pass by The Temple, one final time. Of all the art and all the experiences I have had this week, my most sincere have happened or began in The Temple. I feel a longing for my wings; I want to see them one final time before they burn.

Radiant as ever, The Temple rises tall amidst the openness, without even The Man to overshadow her. She is perfect in her beauty. She asks for nothing, except love and forgiveness. I have nothing to offer, but love and forgiveness. She is my muse, my medicine. She has taken me deeper into human emotion than I ever thought possible. She has shown me the depth of suffering, and the depth of love, and how, although they are hopelessly intertwined, there is always hope. There is always a silver lining. There are lessons in pain and beauty, in suffering, and there is always a choice. We can choose to hold on to our pain or we can choose to reach beyond. We can choose to hold onto familiarity or we can choose to grow. We can choose progress, even if it comes with painful release.

I choose love. I choose life.

My wings have become my symbol for my own release. I created them to protect me, to carry me to places I didn't know I was capable of reaching. And they did both. They kept me safe, even as they pushed me higher. For this short week, that has impacted me more than a full year, they were my tool, and also my crutch. And then, I released them. Now they lay, in sacrifice and submission, in this temple. I have to see them once more.

When I left them, while it was a conscious decision, it was also based on my snap judgment. I was afraid that if I overthought it, I would question it, so I left them on the first ledge that called to me. I find their final resting spot, on an altar on the 6:00 centermost entry way to The Temple, if you were to enter from the direction of where the The Man used to be.

A woman kneels in the dust in front of them, both hands holding them, and head bowed. She is crying. Her whole body convulses with the power of her tears. I stand back, as I watch, confused. Finally, I inch slowly towards her, and then gently touch her shoulder.

"Are you okay?" I ask softly. "Excuse me. But those are my wings. Are you okay?"

She takes a moment to center herself before releasing the wings and grabbing my hands and staring deep into my eyes. "These are your wings?"

I nod.

"You left them *here?*"

I nod.

"This is my best friend Sarah's memorial altar. Why did you leave them here?" I look around. More writing:

Sarah— remember that time on the lake?

We lay naked on the docks and counted

the shooting stars?

Every star we got a wish, and I always

wished for something selfish —

But YOU, all of your wishes

were for others.

All you wanted was to show the

world the kindness it had never

shown you.

"I didn't realize . . . I just picked a spot that felt right. I didn't look at what was below. The whole temple is full of beauty. It wasn't conscious, it just was what felt right." I sink down to sit next to her and hold her hands.

There was never a time you weren't there for me. There was never a time I was afraid to call you for help. You were my angel. I hope you knew how much you ~~meant~~ still mean to me. You always will.

"This is my friend's memorial. She died earlier this year, and this is where we left what we had of her to say good-bye." She releases one of my hands to wipe a tear from her eye. "She was my soul sister."

If I learned one thing from you, it is to celebrate every moment I breathe.
Your life was a celebration of beauty.
You leave smiles, altars, and flowers.

A tear drips down my cheek now, as I take in the altar. There, under the wings that I feel I callously left, are photos, letters, and memorabilia from this woman's life. "I am so sorry, I didn't realize where I was leaving them. She is beautiful." Now, I am crying, too. "These wings have been my magical guides this whole week. I made them from scraps, and took them everywhere with me. I wanted to leave them where they would burn proudly. I am so sorry." I choke as I speak these last words. I never meant these things of beauty to disrespect anyone.

you were always an angel.
Now you get to fly with them.

"No! You don't understand! This altar was created to honor her! Every item you see is placed here by a friend or family member with love, and each one represented who she was in this life. Now, she has left us." She takes a handkerchief from her pocket to blow her nose, and then offers it to me. I do the same.

There will never be anyone in the world like you. For the rest of my life I will remember your sweet laughter, your kind eyes, and the way that you lit up a room. Now whenever I look up at the night sky I'll find the brightest star and think of you.

BURNING WINGS

"I came back today to say one final goodbye, and lying here are these wings." She takes both of my hands in hers and looks deeply into my eyes. "These are the wings that she would choose. These are the wings that she would create. These are the wings she would wear. When I saw these wings lying here, I knew that she was an angel and she had flown to heaven. You built her wings. Thank you. Thank you so much."

We cry together, two strangers wrapped around one another for comfort, inside of a sacred temple on top of dust, in the middle of the desert. She thinks she cries for her friend, but we really cry for the same things: the pain of being human, of living and loving fully, of knowing that for every high, a low may follow. *Life is just beauty and pain.* I feel another presence approach, and looking up realize it's another of Sarah's clan, come to mourn too. So I leave them together, cradling each other, savoring their last time with Sarah's altar, before she burns, with my wings.

I've saved the rest of my bag of mushrooms for The Temple burn. My heart is fully open and vulnerable. Now, I turn my gaze upwards, both symbolically and physically, to my third eye. I have one more night to push boundaries and shatter illusions. I want to go out with a bang. I look at the last of my fungus. It's a lot: perhaps an eighth and a half.

As the sun sets for the final night, I meditate on top of the van. I'm not very good at meditating; mostly, I try to sit still, and pretend I know what I am doing. The thought of silencing my mind in stillness confounds me. My mind, as I know it, has only experienced true calm when my body is engulfed in movement. During short intervals of dancing, I've found true mental peace. During orgasm, there are no words. Making my wings, I became so immersed in every tiny stitch and bead, that there was no room for anything else. Here, my mind races, how can I silence the memories of the week?

So instead, I pray.

Spirits, help open my third eye. Help me find my true self. Take me deeper, even if it means darkness. I trust. I am open.

I eat three mushrooms, chewing them slowly and thoroughly before swallowing them, resisting the urge to gag, and embracing the mild repulsion I feel from their taste. It's a strange thing to feel aversion and yet welcome the unpleasantness, trusting that it has a divine purpose. Suffering is a part of life; wisdom and compassion are choices. It feels sacrilegious to be comparing my eating psychedelic mushrooms on top of a van at a heathen festival in the desert, to any sort of holy journey, and yet, to me, that's what it is. How else to describe the wise men and women whom I have met? How else to describe the religious experiences I've had? How else can I quantify this dismantling of self, except for "holy"?

"Yo! Fun Fairy!" I turn my head to see who is calling me, and as I do, the shells in my hair smack my face. I laugh at the sensation, and then smile, as I see Spruce Man. My co-conspirator! Where has he been?

BURNING WINGS

"Spruce Man! I've missed you!" He climbs up onto the van to join me, and we hug for a long time. "I've missed you." I say it again to make sure he knows that I mean it. Spruce Man has a funny way of always being there and, I'm ashamed to admit, I have taken his presence for granted. Compared to the disruptive and vivacious personalities we're camping with, full of drama and theatrics, Spruce Man is calm and zen. He is a constant friend: never requiring maintenance or demanding excess attention. He simply is who he is, and he goes with the flow of life rather than fighting it. I imagine him as a monk in a past life, or as a lamp lighter in this one: relaxed and at peace with life, even as chaos surrounds him.

"Hey, Fun Fairy! Where have you been? I lost you at the burn last night."

"Where have I been? I've been everywhere! I fire danced at dawn. I found a gnome for Taylor. I left my wings in The Temple." I remember my wings again, and feel a tinge of sadness. Their loss is a reminder that time is moving. "Want some mushrooms?"

"Your wings? You left them? Well, you'll have to be our fairy without your wings. I think you'll be fine." He helps himself to two, and sips out of his stainless-steel coffee cup to wash them down. He offers it to me "Whiskey and ginger?" I take a few sips of his drink, and light up a cigarette.

"The sunrises and sunsets move me the most here." The sky is pink and blue, and as my three mushrooms begin to kick in, the colors pulsate to the omnipresent thudding bass music from a few camps down.

"They are the bookmarks to night and day. They remind us that time is real."

"Is it, though? I had an epiphany earlier—that there is no time and every moment exists at once." I consider what I just said and laugh. "Listen to me! I sound like a hippie! On one hand, I want each moment here to last forever; at the same time, I look back on the week and see so much change and progress has happened. I've partied my face off with so much magic here, and with so much depth. I want it to last forever, and yet, it feels arrogant to try to pin something like this place down and keep it." I sigh.

"The impermanence hit me as The Man burned. I realized that this week is going to end and we will leave. Back home. Our *real* home." He takes my cigarette and smokes it with me. The sky is darker now.

"I felt very little as I watched Him burn; I'm very sad about The Temple. She has been my safe place this week. I wish there were a way to keep her."

"Have you ever heard of Tibetan sand mandalas?" Spruce Man asks.

"No, I don't think so. I'm kind of getting into Tibetan Buddhism. But I'm really bad at meditating. Or staying sober."

"So, Tibetan sand mandalas—you know what a mandala is, right?"

"Yes . . . Like sacred geometric patterns? They're usually in circles or squares? And symmetrical? I saw them in a fire last night." My vision is starting to swirl. There are mandalas in the sky again.

"Exactly. So, Tibetan monks will create these incredibly

intricate mandalas, made out of sand. They have trays of multi-colored sand, and they meticulously place each grain onto a large board or table." He paused to take another drink. I eat another mushroom.

"They spend a long time, sometimes weeks, immersed in prayer and meditation, creating these incredibly intricate, giant mandalas. Using sand! Fucking sand! Tiny granules of colored sand!" I laugh. I imagine creating a mandala out of playa dust. I think back to creating my wings, and how I was able to find peace and stillness, going into a state of meditation I couldn't achieve without a tedious task.

Spruce Man continues. "The point is, that after they finish, they destroy it. They spend all this time building this perfect divine piece of art, and then they blow it away! It symbolizes life, always in flux. Life is always moving. There is no permanence, so why pretend?"

"Just like Burning Man." Now I understand.

Nothing is permanent. Except for a moment. Like the ecstasy of now. "And so, in releasing The Man or The Temple, we accept the impermanence of life. We are living in the present. Trusting in life."

"Something like that, exactly. Don't get me wrong—I'm not ready to go home! But hell, a real bed and a real shower doesn't sound half bad." He shrugs.

Now the sunset has completely dissipated into the lights of the night. The Temple. She burns soon. "I need to get to The Temple. Are you coming?"

"I need to regroup. Want to wait?"

"No. I'm sorry. I need to be there, and maybe this is

something I should do alone." We hug for a long time up on that van. Stars above, lasers surrounding us, and the dust below. He, too, is one of my teachers. I should never take anyone for granted, let alone someone like Spruce Man, who is wise beyond what he projects, at first glance. Somehow, the playa attracts the perfect people and lessons to me, just when I need them.

One week ago, Spruce Man and I were packing his van, impatient to get to this place, wondering what the week would bring. We had parties and drugs on our minds, and were eager to explore this magical city. Now, on the last night, we hold each other, basking in a week of individual, mind-bending experiences, that have taken us far beyond what we expected. He was my partner on this expedition; it was with him I experienced my first sunrise. Now, we have spent our last sunset together. Although we lost each other during the week, we always find each other again; and through this last conversation, I have gained new clarity: to embrace the inevitable destruction of what I hold so dear— rather than fight it.

Grinning stupidly, I leave camp for The Temple. I am usually cold; tonight, I am strangely hot. I wear a long-sleeved turquoise wrap top, silk wide-legged gypsy pants, a big green velvet cabbie hat, my hand-sewn pocket belt, and my black boots. I have a bright pink sarong that a friend brought me from Mexico, and a water bottle. My boots are stocked with a flask, my remaining mushrooms, and what is actually my last pack of cigarettes, found miraculously under a pile of tutus. My tiny green fairy sits weightlessly on my right shoulder.

Like last night, The Temple is surrounded by people and cars and bikes. Unlike last night, there is a reverence. Rather than the loud voracious voices and yells, there are murmurs and chatter. Instead of the hard bass and house music, there are slow ambient tones, playing from the few sound systems on. I weave into the crowd, unsure of where I am going, ending up a few hundred feet away from the inner circle, closer in than most of the large art cars. I look around for somewhere that looks safe, while chewing on a ribbon braid from my hair. I walk a little farther along the same circumference, finding myself next to a vintage convertible with the top down. As I lean on it to rummage in my boot and grab my flask, a man offers me a seat in the back. I hop in and cozy up, sitting on top of the back seat; he joins me.

He is a purple wizard, and has a long white beard to match. His name is Frank and he happily accepts my flask, inquiring about its contents.

"It's called Fernet Branca; it's an Italian liqueur made from herbs. It's bitter and weird, but I love it." Fernet is one of those things that inspires either intense love or hatred, and for me it is love.

"I like it. Thank you, sister. How has your week been? Have you visited The Temple?"

"The Temple has been my sanctuary. Without her, I don't know if I understand this place." I eat another mushroom: I am very high now. My vision is blurred, and full of a kind of movement, not usually seen in this dimension.

SUNDAY: *The Last Sunrise*

"They called her 'The Temple of Forgiveness,' and I think I have forgiven. Past loves, and also, myself. Have you ever felt guilty for suffering?" I regret my words as they exit my mouth. Usually, mushrooms stop me from speaking, instead opening me visually and rendering my voice useless. I'm surprised that I am coherent, let alone exposing my vulnerability. And what do I mean by *feeling guilty for suffering?* Do I feel guilty for suffering? And then I realize that I do.

I feel guilt for my pain.

I've always wanted to be nothing more than happy. I want to project and share joy. I feel an intense obligation to be blissful. I've been hiding my heartbreak and pain from the world and myself. At least until the drugs and the parties fade, and I'm left again with myself.

I feel guilty for suffering. I feel guilty for having my heart broken. I have to forgive myself for my pain.

"Guilty for suffering? Yes, I imagine I have. What a strange concept! To feel more pain through guilt for the pain already inside? It's a strange cycle, and one that you must break to fully heal. Others may give you reasons for suffering, but ultimately, it is you that chooses to suffer." He pauses, with a thoughtful look in his eye. He strokes his beard, as only those with wizard capes and white beards can do. "May I have another sip of that elixir of yours?" I again offer him my flask; he takes two small sips before handing it back.

"They say that suffering is a choice. I believe that those who live from the heart choose suffering, along with joy. When we open our hearts fully, we do so with the understanding that we may feel pain.

"Have you ever heard the word 'sentient'? I just learned it and it may be my new favorite word. It's an adjective describing a conscious perception or empathetic understanding. As we become awake we become sentient. Our capacity to feel and identify with others increases. Feeling moves from perception and integrates with the soul, and it causes emotional ruptures, like a volcano spewing lava from a seemingly dormant local. The heart chakra, in Sanskrit *Anahata,* is the epicenter of this. Touch your heart, not the heart on your left where it physically beats, but the heart energy center in the center of your chest."

I bring my hand up, hypnotized by his words. My dirty hand falls just between my breasts but slightly up from them. My hand naturally pulls away so just my pointer and middle finger touch this place. They begin to gently make circles there, feeling the hard ripples of the bone first, and then feeling an energetic orbit escalate.

"I feel it." I whisper, eyes still closed.

"Yes, the *Anahata* is the midpoint of the seven major chakras. It is the center connection of the timeless infinite divine soul with our current earth form.

"The heart never lies. The mind and emotions? Maybe. They don't mean to be untruthful; they are error prone. The heart is pure. The problem, of course, with this is that we must function here on this planet, in this life, in this form." Again, he pauses to stoke his beard.

A tiny fire begins to burn inside The Temple. There are no fireworks. There is no need to glorify her. She is glorious without adornment.

He continues: "Circumstances of all karma: our bodies, our upbringing, our learned behavior . . . These can work against the heart, so it is tested to its fullest potential. Our hearts are the doorways to our souls, and our souls are ageless, but yet we must fight to maintain them." The fire slowly spreads; a few small cheers erupt from the crowd. His voice grows softer.

"Our souls, they enter the human realm over and over and, through the hearts, they recognize kindred spirits. The purpose is simple: to love unconditionally." His voice is still low, and now, it takes on a deeper tone, as if to emphasize his point.

"The real question is: how to love unconditionally, when your love isn't wanted?" A single tear drips down my cheek, as I speak. My fairy wipes it away.

"The action of love is more complex than a simple thought. The human condition tries to dissolve the heart. But as I have already told you, the heart is as ageless as the soul, and so each test of heart's purity is simple karma returning so that you may rise above it."

"Logic competes with the heart's purpose," I say softly as my hand once again begins to massage my heart energy center. I can feel pale pink light grow there, and a tiny sphere begins to spin.

When Frank speaks again I hear it as though I am under water. "'Logic competes with heart's purpose.' Sigh, yes it does! And, for good reason. When we are shown abuse and fear and hatred, it feels demeaning to continue to love and offer ourselves to another."

I feel the warmth radiate from my heart up and down my body through the center line, spiraling like a DNA helix. I breathe into it as I still rub that spot on my chest, and its colors are a rainbow.

"So, how do we honor our soul connection and our heart's desire, to love freely and without restraint?" Frank is still talking, and I don't think he is speaking to me anymore, he is in his own trance and has become a conduit for wisdom, lost in fire and energy.

The fire in The Temple spreads. I watch the place where my wings lay as the fire consumes it.

I eat another mushroom.

"How do we balance our love against human frailties, like deceitfulness or dishonesty or jealousy? How do we continue to love?" The rainbow fades as the pain returns. My cheeks are covered with salty tears, tears I thought I had long since used up.

"How can we not? Yes, pain is real. Yes, suffering is real. Yes, people can be cruel. And, what is the alternative? To become jaded and dark? To wallow in our sorrow, and pass it along? Why would you want that?"

His gaze is fixated on The Temple, burning. He pauses to glance at me, and sees my tears. He does not offer physical sympathy, rather an emotional presence that is worth more than a million hugs. The fire in The Temple grows higher, roaring into the second level.

"I want to love. Even if it hurts. Even through the darkness. I want to be the light. I never want to treat people like

I have been treated. I never want to be the source of that much pain."

"Each and every one of us, is part of a chain. Each interaction we share with others, has the potential to spread love or hate or anything in between. When others offer us these things, we can accept them, or not. We can pass them along, or not." The flames grow larger still; now, the full first level is engulfed—the level where the words and prayers and confessions of thousands lie.

"When we pass them along, they grow stronger. So, when you accept hate, and then pass it along, it is stronger because you spread it. And the same with love. When we receive kindness, and pass along its essence, we tap into the divine, and the more we spread it, the stronger it becomes. Now, I am not saying that because we pass it along we lose it within ourselves; rather, we multiply its spiritual intensity through proliferating it."

"So, we can take the joy or pain or peace or hate or beauty we receive and multiply it?" I am so high, I can hardly keep track of his words, and yet I need them. He is validating everything I believe, inside of me, and expanding upon it, in ways I have not been able to fully describe. The flames spread to the second level of The Temple. My fairy tries again to wipe away my tears, too copious for her tiny hands, so, she begins to glow a soft green light, and allows it to engulf me.

"In simple terms: *yes*. Every single person you will love in this life, or that will love you, will imprint on your soul, forever. The love you share is a tiny seed that blooms continuously. The purest love will still leave scars and cause pain and, after that initial burn fades away, the remnants are still beautiful and the scars heal cleanly.

"It's the dark, sticky, unrequited love that can get messy: the fearful love, that leaves infected wounds, that scar up in raised welts, that will never fully heal. Those are the kind of heartbreaks that take whole lifetimes to get over." I think of *him* again. He has a heart-shaped burn mark on his hand, to remember me. I have the shards in my heart, the ones left contaminated, filled with pus, dark shadows, and hot, sticky blood.

The Temple burns brighter and, I swear, there is blood coming out of her wood, like sap.

"We never fully heal. It's an illusion. We transmute the energy, we don't dissolve it." The third and topmost level of The Temple catches fire, and still, giant, silent tears cascade down my face. She is majestic, as she burns. With all of her on fire, I can fully appreciate her intricacies. As she burns, I do too; not the deepest parts of me, just the ones that have been shrouded in illusion.

"Energy can neither be created nor destroyed; rather it transforms from one form to another." He smiles sadly. *He too has loved and lost.*

"Going beyond this concept, energy has the power to multiply, and you also have the power to choose what you allow to multiply, within yourself. Just because you are faced with pain or hatred, you don't have to deny it, you don't have to pretend you don't feel it, you don't have to relinquish it. You do have to decide if it is something you will pass on, remembering the law of multiplicity. Perhaps the guilt you feel, for your suffering from someone else's passing pain to you, is your refusal to pass it along. It is your way of dealing with internalizing it, so it stops with you. This is a noble cause for suffering, but not mandatory. You must find a way to turn the pain it into medicine. *Do not let it multiply within you!*"

The smoke from The Temple contains thousands of prayers. Every heartfelt word offered burns just the same. No matter who has offered pieces of their soul to that wood, they now incinerate together. There is no order or class, there is just pure reverence. My words, along with the unnamed others', burn.

Countless altars, dedicated to the deceased, are no more. The corners of Sarah's altar would curl, as it ignited. When my wings burned, would the yarn ignite or melt? How would the stones fall from the burning webbing? Landing on more embers, on more burnt memories? The looms, burning as well, would have illuminated the shape of the wings, just as the outline of The Temple became so illuminated to me. The glow sticks wouldn't burn, they would melt, perhaps the last part of the wings added will last the longest. If my fairy could burn, would it hurt her? Is she as invincible as she appears?

Gracefully, The Temple finally collapses. Now the crowd rises in vocal appreciation. She is mighty, but she is no match for the force of the fire. She surrenders herself, to illustrate the endless flux of life. She is grander than any church or chapel ever could be to me. She was designed long ago, built three stories high in under a month, and for one week, she served as a holy place for me and for my new community. She was as a meeting place, as a place of solitude and release. She taught me that every being alive contains love, and that all are worthy of forgiveness, no matter the pain they caused. She took our pain, and died in sacrifice.

With her sacrifice, I decide to forgive him, and to forgive myself, even if it takes a whole lifetime.

Her flames begin to dim. I must go to her. I am so hot. I eat another mushroom. My companion, Frank, has left. My fairy hovers above my head. I can feel her light, even as I do not see her tiny body. I take off my shirt, tying it around my belt, and I would take my pants off as well if I thought I could get them off over my boots. Once again, I acknowledge how high I am. I can almost levitate outside my body, and appreciate the absurdity of needing to dance around the fire naked. Faces swirl around me. The sky above me pulses, releasing near to me, then pulling back up. I look down at my hands, and see a rainbow collage of color. The fire is ahead and it wants me. I rush towards it, doing my best to weave around and respect those still sitting, needing her, craving her. Her smoke is my magnet.

When I get close, the barrier has been released, and there is no one to stop me from getting to her embers. The crowd naturally forms a clockwise circle around her, looping in and out of itself, like the ribbons on a May pole. Except there are no tangible ribbons to leave a mark, there is only energy. The auras from every individual around the giant open bonfire of sacred wood and offerings, float up into the sky, creating a new visual that rivals the patterns of the smoke.

As I weave through the crowd, topless, my sarong trailing behind my outstretched arms, I look deeply into the faces I encounter, seeing their love and their pain. Each radiates its own aural field. Some are white, some are purple, some are red . . . Every color of the rainbow, I encounter through its essence. Each face is unique, and each is the same. Two eyes, a nose, a mouth, and an aura. There is something familiar about each one. They flash bright, as they turn towards the fire, and they grow dark as they turn away. I make eye contact with a woman, and hold it for a few seconds longer than necessary, before I realize I am staring into my own eyes. I turn to the next person, who has my face, too.

They are all me. We are all just mirrors.

My fairy flies with me, hovering next to my face. I look over at her and now, finally, I can focus on her face. It is also my own. She stares deeply into my eyes, and finally I understand, *she was me all along.*

She's just another illusion, even though all illusions are just illusions.

She smiles, and then in a flurry of light, dives into the burning embers. A tiny fire erupts where she disappears.

I no longer need her.

The fire is wretchedly hot, and I embrace its power. Sweat drips down my forehead and trickles down my chest, forming a rivulet between my small breasts. I revel in it.

Water and fire. I am complete. I am whole.

Halfway between lost and found. That's how I came here, wanting to push boundaries, to challenge the world, and still to belong to something larger than myself.

I have pushed boundaries, I have challenged *my* world, and I have found something to belong to, larger than myself. I am still jaded by my suffering, and becoming increasingly at peace. I am still as optimistic as I was, now wiser; no longer in spite of pain, now, in harmony with its inevitability, and trusting in myself to rise above it.

When the light becomes too much for me, when I grow too hot, I turn outwards, towards the open playa. After a few spins around the fire, the city's map becomes unrecognizable to me: there are just the embers, and the outside world. Camp could be in any direction, within three hundred and sixty degrees: it is all the same, now.

When I leave the fire's inner circle, even surrounded by people, I find darkness and coldness. At first this is revitalizing, but quickly I become chilled, and dance back, into the inner circle of true devotees, hugging the remains. Yes, the dark and cold are real. I feel them, and I appreciate them, in a new way. They are refreshing even, especially when I am overwhelmed by the fire. I stare into the tiny fires, still burning amongst the embers, and see in them again the endless suffering and devotion of so many people. There is heat in the light, and there is cold in the darkness; each has its purpose, and its beauty.

The darkness seems to tug at me, and I feel its draw. It is rough but real, showing the shadow that lurks behind the light. I turn back to the fire. I accept the darkness, but I know I will always choose the light.

))☼((

I leave the fire with no concept of direction. The Man is gone. The Temple is no more. I can't tell where the city is.

I am far out into the deep playa. The lights of the art cars bewilder me. The mushrooms have turned them into a collage of glowing spots, and I'm looking at them through a wet pane of glass.

I am cold. *So cold.*

My feet hurt.

I want to go home. What does that mean, anymore?

This place is supposed to be my home, and yet I have witnessed its dissolution.

I have seen my sacred places burned before my eyes, the ashes blown away in the wind.

I walk slowly, dragging my feet on the playa. Every direction I choose is wrong. If I could find 9:00, I could find my camp; if I could find 2:00, I could find friends. I can't find anything, besides confusion.

There is no home. There is no easy answer. There is just a blind trust, that it all has a purpose, that I wouldn't be here for nothing.

It can't be for nothing. It must mean something.

Everything has changed here, and yet, nothing has changed. I've come so far and yet, I'm still a lost fairy, trying to find the light in the darkness.

BURNING WINGS

There are so many false lights, false prophets, false hopes.

I keep on thinking I understand it all, that love and life make sense. Then again, the clarity vanishes like it never existed in the first place: blown away, like colored sand after the mandala is completed.

A tiny voice inside of me cuts through the pessimism and says, *trust, trust, trust.* Trust in what? Each plateau I find, leads only to more mountains. Each dismantling shows me more illusion.

There are no real ends, just infinite beginnings.

Then, I look up at the distant heavens, beyond the artificial lights. The sky has begun to lighten.

Another sunrise is coming.

It is almost tomorrow.

Another day will soon begin.

It wasn't my last chance, after all.

The End

(until next year)

BURNING WINGS

NOTES ABOUT *Formatting*

CREATING THE LAYOUT FOR BURNING WINGS quickly turned into its own project. I wanted the pages to take the reader on a journey, without distracting from the imagery the words presented. When my art director, Eli, was told I wanted to use 30 different fonts, along with more of Marie's custom illustrations throughout the book, he laughed, shook his head, and then he taught me how to use InDesign.

So, there I was, a month out from launch, recovering from COVID-19, and formatting my own book on a new program. I kept on telling myself that since Burning Man was canceled this year, this work was replacing my usual art project and pre-production stress load.

The uses of handwritten fonts as my character reads the writing on the temple walls pays homage to what it is really like to walk through a temple at Burning Man. Some are purposefully meant to be difficult to read, allowing the reader to choose whether to commit or move on.

The interior illustrations are also by Marie, created for the original edition, which was never published, but gifted at Burning Man in 2017. Those few hundred copies of playa editions have now made their rounds through multiple Burning Man's and various festivals, and I've received stories about them being read onsite.

With those images in mind, I purposefully decided to keep

both the text and spacing larger than I would expect from a literary novel, so that these weary imaginary burners and festival goers didn't have to strain their eyes (which I imagine were also very sore from late nights with lasers, fog machines, and dust).

I'd also like to acknowledge Marie Poliak again for the incredible cover art. The intention for the cover was to show the playa itself, and elude to Burning Man, without actually showing the man or other iconic imagery. The intention for "the girl" as we began to call her, was for her to both emanate Burning Man culture and for her features to be abstract enough for anyone to find themselves in her. She had to be youthful but powerful, classic but intriguing, beautiful yet interesting, and she had to look like a warrior of the dust. I think we nailed it.

I'm proud of the piece of collaborative art you hold in your hands today.

-Kyra

BURNING WINGS

ABOUT THE *Author*

KYRA BRAMBLE IS ONE OF THOSE PEOPLE who lives and loves fearlessly, and that attitude is reflected in her writing. She is a writer, globe-trotter, die-hard burner, queer celebrator, in-demand holistic chef, yoga teacher, and entrepreneur. Raised in liberal northern California with roots in New York, she spent her twenties based in San Francisco before moving to Maui, where she currently lives.

A book worm since childhood, she views words as passports to the soul, and a conduit to share the intangible yet ubiquitous emotions that all humans experience. Her intention as a writer is to blur the lines between revelry and spirituality, and to pioneer a new genre of female-centric counter-culture writing.

Burning Wings is Kyra's first book, a no-holds barred story of the intense spiritual awakening that can occur amidst the madness and epiphanies of drug culture, all through a contemporary female lens with signature Gonzo flair.

Made in the USA
Monee, IL
07 April 2021

64998523R00164